WHETHER I'LL LIVE OR DIE

STACY EATON

NITEWOLF NOVELS

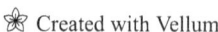 Created with Vellum

DEDICATION

To those who fought and won;
To those who fight daily but are afraid to take the next step;
And to the memory of those who never got their freedom.

ACKNOWLEDGMENTS

This story has been growing for a long time, and it is my wish to acknowledge the victims and their families first. This is your story that I share, your heartfelt fears and pain that are marked on these pages. I have written *Whether I'll Live or Die* for you.

For those of you who were victims and found a way to freedom: I am proud of you.

For those people who lost their lives or were too afraid to walk away and died keeping a secret so horrifying on your shoulders: You will not be forgotten.

To all the people who live in fear and pain of what will come next: May this story give you the strength to reach out for help and find a way to live a life you deserve.

To my husband Jason, who is my Colton, the one who loves me for what I am and would never think to raise a hand to me or to verbally assault me in any way: You are an amazing man, and I love you from the bottom of my heart.

To my daughter whose patience was unmatched each time I said, "Give me just a few more minutes": You are the most precious little girl in the world! Grow up strong and don't ever let anyone do anything to you that does not feel right.

To my parents who stood beside me through so much, who were always willing to open their home in times of trouble, who never judged me as I grew, and who always loved me for what and who I am: I love you both dearly and can never thank you enough.

There have been so many people who have encouraged me, supported me, and listened to me go on and on about this story. I can never thank you enough for allowing me to throw ideas out and to have your feedback.

A special thanks to Natasha Brown for her amazing ability to put my cover art together and make it so incredibly special.

And last but not least, to Dominique Agnew, my editor: Your ability to see my vision and to help me put the words to their best usage was amazing. Your questions and your ideas to improve the story while never trying to change my voice will always be appreciated. You made a very tough story flow, and it is with a special thank you that I now give my readers *Whether I'll Live or Die*.

FOREWORD

The color of the skin or the age of the body does not matter; nor does the square footage of your house or the type of car you drive; nor does race, sex, and economic status. Domestic violence touches all people without prejudice, tears them down from the inside out, shatters their hopes and dreams, destroys their self-esteem, and causes embarrassment beyond repair.

Every nine seconds in the United States, a woman is assaulted or beaten: at least six women every minute of the day; four hundred women in an hour; nine thousand six hundred women every single day.

Women are not the only victims. Estimates say that one in four domestic violence episodes involves women abusing the men in their lives. Very few men will report this abuse, feeling the authorities will not believe them and embarrassed that they were victims of a woman abuser.

No matter the method—verbally, mentally, or physically—abuse takes away choices, and burdens the victim with unwanted fear and stress.

Abuse controls life, changes the very character of its victims, and teaches children that it is acceptable to act this way. A male child who views abuse to his mother is twice as likely to abuse his own partner when he grows up.

There is no reason not to find a way out. There is absolutely no excuse for not trying to get help. Do not allow the lack of money to keep you from seeking assistance. Do not allow your abuser to threaten that he or she will remove your children from your care because you seek help. Most people cannot escape alone, they need people and resources to help, and there are organizations that exist solely for this purpose.

If you or someone you know is being abused, please contact the National Domestic Violence Hotline at 1-800-799-SAFE to get the help you need. Do not wait a minute longer.

PROLOGUE

$\mathcal{I}$ thought I was strong, that I could take on the world, that one day I would grow up to be someone special, someone that people would look up to, someone that people would talk about, that I would leave a footprint on this world.

Little did I know just how weak I was and how hard I would have to fight to become that person.

CHAPTER ONE

AMANDA

I closed the back door to my Chevy Citation and slung my gym bag over my shoulder. I wiped the perspiration off my brow as I set my sights on the glass doors of the building.

The place didn't look like much on the outside, just a tall beige concrete industrial building. It's what's on the inside that counts, I thought to myself as I pulled open the door. The whoosh of air conditioning descended in a welcome wave, refreshing my hot skin.

I embraced the sweet and musky scent of sweat emanating from the weight room. The sounds of metal clanging from down the hall echoed off the walls toward me. Hypnotized, I followed the sound.

The fluorescent lights that lined the hallway buzzed quietly as the sounds of the metal on metal got louder, slowly drowning out the noise of the lights. I approached the archway to the main area and slowed. A butterfly took flight in my belly as I peered cautiously through the gap in the cinderblock walls.

The room took up most of the industrial space of the building. Large halogen lights high in the ceiling brightened the room so it was easy to navigate the machinery. My eyes traveled quickly over the after-work crowd, and I swiftly released the breath I'd been holding.

Relieved that I didn't see him, I crossed past the opening to head to the locker room. Chewing the corner of my bottom lip, I rounded the corner and slammed right into a solid body, an *oomph!* escaping my lips.

A hand grabbed my arm in a vice, squeezing my bicep. My heart rate began to increase.

"Steve!" slipped from my lips as I bit back the words of pain. "You scared me!" His grip intensified around my arm, and I clenched my jaw to hide the pain.

"Where have you been?" he sneered down at me as his face came closer, his dark brown eyes closing into a squint.

I blinked in confusion. "I just got here; I was a little late getting off of work."

My fingers began to feel numb on my left hand, but I would not give him the benefit of knowing how much discomfort his hold caused. As his mouth opened to speak, the odor of bitter coffee struck my face. The sound of footsteps echoing on the walls caused him to look over my head. He released my arm instantly and stepped back.

There was no doubt in my mind whose shoes approached us. I flexed my hand slightly by my side but never took my eyes from Steve's face.

Mark stepped up beside me, just close enough that his arm brushed against my shoulder. I looked up to see his jaw clenched, the muscle on the side ticking like a second hand on a clock. I glanced back to Steve and took in the anger etched on his face.

"Steve," Mark's voice was deep and gruff.

"Mark," replied Steve's deeper voice.

They stood almost nose to nose around five foot ten or eleven each, their shoulders stiff and wide enough to block out the view of an entire room.

They sized each other up, never breaking eye contact with one another. Clearing my throat quietly, I tried to break up the mounting tension.

Mark's eyes flicked to me quickly, although his face didn't move, "Mandy, go get dressed. We have a busy routine tonight."

Thankful to have been released, I nodded and sidestepped Steve to go the last ten feet to the locker room. As the door closed slowly on the scene behind me, the muffled thump of my gym bag as it hit the tile floor filled the quiet room. I sank to the bench, allowing my face to fall into my hands. This needs to stop, I thought.

Unzipping my bag, I relaxed at the sound of the metal on metal. I needed to forget about Steve and start focusing instead on what lower body routine Mark would put me through. I kicked off my sneakers and wriggled out of my jeans to put on my workout gear. Before tossing my work clothes into my bag, I pulled out my weight gloves, straps, and leather support belt that would protect my lower back and internal organs.

I pulled my long blond hair up high and tight on my head, hoisted my bag into my locker, and then spun the dial on my lock, turning to make my way to the main floor. Mark stood right where I expected him. Glancing around, I didn't see Steve, and my shoulders relaxed. I smiled as I stepped in front of Mark, hoping he would skip the lecture, his intense green eyes watching my every move. I knew he was about to say something, but I really wished that he wouldn't.

Mark was not only my friend, he was my trainer. We had met several months ago when he'd noticed the potential I had to body build. Like almost every other woman in the gym, I had already noticed him, so to know he'd been watching me had seriously surprised me.

Mark was nine years older than I was, making him twenty-eight, and I had found myself more than once fantasizing about him. I was pretty sure every hot-blooded woman in the place did. I mean, how could they not? He was unbelievably built, with the sexiest emerald eyes and square-jawline I had ever seen outside a magazine.

Smiling shyly, I hoped my infatuation didn't show on my face as I waited, bracing myself for what he would say. Absently, I pulled my weight gloves on, fastening the Velcro tightly around my wrists.

"If I ever see him touch you like that again, I'm going to kill him, Mandy." His words embarrassed me, and my eyes went to the ground. Glancing to my side, I saw Jeff and Bob watching us. I knew they had heard the threat, too. My cheeks warmed slightly. Mark waited patiently for his words to sink in. I nodded just once, bringing my eyes back up to his. What was there to say?

He held the contact for a moment longer. His intensity overwhelmed me, so I looked away awkwardly and began buckling up my weight belt, trying to prepare for the workout he was about to push me through.

Ninety minutes later, my leg muscles screamed as I lowered myself into my car seat. I relished the pain that radiated through my muscles after a workout: the burning and the way the muscles quivered as they started to heal themselves from the torment I put them through by choice. I loved the way I felt after a workout. Smiling as I put the car into reverse, I concentrated on keeping my foot from bouncing off the brake pedal as it shook from the slight exertion.

I made it home safely, though my legs wanted to give out on the two flights of stairs I climbed to reach my apartment. The smell of the moldy carpet in the hallway always wrinkled my nose, so instead, I tried to focus on the pale-yellow paint peeling from the concrete walls. This definitely wasn't a first class joint, but it was my first apartment, and I was proud that I could afford to live on my own.

My stomach rumbled loudly as I unlocked the heavy-duty brown metal door, dropping my bag on the beige carpeted floor just inside. I headed to the kitchen immediately, turned the dial on the mustard-colored stove, filled a pot with water, and placed it on the warming burner. From inside of one of my dark brown cabinets, I found my box of store brand pasta and set it next to the stove.

Sally jumped up on the counter, meowing and begging to be petted. "Hello, Sally, did you miss me?" I crooned to the fluffy bundle of whiteness as I scooped her up and walked into the small living room. I glanced around at the bare walls. I really needed to hang a few pictures. Stark white surrounded me, a vivid backdrop for my heavy pine furniture. I turned on the television and plopped down on the sofa cushion, kicking my feet up on the scarred coffee table. Sally continued to purr softly as we sat together; she twitched her tail at me when I put her aside a few minutes later to add the pasta to the boiling water.

I poured an already-open bottle of pasta sauce into another pan; letting it cook on low while the pasta boiled. A half loaf of French bread sat on my counter, and I picked it up along with a bread knife and plate. I carried them back to the living room, set them on the coffee table, and began to cut the bread.

A knock sounded at my door just as I took the first bite of the flaky crust. Sally raised her tail and shot down the hall. Skittish cat, I thought to myself as I stood up.

I set the plate and knife down on the coffee table where my feet had been and went to the door, pulling it open without looking through the peephole. In hindsight, this was just the first of my mistakes.

The door swung inward forcefully. I lost my balance trying to avoid the door and fell back over my gym bag. A thump vibrated through my head as it struck the leg of a dining room chair. Momentarily stunned, I looked up into the face of a very angry man.

"Steve, what are you doing here?" I asked, getting off the ground as quickly as my shaking legs would allow me.

"You were supposed to wait for me tonight. We had plans." He pushed the door closed behind him with a loud metallic bang, not very unlike the sound of a jail cell closing. As I rose to my feet, I remembered him telling me about some new place he wanted to take me.

"I'm sorry. I completely forgot." The look on his face now had more than my legs shaking as he stepped directly in front of me. "I'll just turn the pasta off, and we can go." As I turned from him, he grabbed my arm in another vice-like grip.

"No, it's too late now," his voice growled as he pulled me to him.

"Steve, stop! You're hurting me." I tried to twist backwards to make eye contact with him, but he reached around and grabbed me by the throat, my arm still held prisoner. My back made contact with the hardened muscles of his abdomen.

"Steve, stop!" I managed to say. He dropped my arm and wrapped his thick arm tightly around my waist.

"Don't tell me what to do, Amanda. You don't tell me what to do. You got that?" The voice next to my ear sounded like it was shouting, but I knew it really wasn't. This voice that, only a few months ago, had lulled me into feeling safe, now frightened me.

I didn't try to fight him; the fear of being held against my will did not allow me to think straight, must less fight. His breath slid past my right ear; I needed a way to calm him down, but my mind went blank. I did not know how to deal with the anger and agitation that had been growing in him recently.

Steve released his arm from around my waist and turned me towards him, his other hand still wrapped around my thin neck. My eyes felt huge as I looked up at his face. Could he not see the fear and pain in my face? Did he not care? His brown eyes were wild.

"You will stay away from Mark. Do you hear me?" This time he did shout at me, and I tried not to flinch. Without thinking, I reached up to pry his hands from my throat.

He picked me up off the ground, slamming my upper body into the wall. My hundred-twenty-five-pound frame meant little to him when he benched three hundred pounds with no problem. My eyes closed involuntarily to the pain that vibrated through my head. My legs caught up to my upper body, but instead of hitting the wall, they collided with the stereo cabinet sitting three feet off the ground. Pain lanced through the back of my thighs as the sharp edges dug in.

His hand still on my neck, Steve held me against the wall as my eyes finally opened. Anger built inside me as I made eye contact with him. Maybe he saw the change in my eyes or maybe he realized how he held me, but he let go and gravity dropped me to the floor. My hand involuntarily flew to my throat as I gasped for fresh air.

I curled the fingers of my left hand into the fibers of the carpet; my lungs burned. What could I do? What could I say to make it better? This was my fault. I knew I should not have forgotten about his plans.

I was able to breathe normally again when I finally looked up at the coffee table; the same coffee table where the eight-inch bread knife sat. The reflection from the television animated the silver blade's surface.

I lunged for the knife, my right hand on the wooden handle as I turned to face him. The tears I had yet to shed welled in my eyes, spilling over and down my face. Nothing could have stopped the anger, pain, and humiliation that flowed through my body at that moment as I thought only to protect myself.

He looked between me and the blade, yet he did not move. Time stood still as we stared each other down.

"Get out, Steve. Get out now," my voice croaked, barely audible over the sound of the television.

His eyes narrowed, but he didn't move otherwise. I saw his nostrils flare as he looked again at the knife.

"Get the hell out of here, Steve! If you don't get out, I'm going to cut you!" My shout got his attention, his Adam's apple moved up and down as he swallowed.

Slowly, he backed towards the door, never removing his gaze from me.

His right hand reached behind him for the doorknob. I adjusted my position, angling my body towards him as he moved.

No words were spoken as he stepped over the threshold. The hinged spring in the door moved sluggishly, so I threw my weight against it and bolted the top lock. The knife fell to the floor of the hallway as I moved quickly to the kitchen, turning off the boiling-over pot of pasta. With the sauce also turned off, I ran into my bedroom and threw clothes into a bag.

Within just a few minutes, I was packed enough to make it through a couple of days. Scooping up Sally on my way to the door, I peeked through the peephole, the metal of the door cold on my heated skin. The hallway appeared empty, and I carefully opened the door, prepared to scream if Steve somehow showed up out of thin air.

The corridor was indeed empty as I ran to the stairs and descended as quickly as I could while holding my bags and Sally, her claws digging deep into my shoulder as she clung to me. Before walking into the parking lot, I looked through the window to make sure the parking lot was clear. Two other tenants were in the lot by their car just past mine. Good, someone to see if something happened, I thought briefly.

As casually as I could manage, I made my way to my car without bringing attention to myself. With my two bags thrown into the backseat and Sally huddled on the passenger seat, I climbed in and locked the door with shaking hands. Backing out of my space, I looked out the rear window to where I could see my building. Two cheap lawn chairs sat on my balcony watching my departure. They knew I would never return, and their sadness crushed me as I put the car in drive.

CHAPTER TWO

NICOLE

*P*ride threatened to overwhelm me as I stood in line with my classmates. It was hot in the auditorium with all the large lights blazing down on us from the ceiling and the body heat emanating from the rows upon rows of people watching; however, that did not affect how I felt at that moment. A trickle of sweat rolled down my neck into the tight collar of my shirt. I smiled.

My hot fingers brushed over the silver metal that adorned my left breast—how slick the badge felt. My hard-earned pride swelled bigger as I realized the accomplishment I was about to fulfill. I closed my eyes to will back the tears. The emotion in my heart cried to be released.

Lowering my eyes to my feet, I saw the bright lights reflected in my boots. My knees shook gently, but not from fear, more from amazement. I am alive to feel, I exulted to myself. I inhaled deeply to stifle the sob that wanted to take over my body. Stepping up behind another classmate, I waited my turn to climb the steps to receive my certificate. The long line of cadets inched forward.

The brass as we called them, the chiefs, lieutenants, and instructors, stood in their own line facing the guests, slowly calling names, shaking hands, and whispering private words as cadets moved along the line.

I marveled at my luck. Another smile tried to form on my lips, but I held it back. Many of my classmates stood in black slacks, a white Oxford button-down dress shirt, and a black tie, but I was one of the truly lucky ones. On this day, I stood out as one of the few graduating with a job already lined up, a hard feat to achieve.

Like only a handful of classmates, I wore a dark blue Class A uniform. My tight-fitting shirt, tailored to fit my curves, sat properly over my bulletproof vest. A pull-away tie was clipped into the front of my neckline, adorned with a special handcuff tie pin given to me by my boyfriend, Colton. The belt I wore around my waist felt tight, heavy, but I welcomed the feeling. It was the feeling of knowing I was dressed to start my job as one of the famous Thin Blue Line.

I glanced into the audience and saw Colton watching me. I couldn't help but return the smile; he snapped a quick picture, winking at me as he lowered the camera.

I reached the steps and heard Jack whisper from behind me, "Don't trip, Nolan." His chuckle made me clasp the handrail more tightly; I took my first step up. I had no intention of embarrassing myself by falling, it would only be made worse as I was the only female in full dress uniform.

I let out the breath I held once I reached the top step. Firmly planting my feet on the stage, I waited for my name to be called.

"Officer Nicole Nolan." Since I had been hired, I was one of the few that got to be called out by a title and not just my name. I walked the stage and shook the hands. As I approached Director Dunn, his smile grew, and he leaned away from the microphone. "I'm proud of you, Nic. You're going to go far. I know it."

"Thanks, Sir." I beamed back, reaching up to take my certificate with my left hand, my right hand reaching under to shake his firmly. Nodding at him again quickly, I turned to the next person in line.

After shaking the last hand, I stepped off the stage, totally forgetting that I was supposed to stop and pose for the photographer there. It didn't matter; I could not have had a bigger smile on my face as I took that first step down the stairs. I had done it.

After making my way to my seat, I clapped for my friends and fellow classmates as they continued. Once we were all seated, and the auditorium quieted down from the final round of applause, Director Dunn started to announce the special awards.

These awards were for special curriculum activities: best in firearms, driving, medical, and overall, and of course the one I got, the most physically fit. Yeah, that's right. I beat out the guys in my class by doing more pushups, more sit ups, by running faster, and by lifting more on the bench press for my age group, twenty-nine and over. Not to mention I outdid them in the hand-to-hand combat training.

Although I might have stepped on some toes when I won the award, I knew that my classmates stood behind me. We had studied, supported, embraced, and pushed each other to do the best that we could since day one of the class.

My name was called. I stood up and walked carefully to the end of the row. My classmates clapped and cheered me on as I moved forward. This time as I walked to the stage, I did it quickly, making sure to stop and smile for the photographer. A few ear-splitting whistles came from the crowd as I descended the steps.

Seated again, I awaited the final part of the program. It all went by quickly, and before long, they were calling us to our feet, saluting us, and saying "Class dismissed" for the final time. Yelling and hugging my friends while I looked for my family, I finally allowed the tears to flow when my parents hugged me and told me how proud they were.

I took a minute to scan the room, observing my classmates among their families, slowly making their way to the door: the door that would lead us to our new careers. Some of them would go far, some of them would fail. Many of them I would expect to see over the years, and a couple I knew I would grieve for as they gave their lives for the duty they had promised to uphold, the duty that said we would serve and protect the citizens and their property as they traveled in and around the Commonwealth of Pennsylvania.

I was now Officer Nicole Nolan, and I was damn proud!

CHAPTER THREE

AMANDA

I drove away from my apartment unsure of my destination. The thought of going to my parents' house bothered me. What would I tell them? I was mortified that I had upset Steve to the point that he had become violent. How could I tell my parents about that?

A few seconds later, I knew the best place to go, for now. While I drove the streets, I thought back to what had occurred in my apartment. If I had just remembered that Steve had wanted to take me someplace, then none of this would have happened. I shook my head at my own stupidity.

Pulling up into the driveway of a small ranch house on the outskirts of town, I saw Mark's car; he was home. My cat sat beside me meowing quietly, not liking the car ride and probably hungry since she had not eaten. Now that my adrenaline finally had come back to normal, my stomach resumed its earlier grumbling sounds as well.

I sat in my car looking at the house, wondering if this was the right choice. Just as I started to put the car in reverse, the front door opened, and Mark emerged.

Nodding once to bolster my courage, I pulled the keys from the ignition and got out. I kept my head down, my hair hanging over my shoulders as I approached him slowly.

"What's going on, Amanda? You okay?" Mark asked as I stopped at the bottom of his cement steps.

Maybe it was the sound of his voice or maybe it was because I finally allowed myself to think about what had happened, I wasn't sure, but as I looked up at Mark, the dam broke and the tears began.

Shaking my head, I tried to meet his eyes, but I couldn't quite bring myself to face him. He saw the tears the moment I lifted my face and stepped down to me immediately.

"Mandy, what's wrong?" He put his hands on my upper arms, my body tensed. The memory of Steve touching me so harshly caused me to attempt to step back. Mark took his left hand off my arm, tilting my chin to look into my face.

A trickle of tears ran down my cheeks as I met his eyes. My hair fell back slightly as he raised my chin and I heard his sharp intake of breath. He was staring at my neck. I felt anger coming off him in waves while he unconsciously tightened his grip on my arm. I winced but didn't pull away.

"Oh, Mandy, what did he do to you?" He pulled me into his strong embrace. Huge wracking sobs carried over my body as I stood within his arms, his hand gently smoothing down my long hair in a calming motion.

Eventually, he pulled away, tucking me into his shoulder as we climbed the steps to his front door.

"Wait," I turned to look at my car, "my cat is in the car." He raised his eyebrows but said nothing as he turned and walked to get Sally.

I walked to the couch as he got her, trying to pull myself together. I felt calmer now that I had released the fear.

Mark came back in, putting Sally in my lap as he sat down next to me. I still wasn't able to look into his face, so my eyes stayed on my lap. My hands twisting around each other as he sat beside me.

"What happened?" he asked quietly.

The thought that I shouldn't have come to Mark's house ran quickly through my mind, and I wanted to lie about what had happened, but he knew something bad had occurred, so how much should I tell him?

"Amanda, talk to me. Tell me what that asshole did to you." I could hear frustration in his voice, and my body started to shake again.

Finally I found my voice. "It was my fault. I forgot about something we were supposed to do, he got angry. It was my fault not his."

"My ass it was your fault!" I flinched at his outburst. "Where the hell is he? I told you if he touched you again I was going to kill him."

I had no problem looking at him now as my eyes flashed to his. "No! You can't kill him! Mark, I'm okay, really. I was just scared. Please don't do anything to him." Sally jumped off my lap, unhappy with my raised voice. I found myself begging Mark in a way, and I didn't know why.

"Don't tell me you are going back to him." He grabbed my chin as he spoke and held it still to keep our eyes locked together.

"No! No, I swear I'm not going back to him. I learned my lesson, but it was my fault," I replied quickly.

"It is never your fault when a man puts his hands on a woman to hurt her! It's never alright, Amanda! That son of a bitch deserves to have his ass kicked!"

"Look, Mark, please, just let it go. I'm not going back to him, and I'm not going back to live at my apartment either. I just want it over with him. I have wanted it over for a while." My voice grew softer as I spoke. He released my chin, and I immediately looked down to my hands lying in my lap.

He was quiet for a minute. When he finally spoke, I was holding my breath. "Fine, I won't, but if I see him come within ten feet of you, I will not give you any more promises."

"Thank you," I whispered without looking up.

His sigh was audible, "You need a place to stay tonight?"

I nodded slowly, "I'm sorry. I couldn't think of any place else to go. If it's not okay with you, I'll just go back to my parents' house."

"No, you're welcome to stay here as long as you like. Actually, I prefer that you do." I glanced up at him and found his eyes back on my neck. His jaw tensed and I swallowed.

"Why do you keep staring at my neck?"

"You haven't seen it?" he asked, surprised. "Go look in the mirror." He pointed down the hall, and I slowly stood up, heading in the direction he pointed. The short hallway had three doors, I could see into the last door to a bed, so I assumed one of the other two was the bathroom. A door to the right stood open, and I peeked in to find it was indeed the room I wanted. I stepped inside, flipping on the light switch. The lamps above the sink shed light on the brown linoleum floor and white fixtures. Two beige bath towels hung from the towel rack on the wall, but the décor didn't interest me. I turned to the rectangular mirror above the vanity.

I wasn't prepared for the perfect purple marks that were already starting to appear on my neck, four marks on one side and one on the other, exactly the size and shape of fingers. Tears filled my eyes again.

My line of vision changed as Mark stepped in behind me, meeting my return reflection. His eyes looked pained, annoyed, and hurt all at the same time. His hand reached out, slipping the hair off my shoulder and around to the back of my neck so he could better see where the four finger marks stared back at us.

With his pained gaze still holding mine, he leaned forward and gently kissed each mark. My pulse increased with each kiss, the tender touch of his lips on my skin caused my heart to thud in my chest.

I was speechless while watching his reflection; Mark had never touched me this way before. While always friendly towards me, there had never been a reason to think he might want something different from me. I stood perfectly still; his reflection spoke volumes to me as the color of his irises deepened into a darker shade. Something akin to shock crossed my mind when I recognized an emotion I had never expected to come from him. I saw passion.

Was I wrong? Maybe he was only trying to make me feel better, like a mother kissing her child's hurts. I watched him and somehow knew it was more than that. My body swayed as his tongue slid up the sensitive skin over the bruises. They did ache slightly, but with his added touch, they felt on fire.

When I swayed, he stepped closer to me, leaning his solid body against my back. Slipping an arm around my waist he moved his mouth to my ear, gently biting my lobe. A small gasp escaped my lips as he teased my ear with his tongue, my hands no longer resting on the counter in front of me, but coming to the arm that wound around my middle.

He broke eye contact with me long enough to pull me around to face him. Pushing me gently against the countertop, he slid his hand down to the small of my back, watching me the whole time.

I raised my chin up; he was not much taller than my five foot five. His face was wide, balanced with strong cheek bones and full lips. Those lips were coming closer to me slowly; he slid his other hand to the nape of my neck and pulled me into him ever so gently.

The shock of this kind of attention from him was enough to weaken my knees. My hands rested on his strong biceps as he closed the gap between us, softly touching his lips to mine. My body leaned into him, wanting to soak up the attention he was giving me.

Without realizing it, I found myself comparing this kiss to how Steve kissed me. It was so different, not harsh like Steve's had become, but almost as demanding in a different way. I allowed the feelings to carry me away for a few moments. The sound of my stomach growling ruined the moment, and we both chuckled as we pulled back.

Maybe getting involved with another person right then wasn't my best idea, but the need to feel wanted and cared for outweighed the risk.

"I take it by the rumbling, you haven't eaten."

I shook my head, not trusting myself to speak.

"Come on, let's get you something. Your workout was intense, you need to refuel." Taking my hand, he pulled me out of the bathroom to the kitchen. As he led me down the hall, my mind raced in circles, trying to process what had just happened, but just going round and round finding no real answer.

I climbed onto the wooden stool at the kitchen island while he pulled out some food. My gaze panned over the kitchen that was devoid of any decoration. The words *bachelor pad* came to mind.

He fixed me a bowl of pasta, mixing in some canned tuna and peas. I was grateful that the food was soft and easy to swallow as the inside of my throat was starting to hurt. We sat on the couch watching television as I slowly ate. When I finished, Mark took my bowl back to the kitchen.

When he reappeared, he announced, "You'll sleep in my room; I'll sleep on the couch."

I shook my head. "No, I'm not kicking you out of your bedroom. I'll be more than happy to sleep on the couch."

"No, Amanda, I insist. You are sleeping in my bed." The way he said *my bed* made my face flush slightly.

"Mark, I really don't mind taking the couch, I'm putting you out enough as it is."

"If you decide to sleep on the couch, then you will be sleeping with me because that is where I'll be," he said it with a smirk on his face. I wasn't sure if he was joking or not, and I shifted slightly under his gaze. Even after the kiss we had shared, I didn't intend to sleep with him at that time, no matter what I felt when his lips had been on mine. I gave in and accepted the use of his room.

"I'll just grab my bag out of my car." I stood up and went to the front door without Mark saying anything further.

I walked over to my car, mulling over his comment about sleeping with him. Where was this coming from? Was he just kidding with me or was he serious? Even with what Steve had done to me, I wasn't opposed to his attention; I just did not expect it.

I didn't expect what I found on my car either. Walking to my driver's door, I noticed something on my windshield. I reached out to remove the slip of folded white notebook paper. I kept my back to the house as I opened the paper. Nausea washed over me when I saw the writing. My hands shook in time with my knees as I read the words:

I'm sorry. You need to come back home. We need to talk.

That handwriting was Steve's. Looking up quickly, I scanned the area to see if he was around. The street was quiet, soft lights shone from inside the other small houses on the block. A streetlamp lit the road, but I saw no cars that looked like his nearby. Nervous to be outside, I opened the car door, quickly pulling out my two gym bags from the back seat.

The hairs stood up on my arms. Was I being watched? I slammed the car door and turned, jumping back when I found Mark standing behind me.

"Oh my God, Mark, you scared me!" I dropped one of my bags, the note forgotten in my hand.

"Sorry. What's that?" he nodded towards the piece of paper.

"This? Oh—it's nothing, just trash from inside the car." I wadded up the note and pushed it into a pocket of my bag before he asked anything more.

He turned to allow me to walk past him back into the house. This would not be the last time I lied to hide something.

CHAPTER FOUR

AMANDA

*I*t felt weird sleeping in another man's bed. It wasn't the first time I had done it, I had slept at Steve's house several times, but to sleep in another man's bed alone felt odd. After what had transpired in the bathroom, I knew that if I asked Mark to sleep with me, he would, but I wasn't about to crawl from one relationship into another. I wasn't that stupid.

I woke up to noises coming from the kitchen and rolled over in bed thinking about what had happened the day before. The noises got louder in the other room, erasing the sleepy feeling from my mind. I climbed out of bed, dug through my duffle bag, pulled out a pair of sweatpants, slipped them on, and made my way down the hall. I smiled shyly as I entered the room, and Mark glanced at me over his coffee cup.

"Morning, Mandy, did you sleep alright?" His voice still husky from sleep, he shifted on the stool that was pulled up to his breakfast bar.

"Yeah, I actually slept better than I thought I would." I wasn't going to admit that his soft masculine scent all around me had lulled me into feeling secure, helping me sleep deeply. I put one arm over my head, the other out to the side, and arched my back stretching my stiff muscles. The hungry look that passed over his features had me turning my back to him; I was not comfortable with the way his eyes had taken me in. The image of a tiger devouring a piece of raw meat came to mind. I suppressed a shiver.

He cleared his throat, "Coffee cups are in the cabinet above the coffee pot."

I pulled one out and poured a cup, carrying it over to the counter near him and pulling out a stool.

"How's your neck feeling today?" he asked softly.

I shrugged and countered his question, "How's it look?"

His fingers slipped over my neck gently as he lifted the hair for a closer examination. "Looks like you should call in sick for a couple of days and take a break from your workout."

I had thought about skipping work, but not my routine. "Why shouldn't I work out? That won't affect my neck."

"No, it shouldn't affect your workout, but I think you should stay away from anywhere Steve might be for a little while."

That made sense; the thought of running into Steve gave me slight nausea. I remembered the wadded up piece of paper in my gym bag. Had he followed me here, or did he just assume this was where I would go? Would there be another note there today? I tensed, suddenly dreading going out to my car. Mark must have taken my tenseness as confirmation that going to the gym wasn't a good idea.

"I gotta head to work, but I put a spare key by the front door. Keep the doors locked while I'm gone. I'll take a break from the gym tonight too and meet you here for dinner around five. How does that sound?"

"You know if neither of us shows up at the gym, people are going to talk." I smiled, trying to make light of the situation.

"Let them talk. I'd kind of like to know how they might feel about that." He leaned over to give me a small kiss on the lips. Surprised at his words, I accepted the simple kiss without comment.

Mark walked out the door shortly after, and I went to the fridge to see what he had to eat. I realized as I peered inside that this really was a bachelor pad, there wasn't much in the fridge: milk for his protein shakes, and some fruit and vegetables that looked slightly old and a bit wilted. Inside the freezer, I found frozen pancakes and some quick microwave meals, but not much else. I made a mental note to stop by the store to pick up some food. The least I could do was repay him for his kindness by picking up some groceries.

I took the phone receiver off the wall, stretched out the knotted cord so it would reach the stool, and dialed the number to work. It rang twice before Dee answered the phone.

"Hey, Dee, it's Amanda," I said quietly into the phone trying to sound sick.

"Wow, Amanda, are you feeling alright? Your voice sounds terrible." Dee jumping into mommy mode immediately did not surprise me, and I had to fight hard not to laugh. She was such a sweet older woman who constantly coddled everyone.

Either I was a pretty good actress or my voice really was messed up. "No, actually I've got a sore throat. I'm going back to bed. Can you let Jim know I'm not going to make it in and might be out tomorrow, too?"

"Sure. You need anything? I can run you over some medicine or soup or something at lunch." I remembered I was pretending to be sick before I gave myself away and laughed out loud.

"No, thanks. I just need to rest." I told her I would call her the next day and give her an update, and we said our goodbyes. One phone call down and one more to go. My shoulders slumped as I thought about making the second one.

I dialed my mother's phone number and felt lucky when I got the answering machine. After the recorder told me what to do, I quickly left a message that I would be staying at a friend's apartment for a few days because my place was being fumigated. Since Dad was allergic to cats, and I'd had to take Sally with me, I hoped she would accept that as a reason to go to my friend's instead of coming home. I finished up by telling her I would call her in a few days. I hated lying, but I wasn't ready to tell the truth.

Having gotten those two things out of the way, I decided I should get dressed and head back to my apartment to get a few more things. The thought of returning made me nervous, but I figured Steve would be at work so it would be no big deal.

The hot water of the shower relaxed the sore muscles in my neck and back. I wore my hair so that it hung down around my face and neck. I hesitated after closing the front door, afraid that I would find another note.

I looked cautiously over to my car and found nothing there. Releasing the air from my lungs, I locked the door behind me.

I became nervous as I walked to my car. I was exposed and hadn't realized how protected I'd been inside Mark's house. Once I stepped out of the door, my protection disappeared. Part of me felt silly, but, silly or not, I could not overcome my fear.

Safely inside my car, I pulled out of the driveway, relieved. The drive back to my apartment went quickly, and the parking lot was mostly empty. Glancing at my watch, I saw that it was almost ten in the morning; most people were already at work. I took a second to scan the parking lot just to make sure Steve's blue Ford Escort wasn't there.

The coast was clear, so I headed up the stairs to my apartment. With each step up, the air around me felt heavier, weighed down with tension. I opened the fire door and stopped midstep. The hallway was empty of people, but in front of my door sat three paper bags.

Maybe the bags contained things that I had left at Steve's house. I got closer and noticed something colorful in the top of one of the bags. A bright bouquet of flowers looking out of place in the dark, dirty hallway peeked out of the bag. I stood staring down at it like it would jump up and bite me. The other bags were filled with groceries, not my belongings.

"You choke me and then buy me groceries? What the hell?" I asked out loud of the dingy-colored walls. I contemplated what to do with the bags and noticed a piece of paper folded neatly inside one of them. I picked it up slowly, afraid to read the words, but not able to stop myself. It was the same kind of paper as before, so any doubt I had about who this was from vanished as my fingers trembled.

Hello baby... I miss you. I know you are sorry about last night, I am too. I picked up stuff for dinner tonight. I'll be over right after the gym to eat and then we can talk. I love you baby... see you then.

Sorry? You know I'm sorry? You asshole, I thought to myself. Not contemplating any longer, I snatched up all three bags and walked back down the stairs, right out the door to the parking lot. I briefly considered putting them into the car and saving myself a trip to the store, but I didn't trust Steve one ounce. Instead, I made my way to the large green commercial dumpster, flipped open the top, and threw in all three bags.

Walking back up to my apartment, I felt vindication for what I had done. I unlocked my apartment door and stepped in, stopping to pick up the knife I had dropped the night before. On the coffee table sat the bread, now hard as a rock. I picked it up, threw it in the trash, and poured the noodles and sauce down the garbage disposal.

After cleaning the kitchen and washing the few dishes, I ventured into my small bathroom and pulled out my makeup. I wasn't one to wear a lot, but I did have some. I found the concealer that I kept for my acne breakouts and spread it sparingly over the bruises on my neck. It wasn't perfect, but at least they didn't stand out quite as much.

Packing up a few things, I looked around my apartment. Four months ago, I had been so excited to be on my own. Now that excitement was gone, and I wished that I still lived at home.

I left the apartment shortly after and knew that the next time I came back, it was going to be to pack up and move out permanently. Storing my things in the hatchback of my car, I climbed into the driver's seat and went in the direction of the nearest grocery store.

It was a quick shopping trip just to pick up a couple simple meals. People who exercised like we did consumed large amounts of protein and carbs, so pasta and chicken were always good things to have around. Throw in a sauce of some kind and a veggie, and you were good to go.

I crossed over the hot parking lot, pushing my cart towards my car. As I thought about cooking dinner for Mark, a smile came to my face as I recalled the kiss we had shared the day before and the comment about people talking. Was this the start of something with him, I wondered, or was he merely trying to make me feel better?

I stored the groceries in the hatchback next to my two gym bags and then went to unlock my door. I froze as I glanced at the windshield. A single red rose and note lay against the hot glass. My heartbeat filled my ears and my knees shook. I looked around immediately. Where was he? Was he watching me? Had he seen me throw away the groceries? On the verge of panicking, I looked back at the flower, afraid to touch it, afraid that it would somehow poison me if I did.

A bead of sweat ran down the back of my neck. I absently followed the sensation as it tickled my skin until it finally hit the collar of my T-shirt. Swallowing heavily, I reached for the note. Unfolding it slowly, I tried to remember to pull in oxygen that I needed to remain standing.

The words leapt from the page as I read them.

Did I forget something when I went shopping? You passed me on the road and I tried to catch up to you, but you were already in the store. Thought I would rather surprise you with a flower to let you know I am thinking about you. Can't wait for dinner tonight, see you then. I love you...

The paper fluttered in my hands as they shook. I dropped the note to the ground and snatched the flower, throwing it next to the piece of paper, stomping on them both. I unlocked my car door and climbed in quickly. I drove straight back to Mark's house without even turning on the air conditioning. By the time I got back, my mind was in turmoil. I could not say if the sweat on my body came from my nerves or the hot interior of the car

Taking the key out of the ignition, I grabbed everything and managed to get it all into the house in one trip. I kicked the door shut behind me and flipped the lock with the tips of my fingers. I set everything on the floor in the living room, and then I sank down onto the couch with my face in my hands.

What am I going to do? How am I going to get away from him? Is he going to keep following me everywhere I go? How do I get the point across that it is over? So many questions swirled in my mind.

The phone rang, startling me; my pulse beat heavily in my ears as I made my way into the kitchen to answer the phone. I brought it slowly to my ear, afraid that it might be Steve.

"Amanda! Where have you been? Why didn't you answer the phone?" Relief filled me as Mark's voice came over the line. The tension in my shoulders relaxed as I heard the concern in his voice.

"I was out. I ran back to my apartment and then I went to the store. I'm fine," I lied, hoping my voice didn't rat me out.

"You shouldn't have gone back to your apartment alone. You sure you're okay?" he asked and his voice calmed down.

"Yes, Mark, I'm fine. Are you still going to be home around five? I picked up some chicken, pasta, a pesto sauce, and fresh salad fixings."

"Yeah, I'll be home around then. I just wanted to check and make sure you were okay. You don't plan on going out again, do you?" he sounded worried, but not as worried as I was at the thought of running into Steve again.

"No, I think I will relax on the couch and just watch T.V."

We said our goodbyes and I unpacked the groceries. Once finished, I settled into the soft plush sofa and turned on the T.V., flipping through channels until I found a rerun of *I Love Lucy*.

Sometime during the afternoon of watching old programs, I dozed off. I woke up to find the room growing dark and heard a noise in the house. Not totally awake yet, my mind went wild with visions of Steve being there. The nerves in my body stretched taut as I listened for more sounds.

Water running and footsteps on the linoleum told me the noises came from the kitchen. I sat up slowly, looking over the top of the couch. At the sight of Mark's back in front of the stove, I fell back onto the cushion with relief.

The VCR next to the television showed the digital time of almost five-thirty. I couldn't believe how long I'd been out. I wiped my eyes with my fists, trying to clear the rest of the sleep away and sat up again. Mark either turned around or heard me because he called out from the kitchen.

"Hey, sleepyhead, you want to come help me cook dinner?"

Smiling, I got up and walked into his small, country-style kitchen. "How long you been home?" I walked over to a stool and sat down, looking around at the pale blue walls while trying to shake the cobwebs from my sleepy brain. The bright overhead kitchen light made me blink a few times until my eyes adjusted.

"About twenty minutes. I got out a bit early. You were sleeping, so I jumped into the shower real quick." He pulled the chicken breasts out of the package and dropped them into a bowl of egg wash. I watched as he pulled the pieces out and put them into a bowl filled with bread crumbs before placing them on a foil-lined metal cookie sheet.

Nodding absently, I climbed off the stool to get the salad ingredients ready. As I came back to the counter with my hands full, I could see Mark watching me out of the corner of my eye. I put all the items on the counter and smiled at him.

He stepped closer to me, so I turned, putting my back to the counter. He put his hands on both sides of me, trapping me between his body and the counter. As he looked down at me, I began to feel uncomfortable and shifted my weight. His hands went from the countertop to my hips.

This attention from Mark was still unexpected despite the events of the evening before. Sure I had fantasized about him, but that was just it, a fantasy. The fact that he had never shown this kind of interest in me before certainly contributed to my discomfort. Not knowing what he was thinking only made it worse. I wanted to ask him what this was about, but my lack of confidence held me back.

He leaned in and kissed me, taking me by surprise yet again. It started off slowly but quickly deepened to become much more than I had antici-pated. He leaned into me, pushing me harder against the counter. My hands rested on his biceps as he wrapped his arms tightly around my waist. The heat of his body enveloped me. I found myself questioning it at the same time that my body responded to it, my breathing coming faster and heavier to match his. The grin on his face when he stepped back appeared secretive. Did he know something that I didn't?

Turning back to the stove, he put the chicken into the oven without saying a word. I couldn't tear my eyes from him at first; I took in the wide shoulders and the way the muscles rippled on his back under his T-shirt. Finally pulling my gaze away, I turned back to make the salad.

What was up with the kisses? I thought. Did he really like me? I had always thought of myself as more of a little sister or a friend to him. Maybe he thought more about me than I had originally considered. I smiled happily as I threw in the cucumber slices. Maybe I had found a guy worth it. Maybe all that had happened with Steve was fate to bring me here. I turned to look over my shoulder. Mark was leaning back on the counter, water glass in hand, watching me intently. I dropped the carrot pieces into the salad and smiled. The smile he returned, while gentle enough, caused the hair to rise on the back of my neck just slightly.

If only I had learned how to understand my body's instincts early on in life, what a difference it might have made.

CHAPTER FIVE

NICOLE

There is always a sense of nervous excitement the day you start a new job. You hope that you like it; you know you want to be able to do it well. I had an additional worry: Most people didn't have the added stress of knowing that they had the right to take away a person's freedom.

I drove into my official first day of work; the butterflies in my stomach fluttered wildly. I wasn't sure why I was so jumpy, I had been riding along with one of the guys for months. Todd had been training me since I had started, and I rode with him twice a week for almost six months. I pretty much knew the streets, knew the paperwork, and could understand what they were actually saying on the radio, which was a feat in and of itself. Plus, I knew how to actually respond properly when I was called.

Even knowing all these things, this would be the first day that I climbed into a patrol car, closed the door, started the engine, and logged onto the computer all by myself. I could drive wherever I wanted in my township. I could stop any cars that drove along the roadway with equipment violations or which were disregarding traffic laws. I could put my own brand-new, shiny cuffs onto a subject that had broken the law, and I could help that person in need.

I pulled up to the garage where we parked the patrol cars and took a deep breath, closing my eyes. "God, keep me safe today and allow me to go home when my shift ends." I nodded to no one and climbed out of the car.

I walked into the garage through the side door and pushed the button that would roll up the door to open the garage. There stood the white Ford Crown Vic Police Interceptor with blue striping to which I was now officially assigned. A light bar extended over the roof of the car fit with red, blue, and yellow flashing lights. Reaching out, I gently touched the top of the door near the roof, just making sure it was really there.

"You going to make out with it or drive it?" a voice from behind me made me jump.

"Todd! Thanks for scaring the crap out of me!" I shook my head, but laughed when he started snickering at me. I guess I did look pretty stupid rubbing the car.

"Well, you ready, Nic?" Todd asked as he came closer. I looked at him and, while I knew I was a rookie, for the first time I felt like an equal and not just a recruit learning the ropes. Not that I knew even a quarter of what there was to know about this job, but being in the same uniform made me feel like somehow I was on my way.

I smiled widely at him and reached back to pull the door handle open. "You bet I'm ready!" I climbed into the car, reaching for the keys that sat in the center console. After starting the car, I got the radio turned on, the computer booted up, and adjusted the seat.

I put the car in gear and grinned. Todd stood watching me, laughing at me as the car rolled out of the garage.

He closed the garage and then walked over to my car. I rolled my window down so I could talk to him, I could have gotten out, but now that I was in the driver's seat, I didn't want to leave.

"So now what do I do?" I asked him as he stopped next to my door.

He chuckled. "Whatever you want, Nicky. Just don't forget to answer your radio and go to your calls—and whatever you do, don't crash the car, okay?" He raised his eyebrows as he spoke, looking at me over the rim of his sunglasses.

The thought of crashing my patrol car on my first day made me sick, "I'll try, Todd."

"Go! Go drive around." He slapped his hand on the roof of the car, and I didn't hesitate any longer.

Wow! I thought to myself as the heavy eight-cylinder engine kicked in as I put my foot on the pedal. "Damn, this thing has some power!" I said to no one.

Within a few miles, I got used to the power and didn't feel like I was out drag racing anymore. Good thing I was in a patrol car, otherwise someone might have pulled me over for being an erratic driver.

I drove the streets, smiling and waving at the people that honked and waved at me. For the first time in a long time, I felt like I really belonged.

A couple of hours went by as I patrolled around, the radio remained quiet in our area. I passed Todd a few times and did the two-finger wave from the steering wheel. He hit me up on the Nextel a few times to make sure I hadn't gotten lost, and I told him not to worry about that. All the miles I had ridden as a passenger in his car had engraved the roadways into my memory.

My Nextel beeped again, "Hey, Nicky, you ready for some lunch?" He asked over the speaker of our two-way cell phones.

"Sure. Where are we going?" I responded back by pressing the button on the side of the phone.

"Let's head over to Robert's Deli."

I acknowledged him and clipped my cell phone back into the hard plastic holder on my duty belt.

When I got to the deli, he was already there, so I made my way in to meet him. He was seated at a small table in the back corner facing the entrance. It was no surprise that he sat that way. There are few cops who ever want to sit with their backs to the doorway. I guess I would have to rely on him to "watch my back" as we ate our lunch.

No sooner had we ordered than the speaker on my lapel mic keyed up and called out my unit number, "Thirty-Seven Paul Three."

My eyes grew wide and Todd looked at me like, *Well, are you going to answer it?*

I smiled and reached for the mic, "Thirty-Seven Paul Three."

"Thirty-Seven Paul Three, you have an alarm at the Prairie Middle School, 460 Martin's Road, coming from the rear kitchen door's motion."

The male voice coming over the radio was steady and smooth as it gave out the location and information about the call.

I acknowledged back as professionally as I could, "Thirty-Seven Paul Three, copy. I'll be en route." I smiled at Todd, he winked, and we both stood up at the same time.

Todd called out over the counter, "Bag up the sandwiches. We will be back in a few minutes to grab them."

We both exited and walked to our cars. Eager anticipation to finally do my job mixed with anxiety in my belly; I climbed into my car after a deep breath.

Todd and I drove down the road about two miles, pulled up and around to the back of the school. I was in front and pushed the button on my computer to let the dispatcher know that I was on location. I knew Todd had done the same thing when a beep came from my computer.

The activation had come from a door that was now standing open. My body tensed as I wondered if the person who had set off the alarm was allowed to be there.

We exited our vehicles quietly, walking to the door side by side. We both stopped when we heard a noise coming from the inside. Todd looked down at me and held a finger in front of his lips, he moved a few more steps closer to the door.

My heart beat heavily against my chest bone as I followed. As he reached the door, he drew his firearm and peeked inside the door. My hand rested on my gun as he stepped into the door and stopped.

"Hey, Peter, what are you doing here?" Todd spoke, holstering his gun. Obviously, he knew the guy. I stepped in behind him as the man replied.

"Todd. Hey man. I know, I know, I set off the alarm and forgot the passcode to turn it off right away. I needed to pick something up that I left here. Sorry."

"Not a problem. Just make sure you remember your code next time." They spoke for a few minutes as I stood there listening. During the conversation, the dispatcher had asked our status, and I replied that we were okay.

Climbing back into our cars, we moved to exit the parking lot heading in the direction of the deli. I pulled out onto the roadway when it was clear enough to do so. Being a cautious driver, I glanced in my rearview mirror and noticed a car flying up quickly behind me. The vehicle obviously was driving faster than the speed limit to catch up to me.

My foot lightened on the accelerator, I looked in my rearview mirror again. The driver was young and he was dancing around in his car, weaving on the roadway as he moved with the music. The heavy bass reached me in my own car as the hood of his car was only ten feet behind mine, way too close to be safe.

"Dude, are you stupid? What are you doing riding a cop's bumper like that?" I said to myself. I unclipped my cell phone from my belt to hit up Todd.

"Do you see this guy on my ass?" I spoke into the speaker.

"Kind of hard not to since he is trying to sit in the back of your car. What do you want me to do about it?"

"Pull the car over, I'll swing back around and give him a ticket for following too closely."

"You got it," he replied, and before I could think of slowing down, his lights flipped on and his siren whooped once to get the driver's attention.

I watched as the driver sat up straight and looked in his rearview mirror. His shoulders slumped as he realized a police car was behind him, and a chuckle escaped my lips.

Todd pulled the car over, and I turned around in a driveway to come back to him. I did a U-turn in the middle of the road and pulled in behind him. Todd sat in his car waiting for me before he called out the traffic stop over the radio to our dispatcher. Todd gave them our location and the license plate of the vehicle.

As I approached Todd on foot, he smiled, "It's all you, girl. Go for it." I took a deep breath, hiking my eyebrows at him in a nervous gesture as I walked past. My first traffic stop. Here goes nothing, I thought as I made my way towards the driver's door.

In the few steps it took me to approach the car, I ran through all the training I'd received: how to approach safely, how to keep my eyes open, how to speak, and what to say. It all swirled through my mind quickly, yet it did nothing to squelch the nerves that ran through every piece of me as I got closer.

"What's up?" the guy said as I approached the window. Okay, I wasn't expecting that.

"Um." I blinked a few times, trying to remind myself of what I needed to do. "Sir, I'm Officer Nolan, were you not aware that you were following a marked patrol car just now?"

"Yeah, I saw ya. I was just jamming to my tunes, is all." I noticed that he was wiggling a little bit in his seat; I thought he might have to go to the bathroom. This movement would come to mean something else to me as I grew into my job.

"Sir, can I see your license, registration, and proof of insurance, please." It wasn't a question, it was a command.

He continued to be-bop in his car, opening the glove box and rooting around in it before pulling out some papers. I glanced at Todd; he stood on the other side of the car. He was watching the guy closely as he moved around inside.

The driver handed me the paperwork, and I told him to stay where he was. I stepped back to the trunk where Todd met me.

"I know this kid, he's a punk," he said to me.

I just nodded, not sure what to say to that and walked back to my car to run his information.

As I sat down in my car, I looked up and watched as Todd pulled open the driver's door, grabbing the kid by the arm. My body went immediately tense. I totally forgot for a moment that I should be doing something. I finally snapped out of it as Todd pushed the kid up against the car. I jumped out of my car, quickly making my way back to him.

Todd looked at me as I approached. "Put your cuffs on him."

My eyebrows lifted high over my eyes. I wanted to ask, What the hell for? Instead, I reached behind me and pulled my cuffs out of my pouch. The snap was stiff; I had to pull hard to release it. With a loud pop, the cover of the case opened, and I grabbed the cold metal with my fingers.

"He's got a bottle of open alcohol behind his seat and a chunk of marijuana up on his dashboard," Todd spoke as I put the first cuff on the guy's wrist with shaking hands.

"What?" My head snapped up.

He pointed to the dashboard. Right there in plain view lay a little pile of a leafy green substance I recognized quickly as marijuana. Damn, I missed that, I chided myself. How did I miss that? Todd pointed behind the driver's seat. Another mistake I made: not looking behind the seat when I approached the vehicle. My attention had been solely on the driver, not the interior of the car. I'd say it was a blond moment, but I'm a redhead, so I chalked it up as a rookie moment.

I shook my head at myself, snapping the second cuff around the kid's wrist.

"Go put him in your car and advise dispatch you have one in custody for Act 64," Todd said.

I did as I was told. Just as I closed my rear door, Todd walked up to me, "I'll go grab our sandwiches and meet you back at the station. Wait here for the tow to arrive, I already called them, then take the kid back to the station and lock him to the bench. I'll be there five minutes after you to help with the paperwork."

I acknowledged Todd with a tip up of the chin as he turned to walk away. I was embarrassed that I had missed not only the alcohol but the drugs, too. I knew it would not be the first time I would miss something, but as I sat in my car waiting for the tow truck to arrive, I swore I'd make sure to observe my surroundings better the next time.

CHAPTER SIX

AMANDA

I woke up the next morning to find that Mark had called off from work. He said he took a vacation day; since work wasn't too busy they let him have it.

The bruises on my neck were getting better, but not well enough for me to head back to work myself. I thought it would be fun to just hang out with Mark and enjoy the day as he suggested.

We ended up heading out to a nearby lake, a place that I loved to visit and just relax. We took my car because Mark decided he would drop his car off for an oil change.

As we pulled down the dirt road to the parking lot, I noticed that there weren't many cars. I kept forgetting that most people were at work. I found a parking spot right next to the trail that led us down the walking path to the fishing bridge and the big rocks that jutted out along the water.

We walked down the trail side by side, and Mark reached over to take my hand. It felt nice to have my fingers intertwined with his, I smiled at him. Still in awe of his attention, I kept peeking at him from the corner of my eye. I wasn't sure why an older and very attractive man like Mark would want an average-looking younger woman like me. He could have anyone he wanted, why not someone more sophisticated and mature? What could he really see in me?

When we got down to the fishing bridge, we found four people out on the end with their lines cast into the water. We decided to walk along the edge of the water a little ways and find a quieter spot. We settled upon some huge flat rocks that pushed out from the bank. We kicked out our legs and leaned back next to each other.

I tilted my face up to the sun, enjoying the warmth of the rays on my skin. It was another warm summer day, but not as hot as it had been. We talked about silly things, his job and mine and lifting weights. Every once in a while we kissed and held hands. He pulled me closer to him at one point so I could rest my back against his chest. Contentment grew in my body, and it felt good to forget everything else that had happened the last couple of days.

After a couple of hours of sitting, both of us not only had sore butts, but stomachs that were competing for the loudest growl.

We made our way back up the trail, talking over where we would eat. Mark had me laughing about something that happened at work when we reached the parking lot. The laughter died in my throat as I looked at my car.

On the windshield, tucked under the windshield wiper, was a piece of white paper. I didn't need to look any closer to know its source. Mark stopped when he realized I was no longer walking beside him. He looked back at me and then followed my line of vision. Before I could think to move, he made his way to my car and yanked the paper off.

I should have run to get the new note, I should have pulled it off before Mark saw it, but I didn't, and it was in his hands. Dread washed over me.

He unfolded the note, looking up at me when he was done. I still hadn't moved, afraid to ask what it said, even more concerned when I saw the look on his face.

"How many times have you gotten notes on your car?" his voice was low and deadly.

How did he know there were other notes? "Who is it from?" I asked, trying to pretend I didn't already know. I walked cautiously towards him.

"You know exactly who it is from, Amanda. How many other notes?" His shoulders were squared off and seemed wider than normal. The muscles on his chest strained against his T-shirt, and his biceps bulged as he crossed his arms, waiting for my response.

I reached for the note. He pulled it out of my reach. "No, not until you tell me how many notes."

I sighed. "Two, well, three if you count the one at the apartment," I said quietly, looking away from him.

"Three notes! He left one at your apartment? Okay, I can understand that one. Where did he leave the other two?"

I blew my breath out in a burst. "When I went back to my apartment there was a note along with three bags of groceries. I threw them all away." I glanced at him, but looked away quickly when I saw the dark green irises boring into me.

"And the other two?" he asked when I didn't answer his question right away.

"The night I came to your house, when I went out to my car to get my gym bag, there was one on the car then."

"That son of a bitch was at my house! I'll kill him." He closed his eyes for a second, inhaling deeply. "What about the third one?"

"Yesterday, when I went to the grocery store; I came outside to find a note along with a rose." I looked down at the ground, kicking a rock with the toe of my shoe.

"So he's stalking you now. This isn't good, Amanda. You need to call the police." He started to walk around the car.

"No! Wait! I can't call the police. My parents will find out about it, everyone will find out about it." I reached out and grabbed his arm as he tried to pass me. Hysteria rose in me.

"Read this one and see if you change your mind." He thrust the note towards me. I took it slowly.

As usual, my hand trembled as I held the paper in front of me, the familiar handwriting dark and scrawled.

You cheating slut! No one gets you! You got that! If you aren't with me then no one gets you! You'll be dead before someone else gets you! You should have come home when I first told you to. You can't ignore me, Amanda. I won't go away.

Cold chills raced down my spine as tears crowded my eyes, threatening to spill over.

"See? Now you need to call the police. This guy is threatening your life!"

"No, Mark, I can't. Look, I just can't go to the police. They won't believe me, and besides I don't have any of the other notes."

"Where are they?" he asked me quickly.

"I threw them out. I didn't want them around. I know that was pretty stupid. *Now* I know that was pretty stupid!" Closing my eyes, I tried to tame the quaking of my body.

"Fine. You don't want to go to the police? Then I'm going to take care of it myself."

I glanced up at him. The look on his face scared me, but not as much as telling my parents.

I nodded. "I don't want to know, don't tell me. Just don't kill him."

"Mandy, I won't kill him, but when I'm done with him, he'll wish he was dead." He walked away, climbing into the passenger seat of my car.

We drove back to his house in silence, the thin piece of white paper resting on the console, a bad omen in the space between us. A heavy weight settled over my heart and mind, our relaxing afternoon all but forgotten.

When we arrived at the house, he went straight to his bedroom. I didn't know what he was doing. Obviously he was still angry, so I left him alone. Walking down the hallway to the bathroom, I heard him talking. I assumed he was on the phone since he didn't seem like the type to talk to himself.

I couldn't make out what he was saying and I was afraid to lean my ear up against the door. I shut myself into the bathroom and looked in the mirror. My blue eyes were large in my face and my hair hung down straight over my shoulders. I looked very young and very scared as I searched the reflection looking back at me.

Oh God, what had I just done? What was Mark going to do? His deep green eyes haunted me as I stared down my own reflection. I could just tell him that I had changed my mind, that I was going to report it to the police after all. Maybe there was some way to keep it from my parents.

I could just imagine what they would think. My mother would cry and tell me she had told me so and that I wasn't careful enough. My father would be disappointed in me, I couldn't bear that. There had to be something else to do. I hung my head, my hair falling around my face like a curtain.

As I stood contemplating my choices, Mark opened his bedroom door. I pulled open the bathroom door just as he was about to knock, his gym bag hanging over his shoulder.

I stuttered, "Wh…where are you going?"

"I'm going down to the gym. I'll be back in about two hours. I want you to stay here, don't leave the house. Promise me you won't leave the house." He reached up, and with more gentleness than I expected, touched the side of my face.

"I won't go anywhere," I managed to squeak out. He leaned in, kissing me quickly once. I watched as he walked down the hallway to the door. I didn't move until I heard an engine start.

I ran to the front door and opened it just in time to see him put my car in drive and pull away from his house. I didn't even notice him pick up my keys as he walked past the table in the entry.

I paced the living room, tried to watch T.V., but nothing I put on could hold my attention. I walked from room to room looking out all the windows, not looking for anything, but having nothing else to do as the time dragged slowly by.

I should have gone to the police. I should have just pulled up my big girl panties and dealt with my problems. My mom would survive. She had survived her own abuse from her first husband, my father. She could tell me what to do. I debated on whether to call her or not.

I had just made up my mind to call when I heard a car door close. I jumped up, running to the door. Mark smiled as he came up the sidewalk.

"You know, I kind of like having someone here when I come home." He stopped when he reached me; I stared at him like he was crazy. How could he just walk up like there was nothing going on and say something like that?

I shook my head to clear my thoughts, "What happened?"

His gym bag landed on the concrete with a loud plop as pulled me into his arms. "Don't worry about it, Mandy." He kissed me with a smile on his face.

How could I not worry? I pulled back from him, "Mark, what happened?" I wanted to ask him what he'd done, but I couldn't vocalize the question.

"Amanda, don't worry about it. A couple of us gave him a message to stay away from you. He got the message." He chuckled, "He won't be coming near you again anytime soon." He reached down and picked up his gym bag, putting his arm around my back to lead me into the house.

What the hell did "gave him a message" really mean? Did I really want to know? I closed my eyes, probably not. Inhaling deeply, I walked into the house with Mark.

He seemed to be in a much better mood, and I sat in the kitchen watching while he cooked up some more pasta and mixed in tuna, a can of cream of celery soup, and vegetables. He pushed a bowl towards me. He kept on talking, not noticing that I just pushed the food around my bowl. I couldn't imagine trying to swallow food at that moment. The conversation was one sided as he shared news from the gym.

It wasn't long after dinner that I told him I was tired and climbed in bed. I couldn't handle the fact that he was in such a good mood. I kept waiting for the police to come and knock on the door. What had he done? Was Steve still alive? Could he have really killed him? Would he be happy if he'd really hurt him?

I knew something had happened; I was sure of it, and the fact that Mark was in such a good mood bothered me, seriously. How can someone hurt someone and then take some kind of perverse joy out of it?

I slept fitfully that night, with constant dreams of being chased and feeling like I was lost in the woods with no way out. When the sun started to rise, I was quick to get up and change into a pair of shorts and a T-shirt. I needed to burn off some of this pent up stress, so I put on my running sneakers and headed for the front door.

Just as I was about to walk out, I heard Mark rustle on the couch. "Where you going?" his voice was very deep, husky. Despite the stress I felt, I found myself drawn to the sexy sound of it.

I shook my head, "Just going for a quick run. I haven't worked out in a couple days, my body is feeling restless."

He chuckled. "Okay, go enjoy your run. You should be safe out there alone." He rolled over and pulled the covers up over his head.

I stared at his back for a minute, his words echoing in my mind. I opened the door and stepped out, the thought that maybe I would be safer outside than inside crossed my mind. I took off at a quick pace without even bothering to stretch, running from the demons I had created.

CHAPTER SEVEN

AMANDA

I returned to the house and found Mark in the kitchen drinking coffee. I walked past him, grabbing a few paper towels from the holder to wipe down my face.

"Have a good run?" he asked, glancing up at me before going back to the paper he was reading.

"Yeah, it was great. I really needed that." I leaned back against the counter. The run had done me wonders; I'd started to feel trapped inside with everything going on. Stretching my legs had brought my body and mind alive again.

"Good. I'm glad. Here," he pushed the paper towards me, "you might be interested in the article on the front page." A cynical smile played on his lips. I glanced at the paper, my heart dropping in my chest as I read the headline, "Freak accident at gym leaves one man in critical condition."

Oh my God, what had he done?

He was still smiling as I glanced up. I shivered inwardly. Swallowing, I looked back down at the paper. I was afraid to put my hands out while they were shaking, but I slowly reached for it anyway.

Sources say that at the Applebrook Gym yesterday around 5:00, an acci-

dent occurred in the upstairs free weight room. Steve Miller, age 23, was working out alone when he attempted to bench press over 400 lbs. The bar fell on his chest crushing his ribs, and then rolled up to his neck causing him to lose consciousness. Reports say that Miller is in serious condition because the bar pressed so tightly to his throat that it cut off air supply to his heart and brain before finally falling off to the side. It is unknown if there will be any brain damage to Miller from the accident.

Employees at the gym state that they always encourage people to work out in pairs and that no one should attempt to lift that much weight alone. They are looking into making it mandatory to have at least one other person present at all times in the free weight room.

I read the article twice before I could peel my eyes from the page. No longer was I sweating, my body had grown ice cold. Mark had a lopsided grin on his face.

"What did you do?" my voice but a soft whisper.

He laughed and then shrugged, "I didn't do anything. I can't help it if he was trying to show off and hurt himself." I straightened up as he climbed off his stool. "Mandy, you don't have to worry about it anymore. Trust me, he won't bother you again."

I stood completely still as he moved around to stand behind me, his hands now on either side of my hips against the counter. With my back to him, I felt his body push against mine, his breath on my ear as he leaned his face into my hair.

"He deserved it, Mandy. He will never come near you again, I promise you that." He kissed my neck after he spoke the words, an uneasy feeling started working its way through my body.

"Go take a shower. I have plans for you today," he said as he kissed my neck again, nibbling on my earlobe gently. He stepped away from me without another word. I left the room without looking at him. I couldn't help but wipe my neck where his lips had touched me as I turned the corner.

After entering his room, I closed the door, collapsing to my knees as they gave out. I knew what I read in the paper was wrong. Without a shadow of a doubt I knew Mark had had something to do with the so-called accident. It had not been a freak accident, it had been my fault.

Part of me was almost satisfied that he had been hurt, but I just couldn't think this was a positive thing. I never wished for anyone to ever get hurt. If Steve had just left me alone, then none of this would have happened.

I don't know how I managed not to break down into tears, but somehow I found the strength to get up and gather some clothes to take my shower.

Walking into the bathroom, I wondered what he had in mind for today. A glance in the mirror showed the bruises on my neck were healing nicely, more yellow than purple. By tomorrow I would be able to cover them up with makeup. I would still keep my hair down to help hide them. I finished my shower and was slipping on my shorts when the bathroom door opened suddenly.

I pulled them up quickly, glancing over my shoulder. "I'm getting dressed." He leaned lazily against the door jamb.

"Don't bother. What we plan on doing today doesn't require clothing." He stepped closer, sliding his hands around my waist pulling my back to him.

What the hell was he talking about? Did he think I was going to have sex with him? I put my hands over his, trying to unpeel them from my waist. His grip tightened.

"What are you doing?" I spoke quietly.

He laughed. "You and me, Mandy, that's what I'm doing." He leaned in to kiss my neck. "I've wanted to do this for a long time, Mandy. You can't deny that you haven't thought about it, too."

Okay, so I had thought about it, even fantasized about it a little bit—well, maybe more than a little bit—but his sudden showing of interest concerned me. Had he not shown interest before because I was dating Steve?

I didn't know what to say, completely taken aback by this type of attention from him and with everything that had recently occurred. Part of me craved the attention from him, wanted someone to care about me. For some reason, I felt I needed love and was willing to lower myself to accept it under unusual circumstances. I quickly suppressed my inner voice and decided to go with the moment as it was obvious he cared about me. Letting me stay at his place and protecting me from Steve, he had to care about me.

His lips moved along my neck with a new intensity that he'd not exhibited before, his hands held me tightly against his body. He turned me around, laying a kiss on me that left me breathless.

Mark broke it off and winked at me, "Come on." He took my hand, leading me into the bedroom. As we got to his bed, he turned around to face me, pulling me into his arms once again.

He pulled me down to the bed with him, my body covering his. Rolling me to my back, he kissed my neck and slid his hands down to my chest. Since he had interrupted my dressing, he had instant access to touch my breasts. He was quick to slide his hands down further, and even though I wasn't completely comfortable with what was happening, I let it proceed.

I supposed I should have been thankful that someone as popular as Mark wanted to be intimate with an ordinary girl like me.

It wasn't long before we were both naked, and he entered into me. I stilled as he filled me. "Relax, Amanda," he huskily whispered in my ear. I tried to, but he was large and the pain as he moved inside of me caused me to tense.

Although I had been sexually active for several years, I was by no way comfortable with the act. To me, it was just something that two people did together, something men wanted more than women.

Mark moved in and out, I kept my eyes closed and held on to him tightly, burying my face in his shoulder, wondering if this time I might experience what others talked about. I didn't know what an orgasm really was, I had never had one, no one had taken the time to bring me there.

As Mark finished, the experience remained the same as in the past, I wondered if maybe I just couldn't. I can't say I was disappointed because I didn't have any idea what I was missing.

Once he finished, he rolled off to the side. His eyes closed, his breathing heavy, his hand resting on my thigh. I watched him. I wanted to say something, but no words came. I remained quiet, silently observing him.

Within a few minutes I realized he must have fallen asleep, his breathing slowed, his body stilled. I took my time to look him over. His chest was wide, with swirls of light blond hair, abs that were incredibly defined. He had the perfect upper body; my eyes drew lower, I couldn't help but blush as I took in the sight of him.

I looked away afraid he would wake up and see me checking him out. I silently wondered again where all this had come from. Mark had always been friendly, but he had never said or even looked like he wanted more from me.

He continued to lie there quietly; I scooted to the edge of the bed, deciding that I would go clean up. I hated the way my body felt after sex. Mark's hand grabbed my arm just as I was about to stand up. "Where are you going?"

"I thought you were sleeping. I was just going to clean up," I remarked embarrassedly.

"I'm not done with you yet." He opened his eyes and smiled another lazy smile. I allowed him to pull me back down.

"Roll over on your stomach," he said as he came up on his elbow.

"Why?" I asked hesitantly.

He chuckled, "Because that's how I want you, now roll over."

I did as he said, rolling over, turning my head so I could see him. He leaned over, kissing me as I rose to my elbows to meet him. Breaking away from the kiss he got on his knees and put his hands under my hips, lifting my buttocks up into the air towards him.

I found myself on my hands and knees, the tip of him sliding against me. I was slick from our previous episode, and he slid right inside. I gasped immediately at how deep he was able to go this way. He groaned behind me as he slid in and out slowly.

"You are so tight, Mandy, so damn tight." He gripped my hips firmly, curling his fingers around my pelvic bone, and slammed into me hard. I moaned, but it wasn't from pleasure.

He slammed into me over and over again, the pain started to fade, and I started to feel some small amount of pleasure. I relaxed, wanting to enjoy it. The moment was short-lived as he finished.

He let go of my hips and bent over me, resting his face on my back, his heart beating fast and hard against my skin. Droplets of sweat ran off his body and onto mine. I drew from his body heat, savoring it until he opened his mouth to speak.

"That was perfect payment." He slipped out of me and fell back on the bed again.

Payment? Payment for what? I looked at him totally confused. "What do you mean, payment?"

He laughed; a sound that I would forever hear in my head, hollow and merciless. "Payment for taking care of Steve for you. I gotta go take a shower and then I have to go meet someone." He got off the bed, my eyes stuck on the imprint his body left on the sheet next to me.

With the sound of the shower running, I curled in a ball. I had just been made to feel like a prostitute. I was a whore, no wonder I got no pleasure from it. Whores didn't get pleasure, they had sex for payment.

I pulled the sheet up to cover myself, curled in a fetal position, fighting back the tears. I wasn't sure how long I lay there before Mark popped his head into the room with a quick, "I'll see you later."

He turned around and walked out without another word. As the front door clicked closed, the tears began.

I cried quietly, thinking about how Steve had beaten me up, threatened to kill me, and then stalked me. Then Mark had used me, playing on my emotions to get what he wanted. There wasn't much difference to me. They had both hurt me.

I cried myself out then showered quickly. Just like after what Steve had done to me, I would never go back. I knew as I hurriedly packed up my things that I could not stay at Mark's house either.

I had no idea how long Mark would be gone; I wanted to be out of the house before he returned. I didn't even leave a note as I closed the door and ran to my car.

As my engine came to life, I wondered how I'd gotten myself into this. Shaking my head, I pulled out of the driveway deciding it was finally time to go home. I needed to be close to my mom.

CHAPTER EIGHT

NICOLE

"*W*ake up, Nicky," a soft masculine voice invaded my dreams. I felt my body being moved slightly. Was that a hand on my hip? Yes, that was a hand on my hip and that was Colton's voice in my dream, only it wasn't a dream.

I mumbled something to him, but even I didn't know what I was trying to say.

He chuckled softly into my ear, "You need to get up, Nicky. It's almost noon. We have to meet Tom and Suzanne at two." He kissed my neck gently. My hair was short so that it granted him easy access to my neck. Short hair was easy to deal with at work, no fuss of pulling it up or having it long enough for people to grab.

I groaned as he kissed my neck again. It was not a groan of pleasure, it was a groan saying, I'm tired leave me alone. I had gotten home late from work that morning. It had been almost seven when I'd walked into the door of my townhouse, and it took me a while to calm down enough to sleep. I had probably only gotten four hours.

Colton bit my neck playfully. I laughed, swatting at him. "You keep that up and I'm not getting out of bed at all and neither will you."

Colton had just moved in with me, about a year and a half after we'd started dating. I'd been in the police academy for a few months when a friend invited me to go to one of the local police picnics. Colton had been there with some guys from his department, and we connected in a way I had never imagined possible. When we weren't working, we spent the majority of our time together, but it wasn't unusual for us to go our separate ways and hang out with our friends. It was a natural relationship, something I never thought I would have.

I always told Colton it was his easygoing nature and positive outlook that helped to balance my constant need to control my own life. Always wanting to be one step ahead of the game and not allowing others to control my destiny had become of the utmost importance to me.

"Forget Tom and Suzanne, I like your idea better," Colton whispered in my ear. I put my arms around him and smiled as I met his bright blue eyes. I was lucky to have such an incredible man in my life: A man that valued the things I did, one that cared about people and cared about what he did when he went to work. I was so proud to have him in my life, and I prayed daily that things would continue to work for us.

"Come on, as much as we both want to stay here in bed, you know we need to go meet them. Did you by chance turn on the coffee?"

"Yes, and while you are in the shower, I will bring your mug up to you." Colton rolled away and walked towards the door.

"I love you," I responded.

"I love you, too. Now go get in the shower before I change my mind and join you." He walked out of the room with a smirk on his face.

I rolled over and buried my face in the pillow. I was so tired but knew I needed to get up. That was the hard part about working a night shift rotation. You get home at six or seven in the morning and get a few hours of sleep. Then the world expects you to get up and join in. I groaned as I pushed myself up.

The hot water along with the scent of strong coffee woke me up. I'd been doing this rotation for a while now, so I was used to it. I might complain about the sleep, but I actually enjoyed going back and forth between nights and days.

Colton and I left the house thirty minutes later, driving the forty-five minutes to meet up with Tom and Suzanne. We were heading to a wine festival for the afternoon. There would be live music and tons of wine with people lying around on blankets relaxing and socializing. It was something Colton and Tom enjoyed doing.

Suzanne and I did, too, but not as much as the men. Before we left, Colton packed a cooler full of cheeses, fruits, and crackers to go with our wine. We didn't need anything heavier since we would be sitting out in the sun all afternoon.

The day went great, the conversation fun. The sun was setting, and people were getting loud and rowdy from the hours of nonstop drinking. We all sat around, joking and laughing at the silly antics of people trying to talk, dance, and communicate in general.

I had stopped drinking hours ago. As the designated driver, I had switched over to soda after two glasses of wine. With only having a few hours of sleep, the decision was easy. If I had continued to drink, I would have been sound asleep already.

While we all relaxed with the music, a couple off to my left caught my attention. A woman stood talking to a man when another man came up to her grabbing her arm. She yelled at him as she yanked her arm free. He grabbed her again, this time trying to pull her away. She kicked him, he responded to that by backhanding her across the face.

That was all I needed to see. I jumped up off the blanket and went towards them. I called back over my shoulder to Colton to call 911. I saw him lift the phone up to his ear.

I was surprised he hadn't gotten up with me, but he was pretty intoxicated, so he probably realized he would be more of a hindrance than a help. Good for him, nothing like one drunken cop trying to deal with another drunk.

The two parties screamed at each other, the woman tried to turn away from the man again. He didn't like that very much; he ground his teeth, took a step forward, grabbed her arm and punched her in the face. Damn! The sound of his fist making contact with her cheek echoed in my ears as I got closer. She fell to the ground.

He got on top of her, sitting on her waist, holding her arms above her head; she tried to buck him off. He had her in weight by about eighty pounds, but if she had known what she was doing, she could have gotten him off. I got behind him and grabbed him in a choke hold. The element of surprise worked in my favor, he was easy to pull off and control.

Once he was off, I dragged him back a few feet; he squirmed trying to get free. Fortunately, he was intoxicated; otherwise this approach would not have worked quite so well.

About six feet from the woman, I let go of his neck, he fell to the ground. He grabbed his throat, sputtering. I hadn't done any damage, but he was playing it up.

"You wanna pick on someone, asshole, pick on someone who will fight back," I said as he looked up at me. "Yeah, not such a big man now, are you?" I continued. "Stay right where you are." The woman's face was red, the swelling had already begun.

Another woman came to her aide, smiling at me as we exchanged glances. By the way she checked over the woman, I figured she was in the medical profession of some kind. I stayed where I was, keeping an eye on the guy who was cursing me under his breath. Sirens could be heard in the distance, he decided to sit up; I stared him down when he tried to stand, his response only a huff and a few swear words.

The police arrived, moving through the crowd. I knew the responding officer and shook hands as they arrived, explaining quickly what I had witnessed. The woman refused an ambulance, saying she didn't want to press charges. I looked at the cop in front of me and told him to file. I would testify to what I had witnessed even if she wouldn't testify to what he'd done. He nodded back, handing me a business card.

He cuffed the guy and took him to his car. The woman came up to me and started yelling, "If you hadn't grabbed him by the neck, he wouldn't have done that." I blinked in surprise, staring at her.

"Are you serious?" I asked incredulously. "I grabbed him *after* he did that to you. I did it to keep him from killing you." I shook my head and began to walk away from her.

"Yeah, well, I was fine. He didn't hurt me. I could have taken care of that myself without the police," she yelled at my retreating back.

I turned one last time, "I am the police."

There were many different types of people in the world: The ones I had trouble stomaching were those that made excuses for people who were abusive. It was not unusual for the victims to make excuses for what happened to them, and it always frustrated me to see them defending their attackers. I wanted to shake them and tell them to wake up—wake up and run.

I walked back to my group and sat down. Colton gazed at me with glassy eyes. It was a good thing he had stayed seated. I wouldn't have been surprised if he couldn't stand straight when we got up to leave.

"You know that was really hot how you did that," he slurred towards me as I crossed my legs at the ankles and leaned back.

"Wow, you could see that far with your blurry vision?" I laughed.

They all joked about what happened, but I found myself pensive, ready to go home. The alcohol helped them find humor in it, but I just didn't, I never had. I continued to sit and look around, listening to them banter back and forth. Scanning the area, I found people looking my way. I tried to ignore them, but it seemed that every place I looked, people stared.

Sometimes they smiled, sometimes they looked away, and sometimes they glared. Finally, I was able to talk my friends up off the blanket, and they began floundering in the direction of the car. The wine, music, lack of sleep, and events of the day had taken a toll on me. I just wanted to climb into bed.

As we approached my car, I observed an older man stumbling to his car, trying without luck to unlock the driver's door. He was beyond intoxicated and fell into the range of obliterated. I unlocked the door to our car with the push of a button and then made my way over to the guy who was still working intently on his lock.

"Hey, you need some help with that?" I asked as I walked up to him.

"No. No, I'm fine," he slurred. When he looked up at me, he dropped his keys. My reflexes were much faster. By the time he looked to the ground, I already had his keys in my hands. He stared at the ground for a long moment, swaying back and forth. When he got around to looking back in my direction, his keys were snug in my pocket.

"Did you lose something?" I asked innocently.

"Where did my keys go?" he asked, the confusion evident on his face. "I just had them." He turned in a small circle; I put my hand out to steady him if he started to fall.

"I think you dropped them over there." I pointed to the other side of his car. Blinking rapidly, he moved to the other side of his car, one hand against his vehicle to keep him upright. I shook my head.

I pulled his keys from my pocket, unlocked the door, and tossed them onto the driver's seat, hitting the lock button on the inside. I closed the door before he saw me. He continued to search as intently as he could manage along the ground.

I watched him for a moment longer, shrugged, and walked away.

Yeah, I just cost this guy money to have a tow company come out to open his car door, but I probably just saved him from killing someone or getting thrown in jail for driving under the influence. To me, it was worth it.

Smiling to myself, I walked back to my car. No matter where I was or what I was doing, my badge was always in mind. Three hundred and sixty-five days a year, twenty-four hours a day, seven days a week, the badge was always there.

CHAPTER NINE

AMANDA

I went to my parents' house and found them gone for the afternoon. That was good. It gave me a chance to get settled. I needed to figure out what I would say to them.

A few hours later, the sounds of car doors closing raised the anxiety level in my body. Here goes nothing, I thought as I walked from my old bedroom. I went to the living room, sat down on the couch, and grabbed a magazine off the coffee table to hide my unease.

"Hey, Mandy, honey, what are you doing here? I've been calling you, where have you been?" My mother smiled as she walked into the house, dropping her humongous handbag on the side chair.

"Hey, Mom. Sorry, I was staying with a friend. They were fumigating my apartment," I cringed inwardly at my lies. "I left you a message. Hi, Dad."

"Hi, sweetheart. I saw in the paper about your boyfriend. What happened?" he asked as he walked into the room. Although he was my stepfather, he was the only man I had ever known as Dad. Seeing his strong wide shoulders made me want to throw myself into his arms. There was no safer place to be than there.

"He's not my boyfriend anymore. We broke up." I stood and went to hug my mother, hoping Dad would let it go.

"Well, good. I didn't think he was good enough for you anyway." He walked into the kitchen. Man, if he only knew, I thought.

"Are you okay, honey?" Mom asked me as she put her arms around me to return the hug. It took everything in me not to break down, but I managed to keep together.

"Yeah, Mom, everything's okay," I said quietly.

"If you want to talk about it, just let me know," she said just as quietly.

"Thanks, Mom." I squeezed her then let go. "Where have you guys been?" I questioned her to move the topic away from me.

From the stories my mother had told me, my biological father had been very abusive towards her, she had told me repeatedly to be careful of the men I dated, fearful that I might fall into the same trap into which she had fallen. There was no way I was going to tell her about my relationship with Steve if I didn't have to.

The question worked, and soon my mother filled me in on everything they had done the last few days. I took a deep breath, thankful they didn't notice the marks that were still faintly visible on my neck.

I gave up my apartment and moved back in with my parents. My life for the most part went back to normal. I went to the gym in the morning instead of after work, trying to avoid Mark.

A few people I bumped into from the evening crowd told me Steve had been released from the hospital without suffering any major medical problems. I was thankful for that, and even more thankful he had not contacted me. I was surprised that he had come back to the gym, I would have thought he would have moved to a different one, but I was told he still came every night and always worked out with a partner.

The only person who ever mentioned Mark to me was Robert from the front desk. He told me one day that Mark wanted to know if I was still a member. I shrugged and walked away without commenting.

It had been almost six weeks since I had last seen Mark. I still felt cheap and used by what he had done. It hadn't been enough for Steve to physically hurt me. Mark had followed Steve's abuse by slamming me down in a whole different way. I had been so vulnerable.

One morning soon after, I found myself absolutely starved even though I'd eaten a big breakfast after my workout. My job at the frame manufacturer was relatively easy. Stores that framed pictures called up and ordered their molding, I took their orders over the phone and entered them into the computer. I finished up the one I was working on and stood up to move around my desk.

All too quickly, the room began to spin; my body broke out in a cold sweat. Black seeped into my eyesight and, before I could do anything to stop it, I felt the floor hard on my knees as I came down.

I started to come around, hearing voices around me and sensing something cold on my forehead. I opened my eyes to find Anne, one of the other data entry clerks, sitting over me holding my hand and pushing an ice pack to my head.

"Hey you, you passed out," her voice spoke softly. I closed my eyes again as a wave of dizziness hit me. After a few deep breaths, I tried again.

"How are you feeling?" she asked quietly. I heard people moving around. A door opened and someone said, "She's in here."

I moved my head so I could see the door as two ambulance people walked into the room. One carrying a big blue bag looked down at me, the other pushed a stretcher.

"Oh, wow," I shook my head and tried to sit up. I winced at the pain in my head. I put my hand up to feel a bump. "Ouch," I said belatedly.

One of the medical guys bent his knees to come down to my level, "How do you feel?"

"Embarrassed," I answered him softly.

He chuckled. "Do you know what happened?" He took my chin in his hand and shined a flashlight into my eyes.

I blinked a few times to clear the bright light out of my eyes, trying to remember. "I was hungry and got up to get a snack. I guess I stood up too quickly and I passed out. I remember seeing nothing but black."

"Have you eaten today?" he asked as he put a blood pressure cuff around my arm.

"Yeah, I ate a big breakfast around eight-thirty when I got to work." I watched him pump up the cuff, feeling the squeezing of my muscles.

"Are you diabetic?" He glanced up at me as he pumped the bulb to inflate the cuff.

"No, not diabetic, but I am hypoglycemic." The cuff got bigger.

"You do know they go hand in hand, right?" His eyebrows went up.

"Yeah, but I only get it once in a while if I skip meals and work out too hard." I rubbed my arm after he pulled the cuff off.

"Your blood pressure is a bit high. How are you feeling otherwise?" He put the cuff down, picking up a clipboard and writing on it.

I shrugged, "Fine. My head hurts where I hit it, and I'm still hungry, but otherwise, I feel fine."

"Well, I think we should take you with us. We'll test your blood sugar in the ambulance and see if you need any glucose. You need to have your head checked anyway. You probably gave yourself a concussion when you fell." He stood up, turning to move the stretcher closer to me.

"Is that really necessary? I feel fine, I really do." I looked up at him.

"You can sign off against medical advice, but I think you better go get checked out."

"Amanda, you should go to the hospital and see a doctor," Anne coaxed me. She was still sitting on the floor beside me.

"I'm fine, see?" I pushed myself up and started to stand. The room instantly started to spin again, hands grabbed me from different sides.

"Yeah, you're fine alright. Lie down, Amanda, you're going to the hospital," the medical guy stated. The room started to blacken again, I closed my eyes. I allowed the EMTs to move me to the stretcher.

I groaned as I lay down, my eyes tightly shut. They buckled me onto the stretcher. Embarrassment burned my cheeks.

"I'll call your mom and let her know," Anne told me as they wheeled me to the waiting ambulance. I nodded but kept my eyes closed. The world still spun nauseatingly.

Once in the ambulance, I started to feel better. I could open my eyes and talk without spinning on the merry go round.

We arrived at the hospital, and I found myself wheeled into a room, a nurse immediately put in an IV. After asking me the routine medical questions, she took several vials of blood from my arm.

I waited to see the doctor, sitting back with my eyes closed, mortified to think that I had passed out at work. I had never done that before. Normally, my hypoglycemia was controllable; it came on much more slowly, slowly enough that I could do something about it. I needed to remember to eat more carbs after a hard workout. That would help.

Forty minutes after I had arrived, the doctor walked in. He asked the same questions again. He wanted to know how I felt, and I told him I was now starving. He smiled.

"I'm sure you are." He pulled up a rolling chair. He took a seat before he continued, "Your blood sugar is fine, a little low, but I'm not surprised."

"Not surprised, why?"

"Well, someone in your condition who has hypoglycemia will tend to have more problems with it around this time," he spoke cautiously.

I furrowed my brow, "My condition?"

"Amanda, did you know you are pregnant?" he spoke quietly, watching me for my reaction.

My mouth hung open as we locked gazes. What had he just said? No, there was no way. My mind raced. When was my last period?

"When was your last period?" he asked me as if he could hear the question in my mind.

"Um, I don't know? They aren't regular. Maybe two months ago, sometimes I skip a month." That was what I had told myself a few weeks ago when I didn't have my period. It's just one of those months; I blamed it on the stress of what I had gone through.

"Well, while you are here, we will go ahead and do an ultrasound to see if we can find out how far along you are." He paused for a moment. "Do you know who the father is?"

I swallowed. It had to be Mark, Steve always used a condom. I nodded slowly, tears stinging my eyes.

He put his hand on my shoulder. "Relax here for a little while; we will get the ultrasound machine ready for you."

I put my head back against the bed. I was pregnant. Oh, dear God! How had this happened to me? I was only nineteen, I couldn't raise a child. The tears slowly ran down my cheeks.

Alone, lost in my thoughts, I wondered what Mark would say. Maybe he would be happy. Maybe he would tell me that what he had said before was only a joke. Maybe he would tell me he loved me and that we would have the child and raise it together as a happy family.

By the time the nurse got there to wheel me to the other room, I convinced myself that everything would be fine. A pretty little picture was installed in my head: Mark and I walking through the park pushing a stroller in front of us.

The technician did the ultrasound, stating that I was about six weeks along. She asked if that made sense, I nodded. Of course it made sense. Six weeks ago was the first, second, and only time I'd had unprotected sex.

They discharged me shortly after, advising me to check in with my doctor soon. I walked out to the waiting room to find Anne there.

"What are you doing here?" I asked when she pulled me into a hug.

"I called your parents, but they didn't answer. I left them a message and figured, just in case they didn't get it, someone should be here to help you get home."

I hugged her back, fighting the tears as I did. Anne was a good person. "Thanks, Anne, I really appreciate this."

She gave me a ride to my car, and I made it home in time to erase the message from the answering machine before my parents got home. I didn't feel like explaining it to them yet.

Before I told them what was going on, I needed to talk to Mark and see what he had to say. I grabbed a gym bag from my room, slinging it over my shoulder. The best place to talk to him was probably at the gym.

With determination and a stomach full of butterflies, I climbed back into my car.

CHAPTER TEN

AMANDA

When I pulled into the parking lot of the gym, I found my palms damp and the butterflies on a rampage. I swallowed hard, climbed out of my car, and grabbed my gym bag. Mark's Ford sat on the other side of the parking lot.

Seeing his car did not make me feel better, it multiplied my apprehensive state by ten. Would he be happy to see me? Would he be upset to hear the news? I had no idea. I opened the front door, inhaling the scent of rubber mats and sweet sweat; it calmed me.

I made my way to the locker room, quickly changing into workout clothes for the second time that day. I didn't plan on lifting since I already had before work. My intent was to get on the treadmill and wait till he finished his workout.

As I walked out of the locker room, I kept my eyes trained on my feet and bounced off someone. Before an apology got out of my mouth, I felt the wall against my back. My eyes flew to the face of the man in front of me, my breath lodged in my throat as I looked into Steve's hate-filled eyes.

Fear like I had never felt coursed through my body, quickening my heart. My hands lay flat and stiff against the cold cement wall. I couldn't speak. I could only stare into the darkness of the brown before me.

He stepped closer, his jaw clenched tightly. I thought maybe I should scream, but he took a quick step back, glancing down the hallway. I followed his gaze; two women were walking towards us.

He looked at me one last time, turned, and moved quickly down the hall in the opposite direction. I didn't make a sound, afraid that he would turn around and come back. I tried to smile at the two women moving past me.

After a few calming breaths, I rolled my shoulders and my neck to release the tension. I pushed off the wall and walked to the workout floor. I entered the main part of the gym and glanced around. A walking track encircled almost a hundred different workout machines in the center of the room. Mirrored walls reflected anyone's vanity, no matter where he or she stood.

The bright blue carpet reminded me of a beautiful summer sky. The cement walls were painted a bright white with stripes and zigzags in hot vibrant colors, creating a vivid and welcoming atmosphere.

Mark stood with three guys on the other side of the room, working on the pull down bar. That was my favorite exercise, but I didn't go to them. Instead, I made my way to the line of treadmills on the opposite side of the workout area and climbed on. I had a good view of Mark as he strained to pull down the three hundred pounds of iron.

His body slick with sweat, his muscles bulging from the exertion, he was physically gorgeous to me, and I couldn't help but watch. My thoughts warred with themselves as I repeatedly took step after step on the rotating belt. The last time I had seen him, he had made me feel like a whore, but the knowledge that I carried his child conflicted within me.

Could I forget how he treated me and move forward with a relationship with him?

When he finished his set, he spoke to one of the guys, then turned to look at me. He raised his chin in greeting, and I returned the greeting with a small smile. My heart fluttered and my response to him quickly reminded me of why I was really here. A quiver started in my abdomen and I looked away.

He didn't come over until he finished his workout. This didn't surprise me because when he lifted, he was all business. Socializing was for a different time. I put about three miles on the treadmill while I watched him cautiously.

"Hey, Mand, what's going on?" he called out as he approached.

My heart flip-flopped once in my chest as he grew closer. He was so damned gorgeous and, to think, I was carrying his child. I absently put my hand on my stomach.

"Hi, Mark. Um, do you have a few minutes to talk?" I stepped off the treadmill, wiping my face off with a towel.

He thought about it for a moment, "Yeah, are you done?"

"Yeah, can I meet you outside after I get changed?" We both turned towards the locker rooms.

He shrugged, "That's fine." I watched him from the corner of my eye as he smiled at a woman who climbed off the leg press machine. A stab of jealousy struck my heart when she smiled back at him. "I'll meet you outside." He turned the corner, then walked faster towards the locker room.

I rinsed the sweat off quickly, changing back into my jeans and T-shirt. My sweaty workout clothes got stuffed in my bag. The sound of the zipper closing filled the air; I threw my duffle over my shoulder and headed out.

I exited the locker room, glancing around the hallway, but I didn't see Mark or Steve. I made my way to the parking lot, scanning over the cars while I walked to mine. Mark wasn't outside, so I threw my bag into the passenger seat. I inhaled deeply a few times to settle the nerves trying to consume me, then I walked over to lean against his car.

A few minutes later, he walked out of the gym heading my way. My hands trembled more the closer he came; I shoved them into my front pockets, never taking my eyes off him as he moved.

"So, where you been?" He stopped in front of me.

I spent a moment wishing he would have walked up and pulled me into his arms. Maybe he could have said he missed me, but he didn't.

"My schedule got moved around at work. It's easier for me to come in the morning," I lied. He shrugged. I looked at the ground.

"You left your cat at my house." The half-smile that crossed his face didn't seem angry.

"Sorry about that. My parents are allergic; I couldn't take her back home." I had thought about Sally often and worried about her.

"No problem. She's pretty cool for a cat; I'll keep her until you have a new place." He glanced around the parking lot. "So what did you want to talk about?" He moved past me, unlocking his car door. I watched the muscles in his arm move when he tossed in his gym bag.

Now that I was here, I didn't know if I could say it or not. The words I'd prepared earlier vanished from my mind. I looked at my feet, closed my eyes, and took in a deep breath.

"What's wrong, Amanda?" he spoke quietly but didn't move any closer.

I released the air I was holding at the same time that I spit out the words. "I'm pregnant, Mark."

"What?" I could literally feel his body tense beside me. "Aren't you like on birth control or something?"

I shook my head, not able to meet his eyes. "No, I'm not."

"Oh, that's just great!" He slammed his car door, I flinched. "And I am assuming you want to blame me for this, huh?"

I looked at him, confused. "I'm not blaming anyone. It happened, I needed to tell you."

He stared at me for a long moment. "How do you even know it's mine? It's probably Steve's." He crossed his arms over his pecs, the expanse of his chest looking bigger than it already was.

I shook my head. "No, it's not his." I looked back at the ground. This was not going how I had hoped, my emotions threatened to let loose at any moment.

"Yeah, and how do you know that?" He snorted once and shook his head when I lifted my eyes to his.

"Because Steve never had sex without using a condom. We never had sex without protection, and the last time we did have sex was over three months ago." I held the tears back.

He turned his back on me and took a few steps away, kicking a rock on the ground. "And why are you telling me this?" he spoke with his back to me.

Why? Why was I telling him this? It was his kid, why wouldn't I tell him this? I didn't know how to answer his question without being sarcastic.

When I didn't respond he turned back to me. "When are you going to get rid of it? Do you need money from me to do that?"

My mouth dropped open. Of all the things I thought he would say, I had never thought it would be those words.

"You want me to get rid of it?"

I wasn't sure if I had actually spoken the words out loud, but then he rolled his eyes before he continued, "Of course you're going to get rid of it. I don't need another kid!" He faced his car and put both hands up on the roof, hanging his head between his arms.

Another kid?

"You already have a child?" I asked as I watched him.

He nodded, "Yep. She's nine."

How did I not know that? Why didn't he ever say anything about her?

"I can't afford to take care of another kid, Mandy. I'll help you pay for an abortion, but if you decide to keep it, I don't want anything to do with it, and I'll sign my rights off." He pushed off the car, eyeing me quickly.

The tears would not stay back now, they fell silently. The fantasy that I had built in my mind had totally disappeared. I didn't know anything about this guy.

"Look, I know where you can get one. I'll even take you there to get it done." He actually put his hand on my shoulder, I shrugged it off. The thought of him touching me revolted me.

I turned to walk away.

"Mandy, wait!" He grabbed my arm, pulling me around to face him. "Look, I'll call my friend, then give you a call and let you know what they say."

Who was this guy who had been my friend, my trainer? Who was this guy who had protected me against Steve, who had actually hurt him to protect me? Or did he just do that so he could extract a price from me, the payment in the form of sex?

"Whatever," I pulled out of his grip, needing to distance myself from him immediately. The tears poured down one after another as I climbed into the front seat of my car. The sobs didn't come until I had gotten down the road and pulled around behind a building. With my car in park, I promptly fell apart.

What a fool I had been! Of course he wouldn't want this child! Hell! I didn't want a child, but part of me didn't want to lose it.

Finally, I dried my eyes, blew my nose, and drove the rest of the way home. In a state of numb despair, I grabbed a glass of water, told my parents I didn't feel well, and went to bed.

When I woke up the next morning, emptiness encompassed me. I skipped going to the gym. I didn't have the energy. All I wanted to do was stay in bed, but I had to get ready for work.

Everyone at work politely asked how I felt. I told them it had to do with my blood sugar and left it at that. Around eleven in the morning, Anne told me I had a phone call holding.

Reaching over absently, I picked up the phone, "Amanda speaking." I froze when I heard his voice. He had never called me at work.

"Mandy, hey, I called my friend, and got the number for the doc I was telling you about. I called them for you, they can fit you in on Friday," Mark spoke quickly in a hushed tone.

Did he really call and make an appointment for me to have an abortion? "You did what?" I whispered into the phone, turning my back away from the door that led into the main office.

"They are able to fit you in on Friday. I will take the day off from work and take you there. Look, don't worry about the money. I'll pay for it." He sounded angry.

"It's not about the money, Mark. Maybe it's not what I want to do." A newfound sense of righteousness began to bubble up inside of me.

His voice rose and I wondered if it could be heard in the room. "You have to, Mandy. You can't have this child. It will destroy you. I told you I don't want another child." He hesitated, lowering his voice, "If you don't, then I'm going to the police to tell them you had us do that to Steve."

My heart almost stopped beating as his words sank in.

"What? I had nothing to do with that!" I practically shouted into the phone, all thoughts of others listening forgotten.

"You knew about it. Do you think the police will believe you are not involved?" Evil poured from his voice. I could never have imagined him like this. "I'll pick you up on Friday morning at nine-thirty." The phone went dead in my ear.

I wanted to throw up, yell, scream, punch a hole through the wall. I set the phone down gently, seething inside as I picked up the order I was inputting. Without thinking, without feeling anything else, I typed in the numbers for the products and processed the orders that needed to be done.

Three days later, I walked out of my parents' house wearing sweat pants and a T-shirt. I climbed into Mark's waiting car, and we drove away. Only one thing was spoken on the way there: "It'll be alright."

I ignored him and stared out the window.

The building we pulled up to looked like every other generic medical building. Red bricks and tinted glass windows circled the one-story unit. How did my life get so screwed up? What did I do to deserve what I was going through?

I would look back on this many years later and wish that I'd had the strength to stop this event—but on this day, I did not.

Mark came around and pulled open the passenger door. I climbed out silently. He took my hand in his as we walked up to the building, pulling open the glass door; I hesitated briefly then stepped inside. I didn't want him to touch me, but I needed human touch at that moment, so I allowed him to keep the tight grasp.

After I signed all the paperwork, I sat down in a chair, staring at the floor. There were no words for what I felt, I was somewhere between hollow and totally empty. I felt nothing as they called my name and I stood. Mark glanced up at me and nodded once, I walked away.

As I walked down the long hallway with doors on both sides, I absently wondered how many other women had been forced there. The nurse led me to a room; it was cold and antiseptic looking. She tried to make small talk, but I didn't respond. After handing me a gown, she walked out.

I pulled my clothes from my body mechanically, carefully folding them and setting them on the blue plastic chair to the side. Pulling the gown over my nude body, I climbed up on the cold table.

The doctor entered a few minutes later, explaining what they would do. I didn't care. I wanted it over. I lay back on the table staring at the white ceiling tiles and fluorescent lights. A shot in the arm made me feel sleepy, but I didn't close my eyes.

The noise and vibration of the machine struck deep within me. All the emotion sucked out of my body. They told me to stay lying down for a little while. I finally closed my eyes as they left me alone. I opened them when I heard the door, from the corner of my eyesight, I saw Mark walk in.

"How are you doing?" he picked up my hand.

I pulled my hand back from his, closing my eyes. He said nothing more, moving away from me until the nurse came back to tell me I could get dressed.

Mark walked out to the hall while she explained what I would feel like for the next few days, closing the door behind her softly so I could dress.

Mark stood in the hallway, arms crossed, apparently lost in his own thoughts as I exited the room. I walked past him towards the exit, and he stepped up beside me. I said nothing as I left the building and went to the car. Once he unlocked it, I climbed in, put my seatbelt on, and turned my head to the window.

He didn't try to talk on the way back to my house. When he pulled into the driveway, I had my seatbelt already off, and I opened the door before the car stopped.

"Amanda!" he yelled as I slammed the door, walking away from him forever. His car door opened and he yelled my name again.

I didn't turn around. He no longer existed, just like our child. I kept walking, into my house, into my room, and fell to the bed. I wanted to cry, but tears would not come. I had cried myself out; I felt nothing. I was nothing but a cheap dirty whore who had killed her child. I wished I were the one who had died.

CHAPTER ELEVEN

NICOLE

*S*ome people dreaded getting up each day and heading off to work. I was not one of them. I knew that each day was going to be different than the last, and I embraced the adventure. There would be days that were similar, days when no serious calls were dispatched—or days when traffic stops kept you busy, but even those were never the same.

That was the biggest lesson I learned as my months grew into years on the job. There was no such thing as a routine call—ever.

I had become comfortable talking over the radio, although I still hated it. I knew the streets well enough I figured I could do them blindfolded if I had to. My reputation was good on the street for treating people fairly, even when they broke the law. My brothers and sisters in blue knew they could always count on me when the need arose, even when asked to do my least favorite task: The Dreaded Female Prisoner Search.

When a neighboring department arrested a female, I would groan inwardly. I would quickly think through the list of on-duty female officers that could possibly get the are-you-available-to-do-a-female-search? message before me. Each time it appeared on my screen, I would scrunch up my nose, but I would respond to do it. After all, it was part of my job.

Today, I found myself on my way to a department north of us to search a female picked up on outstanding warrants. When I arrived at their station, I reached over and grabbed my leather and Kevlar gloves from my duty bag, locked my car, and walked into the front door of the station. The dispatcher buzzed me in so I didn't have to stand in the lobby with the loud and obnoxious citizenry.

Did family members ever accept that the people they loved could do wrong? I was shaking my head as I walked past the heavy metal door.

"Whatcha got?" I asked Andy who was standing inside waiting for me.

"The usual, Nicky. She is pretty cracked up right now, skittish, so be careful. I'll be outside if you need me." We walked down the hallway to the processing area where the prisoner was locked to a bench.

"Anything special you're looking for?" I asked, just in case.

"Nope. Just the usual drugs and weapons." We got to the door and walked to a bank of small gun lockers beside it. Taking my firearm out of my holster, I placed it into the lockbox. I pulled the key out and hooked it to my belt. We weren't allowed to carry weapons back to processing; we would be standing too close to the prisoners in a confined space.

Walking into the processing room, I observed a heavyset white female with wild eyes. Oh, yeah, she was wound up on something. Andy gave me a knowing nod, stepping outside to give us privacy.

I sighed. I hated this part. I took one step closer to her. The putrid smell of someone who had not had a bath reached my nose. It was bad enough to make my eyes water. I reached down for my keys on my belt to release the cuff on her wrists.

"I'm Officer Nolan. I am going to be searching you. What is your name?" I was polite but authoritative in my tone.

"Rhonda," her eyes traveled over me while she answered my question. I tried not to physically gag, motioning for her to stand up.

"Turn around so I can take off your cuffs. Do not try to fight me while we do this. Are you going to cooperate? Or are we going to have a problem?" I reached for her wrists.

"No problem. You a dyke?" her back was to me while she spoke.

I chuckled. "No." It was not the first time nor the last time that question would be asked. Many people thought female cops were gay just because they did a Man's Job.

I removed the cuffs from her wrists, slipping them into the back of my duty belt as I stepped back. She turned, "It's okay if you are, I'm into women, too."

The thought of this nasty, sweaty, stinky, cracked-up woman attempting to touch me turned my stomach. Somehow I kept the disgusted look off my face. "Sorry, you have the wrong equipment between your legs." I continued before she could say anything to counter me, "Rhonda, have you ever been arrested before?"

"Yeah, I know whatcha gonna do." Her use of slang showed she was not well educated. She shrugged, looking at the floor. I asked her if she had anything on her person that would stab, cut, or injure me in any way, she grunted without looking at me. Wary of that response, I knew to be even more careful during the search.

She removed her shirt when I told her to, a dingy white tank top with missing sequins in the design. I absently wondered how long she had been wearing it. She put her hand towards me, I told her to drop the top on the bench. Seeing how dirty she was, I reached behind me for a pair of Nitrile gloves. I grabbed the large size so I could pull them over my leathers.

Picking up her dirty shirt, I glanced over it quickly. Not much to it, so not much of a place to hide anything. I dropped the shirt down to the bench and told her to remove her pants. She looked up, a little smile on her face, "You sure you don't want to try me out." I locked down my jaw to hold back a gag reflex.

"No, remove your pants, please." I waited while she shimmied them over her large hips. The smell in the room grew stronger when her pants slipped down; we called it rotten crotch. It was an all-too-well-known smell to cops who arrest crack whores and prostitutes who didn't clean themselves properly. My stomach churned, I tried not to inhale through my nose.

The pants dropped to the floor, I turned my head away from the puff of air it released up to me. I refused to allow weakness to show in front of her and swallowed the bile that had risen.

Squatting down quickly to retrieve her pants, my hand felt around the pocket area, lightly searching for sharp objects. After confirming there were none in the pockets, I removed the contents: cash, a lighter, and a small clear baggie with a rock in it. Crack cocaine, bingo. My eyes met hers; she shrugged.

I set the contents on the counter behind me and ran my fingers around the waistband. Something hard under the fabric caught my attention. Gently moving my fingertips over it, I tried to picture what it was. I turned the waistband inside out; a small slit could be seen in the material. Moving the fabric around, I was able to release the straight razor concealed inside the pants. Nice, I thought. I set it down on the counter, making sure to keep the counter between the two of us.

I checked the rest of the pants, finding nothing else. I put them gently down onto the bench so no more stink would escape. I told Rhonda to remove her bra.

She was big busted, so after she removed it and set it down, I had her lift her breasts up so I could make sure there was nothing hidden under them. She had bruises covering her breasts; a few looked like bite marks.

"The marks on your chest, are they there because you consented to them?"

She inspected her breasts, "Yeah, I like it rough." Her smile showed me her stained teeth.

I nodded to her once, "Do you have your period?"

"Nope. Why you into dat shit?" If I hadn't been sick to my stomach before, I truly was now. I didn't give her an answer.

"Take your underwear off, please." I waited.

Her pink cotton grannie panties had seen better days, and I steeled myself to the intense stench I knew was coming.

Immediately, I told her to assume the position. She spread her feet and squatted down, giving two deep coughs. As she coughed, something dropped from between her legs and rolled across the floor. We both watched it roll.

"Where'd dat come from?" she acted surprised.

"Gee, I wonder." Nasty place to hide your crack pipe, I thought. Shaking my head, I advised her to get dressed again. I reached down for the small metal pipe on the floor and picked it up with two fingers, sliding the nitrile glove off my hand and around the pipe. I used the other glove to do the same thing with the blade, being careful not to cut myself.

I cuffed her ankle to the bench once she dressed, then I reached back for the cuffs I had placed on my belt and slipped them on her wrists, picking up the two gloves along with the little clear baggie. I looked over my shoulder at her, "Thank you for cooperating." She hung her head in defeat. She knew she was spending the night in jail.

I walked into the squad room to meet up with Andy. "Be careful with this one, there is a razor blade in it." I handed him one glove. He nodded and took it from me carefully.

I smiled at him as I handed him the second glove. "Pipe," was all I said.

"Where was the razor?" he asked.

"In the waistband of her jeans."

"And the pipe?" he pulled that glove from my hand.

I smiled a very twisted smile, "Where do you think?"

I saw the answer register in his mind. He dropped the glove to the floor. "That's gross."

I laughed along with several of the other guys. Andy was one of the newer ones here; he wasn't used to that hiding place, yet. I had learned that one right off the bat.

"Also, here is her rock. She must have just scored it, looks whole. It was in her right front pocket." I dropped it on the desk next to us. Andy was looking down at the glove on the ground.

"It's not going to bite you," I laughed again. "You guys need anything else?"

"No, that's it, Nicole, thanks for coming down to help out."

"Sure, anytime." I retrieved my handgun from the lockbox so I could make my way back to my jurisdiction.

I thought about the woman I had just searched while I drove up the hill. I wondered how she had gotten involved with drugs. She was probably doing the whole prostitution thing to keep up her habit.

I sighed. There were so many women out there that had no self-esteem —women who thought they would never be able to make something of themselves so they turned to alcohol, drugs, and sex. It was sad, but unfortunately it was life. It was a hard life, and I was very grateful my life had not ventured in that particular direction.

CHAPTER TWELVE

AMANDA

"Hey, Aunt Sara!" I yelled down the stairs, my hand sliding over the freshly-polished wood banister.

"I'm in here, Amanda," her voice echoed through the hall from the kitchen. I moved in her direction and smiled when I found her standing at the counter, a glass of wine in one hand, a book in the other.

"Hi, Aunt Sara, another rough day at work?"

She sighed heavily, "These days, it seems like they are all rough." She smiled before continuing, "You going to be home for dinner?"

"No, actually, I'm going out with Angela. We're going to the movies."

"Good!" she laughed. "Justin is gone tonight, too. I didn't feel like cooking. Now I can go collapse on the couch and read."

A year later, I was still glad I had made the rash decision to move to my aunt's in Michigan. I had needed a change, and I had needed it quick. Knoxville had gotten way too small for me. My aunt had a spare room and a good college nearby; it was the perfect way to start over.

"Sounds like a good time." I chuckled, kissed her cheek, and said goodbye. I climbed into my car, started it, and made my way to Angela's house.

Angela was waiting on the front porch for me; she was never on time for anything, so this was a surprise. I looked at my watch to make sure I wasn't late—nope, right on schedule.

She settled herself into my car, her brassy blond hair bouncing. "Oh, we are going to have so much fun tonight!"

"Angie, we're only going to a movie. You act like we are going to some huge party or something." I pulled out of her driveway towards the main road.

"Well, I have a surprise for you." She appeared to be bursting with excitement, and it immediately made me nervous.

At the stop sign, I looked in her direction, "I don't like being surprised, Angie, you know that."

"Oh, come on, Mandy! Relax, you are going to enjoy this one! Trust me, just this once, trust me!" she actually giggled. The twinkling sound it made brought a smile to my face.

"Whatever, Ang. Are we still going to the movies?"

"Yes!" she happily clapped her hands beside me, and then turned up the radio so talking would be difficult. I kept my mouth shut, watching traffic as I drove to the cinema. After parking, I noticed Angela intensely scouring the area.

"What are you looking for?" I asked as we got out of my car.

"It's not a what. It's a who." She eyed me quickly and then went back to searching.

"Who are we meeting? Rebecca?" I stepped beside her. The smile that captured her face could only mean one thing: a man. I followed her line of sight to two guys standing by the beige stone wall talking amongst themselves. Damn—she had set up a blind date for me.

"You are so dead, Angela," I mumbled beside her.

"Oh relax, Mandy. You have been here almost a year and you have yet to go out on a date. I thought it would be fun to just go hang out with these guys." She bumped her shoulder into mine as we walked.

I shook my head. It wouldn't help if I said anything or not. Angela had her mind made up, and as we walked, I looked up from the pavement. I noticed the two guys were watching us approach. It was too late to turn back now.

"Stop sighing, Mandy. Try to look happy and excited," she whispered as we got closer.

Easy for you to say, I thought to myself as we stepped up on the side-walk next to them.

"Hi, Todd!" Angie walked up to the shorter of the two. I remember Angela talking about meeting a guy named Todd a few months back. I smiled at him as she introduced me to him.

We shook hands and exchanged the normal pleasantries. Todd stepped back and motioned to the guy beside him, "This is Josh. Josh, this is Angela and Amanda."

"Nice to meet you, Josh," Angela replied, walking to Todd and slip-ping her arm around his waist. The possessiveness of her touch with Todd made it obvious to both Josh and me that we were stuck with each other for the next few hours. I turned to him when he spoke.

"It's nice to meet you, Amanda. Do you go by Mandy?"

"Whatever works for you is fine." I didn't expect to see him again after tonight, so he could call me whatever he wanted. Politely, I put my hand out to shake his. He stepped closer, reaching for my hand. I was surprised at the warmth in his eyes and the softness of his touch. It wasn't a limp handshake by any means, but his hands had pleasingly-soft skin.

Not sure what to say, we turned back to listen to Angela and Todd. They were whispering quietly to each other, their foreheads low and touching, smiles adorning their mouths as they spoke. I wasn't one for public displays of affection, so I stepped around them to move to the ticket window.

"Not into public displays of affection?" Josh spoke my mind from just behind me.

I laughed. "I have no problem with PDA, I just don't need to stand two feet away and ogle it."

He laughed beside me, the sound quite sexy, slightly deep and jazzy to my ears. "I agree. Why don't we buy the tickets and then we will drag them into the theater."

I started to unzip my purse as we approached the glass.

"Put that away, this is my treat." His smile radiated over his face.

"Josh, you don't need to do that. I don't mind paying for my own ticket. I'm sure you got roped into coming out tonight anyway."

His look changed to a serious one before a sweet smile captured his lips, making his eyes sparkle. "Actually, I volunteered to come out. Well, that's actually wrong. It was more like my idea."

"What, you wanted Todd to set you up with someone?" I laughed again thinking that this guy shouldn't need a blind date. He was good looking, I'm sure he had plenty of women to choose from. He paid for the tickets before answering me.

"No." He handed me the four tickets while he put the change in his wallet. "No, I wanted to meet you."

We were walking back to Angie and Todd, and I stopped, peering up at him curiously. "What do you mean, you wanted to meet me?"

His laughter caused a small thrill to race up my spine. I stood at his shoulder height, so I had to look up into his face. His green eyes were bright as the side of his mouth quirked up in a smile.

"I saw a picture of you with Angela. I told Todd I wanted to meet you. You looked like you were a lot of fun."

I narrowed my eyes at him. "I'm not going to sleep with you, if that's the fun you are thinking."

He threw his head back and laughed. "I didn't mean that kind of fun! I meant you looked like you'd be fun to hang out with." His laughter still filled my ears as he took my arm gently above the elbow. "Come on, we need to get the other two, or we won't have time to get junk food before it starts."

If it hadn't been for his honest laugh, I might have been embarrassed. I had been completely truthful with him: I had no intentions of sleeping with anyone—not anytime soon. He winked at me when I looked back up to his face. A small smile reluctantly found its way to my mouth.

Angela and Todd walked ahead of us, holding hands and standing close. For a moment, a wish crossed my mind that I could have a relationship such as theirs. I pushed the wish away quickly.

With our arms loaded with junk food, we made our way to the theater. Todd pulled Angie up near the top row of seats, obviously wanting to be alone. Josh and I settled into seats about halfway up.

Seated alone with him, I began to wonder if this was really a good idea. My stomach flip-flopped as I nervously reached for my soda. I pushed a handful of popcorn into my mouth, unsure what to talk about. Josh didn't seem to have that problem. He asked me questions about my workout routine. It was obvious by the look of him that he worked out, too, his jeans tight over his legs and his T-shirt hugging his biceps and chest.

I had not allowed myself to look at a man this way in a long time, but something began to stir inside of me that I had long ago buried.

We shared conversation about our routines until the lights started to dim. I found myself slightly frustrated because I was enjoying our conversation and didn't want to end it quite yet.

The soon-to-be-released movie trailers started to play, and as hard as I tried to pay attention to them, I was more interested in the chemistry that seemed to be flowing between our two seats than what showed on the screen. When the lights had been on, sure I could see him, but why could I actually feel him better as the theater grew darker with the featured presentation?

My attention strayed from the silver screen for most of the movie. I was very conscious of his movements beside me. Our legs more than once touched, which always brought us to glance at each other. With the light of the screen shining on one side of our faces, we held the gaze for a second or two then turned back to the screen.

By the end, I found myself wanting to press my leg against his completely.

The final credits began rolling; we picked up our trash and made our way out of the row in silence. He stopped at the end to wait for me to step out, taking my hand as we descended the stairs. Again I noticed how soft his hands felt, even though his grasp was firm.

We exited the building, stopping against the wall to wait for Todd and Angie. His hand still holding mine gently, he pulled me to stand beside him. Our eyes met as we waited. A soft smile formed on his lips as he bent slightly and placed a kiss on my forehead.

"I'm glad you came tonight, Mandy," he said quietly.

I smiled up at him. "Me, too," I replied honestly. There was something about him that I liked, something that seemed to connect us. I wasn't sure if I liked that or not, as my past relationships had turned out so badly, but part of me wanted to enjoy it and just have fun. It had been a long time since I had done that.

Angela and Todd walked over to us; Angela noticed right away that our hands were together, and a smile lit up her face. I smiled back at her before we all walked to the parking lot.

We ended up eating at a local diner, cozy in one of the back booths. The diner wasn't busy, so that was probably why the servers left us alone to just sit and chat for several hours after we ate, stopping by every once in a while to freshen up our drinks.

Josh sat close to me, a couple of times putting his hand on my leg briefly. When he did, I could feel the skin under my jeans warm. By the end of the night, his arm was wrapped around my back, pulling me close to him. I felt lightheaded with pleasure.

As we left the diner, Todd and Angela walked over to Todd's car for privacy. Josh walked me to my car. I put the key into the lock. As Josh pushed my hair away from my neck, I froze with my hand on the keys. He bent down and slowly kissed the side of my neck.

I released the breath I held, turning to face him. The soft curve of his lips held my attention as his hand lifted my chin. He stepped closer, watching me intently.

"I wanna see you again, Amanda." The gentleness of his voice caressed my senses as his eyes traveled over my skin in an almost possessive way.

"I would like that." My knees were weak as I got lost in the green of his eyes. The shadows of the overhead lights hid the rich features of his face, I yearned to reach out and touch them, but I held back, afraid to make a move.

"I think we have something here, something special, Amanda." His mouth moved closer to mine, I licked my suddenly-dry lips slightly and felt my heart race as he moved in.

"I wanna see where it goes." He stopped just an inch from my mouth. I couldn't speak.

He closed the space between us, his lips as smooth as his hands when they connected with mine. His tongue darted out to lightly swipe over mine. I found myself not wanting to resist, and I leaned into him when he pulled me closer. Our tongues meshed together as I gave in for those few brief moments. He pulled back, his eyes still closed as he appeared to savor the moment.

"I'll call you tomorrow," he whispered before he gave me another small kiss.

I nodded at him, not sure I could speak. He let go and turned from me when I realized that he hadn't asked me for my phone number.

"Hey, do you want my number?" I spoke as he stepped away.

He chuckled, looking over his shoulder. "I already have it. I've had it for a couple of weeks." His grin warmed my heart. "'Night, Mandy, have sweet dreams about me."

I watched him walk away, appreciating the view of his gorgeous body as it moved. Oh, you can bet those dreams are going to be sweet, I thought. I grinned and giggled to myself as I slipped into the driver's seat.

The loneliness of the past year seemed to fade away almost immediately. I sat waiting for Angela and thought about how I had avoided getting to know anyone but her since I had moved here. Maybe it was time to get back out there, try something new. Maybe if I go slowly, I thought, things will be different this time.

My smile faded as I wondered briefly if this would end up like my past two. Would I be strong enough to make it through? Would I see the signs ahead of time? Could I protect myself? Sighing to myself, I knew that only time would tell.

CHAPTER THIRTEEN

AMANDA

The months moved on to a year, my relationship with Josh grew swiftly and lovingly. We were together constantly, always out and about, always finding new things to do. I loved being with him and knew that he loved our moments together just as much.

My job as a secretary was only a half mile from the warehouse where he worked, so we often spent our lunch hours together, sitting in a park in the center of the industrial park. The nights when I took my business classes, he would drop me off and deliver me home after classes. Many nights, he sprawled out on the couch while I sat on the floor doing my homework on the coffee table.

On one of these evenings at home, after I kissed Josh goodnight, I closed the door and went to pick up my books off the floor. I heard foot-steps on the wooden stairs, surprised that someone was up this late. My aunt's slippers shuffled over the cream carpet in the living room, her long pink robe swirling around her feet.

"Mandy, do you have a minute, honey?"

I saw apprehension apparent on her face. She passed me and walked into the kitchen, flipping on the overhead light. Concerned, I followed her and sat beside her at the small round kitchen table near the bay window.

"Aunt Sara, is everything alright?" I searched her face, looking for something that might tell me what worried her.

"Honey, everything is fine with me. I'm a bit worried about you, though." She laid a hand on my arm that was resting on the glass table.

"Worried about me? Aunt Sara, I'm great!" I laughed, putting my hand over hers. "Why would you be worried about me?"

"Well, you spend so much time with Josh. No matter where you go, he's there. I'm concerned that he doesn't give you enough space." She squeezed my arm, and I laughed.

"Aunt Sara, Josh is the best thing that ever happened to me! I love spending every second with him. Don't worry about me! I have never been happier, really!"

She watched me for a moment longer, "Okay, if you say so. I just think that maybe you should try spending a little bit of time alone every now and then."

"Aunt Sara, please don't worry. I really am happy." I stood up and kissed her cheek, then walked to the stairs to head up to bed.

As I climbed in bed, I thought back to what she had just said to me. Did she really think that Josh didn't give me enough space? I didn't need space, I loved that we spent so much time together. I loved that Josh wanted to be with me through everything and anything. I smiled to myself as I snuggled down into my bed and closed my eyes, happy to have found love at last.

"So…I have a surprise for you," he said over the phone.

"A surprise? What is it?" I giggled into the phone.

"There is a reason they call it a surprise, you know. I'll tell you after work." I heard his laughter echo through the phone line.

"I have class after work, so your surprise is going to have to wait." I loved when he surprised me, so I was a bit disappointed that I had class tonight.

"Skip class tonight! I promise I will make it worth your while." his soft sexy voice purred through the phone and sent chills down my arms.

"You know I don't skip classes, Josh," I chuckled. This must be one big surprise for him to try and get me to skip class. He'd never suggested that before; he understood how important my classes were to me.

"Oh, come on, Amanda, you can miss one! It's a surprise—a huge surprise! I can't wait until tomorrow night to show you." His voice was eager and quick as he spoke.

"Wow, this must be one heck of a surprise! Fine, I'll skip tonight if it will make you happy, but this better be good!" I laughed as he yipped into the phone. I could imagine the grin on his face as we said goodbye.

As I sat inputting an order for work, the concern my aunt had voiced drifted into my thoughts. She had no idea what she was talking about, every second I spent with Josh just got better.

The rest of the afternoon flew. I walked out of my office a few minutes after five to find Josh leaning against his shiny black Camaro, in his hand, a single red rose. When we saw each other, the smile on his face spread from ear to ear and lit my heart on fire. I ran to him, jumping up into his arms. He caught me easily, wrapping his arms around me and holding me tightly.

"I love you, Amanda," he whispered in my ear as I hugged him. I pulled back enough to look at him, my legs and arms wrapped around him.

"I love you too, Josh," I whispered before I leaned in to kiss his supple lips.

He let me slide down to the ground after the kiss, handing me the flower. I lifted it to my nose, gently sniffing the soft petals as they tickled the underside of my nose. He took me by the hand to pull me away from the car so he could open the passenger door, holding it open as I climbed inside.

He practically sprinted to the driver's door and got in. He pulled a strip of cloth from the back seat, holding it out to me with a mischievous look on his face.

"What's that for?" I asked before I reached for it.

"It's for your surprise. You need to cover your eyes." He wriggled the black blindfold in front of me.

His excitement trumped the uncertainty I felt. I reached for it. "Do I have to put it on now?"

"Yes, you have to put it on now," he laughed. "Don't worry, you are going to love it! Relax, you look like I'm going to make you walk the plank or something."

I lifted the blindfold up to my eyes. "Fine. For you I will do this, but only because you said I'm going to love it, so you better be right."

"Trust me, Mandy, I'll never do anything you won't like." His voice grew husky as he spoke, causing my stomach to flip at the love and excitement that I felt.

He waited until I had the blindfold on and put my hands down.

"Can you see anything?" he asked.

"No, I can't. Now get moving before I take this thing off or fall asleep." I felt him turn in his seat as he started the car. I sat patiently beside him, wondering where we were going, trying to get him to give me hints, but he refused.

Josh was asking a lot of me. My previous experiences with men had left me not as trusting. His patience and love were what allowed me to get through his surprise and this blindfold. Even after a year together, we had not had sex. Every time we got close, a part of me freaked out, yet he was always so sweet and told me he understood. He would say that one day when I was ready, we would, and it would be that much more incredible.

He knew I was not a virgin, but I had never explained to him about my past. No one knew, not even Angie. The fact that he respected me for this and did not pressure me, made my love for him swell in my chest each time.

Ten minutes later, the car stopped and he turned off the engine. I giggled at the sound of him taking a few deep breaths.

His car door opened and closed heavily, rocking the car. I could hear his footsteps as he walked on the pavement, which meant he'd left the windows down. We must either be in a safe place or we weren't going too far from the car, I thought as I waited for my door to open.

I turned my head in the direction of the door and started to get out. His hand came down to mine as he helped me stand up. I felt his hand shaking gently. This surprise must be big for him to be nervous.

"Okay, can I take this off now?" I reached up to pull off the blindfold.

"No, not yet, keep it on for just a couple more minutes. Come on, we have to walk. I won't let you trip over anything, just keep walking straight." Soft grass under my feet gave way back to hard cement as he edged me forward.

"How far are we walking?" Uncomfortable about walking with a blindfold on, I briefly wondered if there was anyone watching us. A blush crept into my cheeks to think that we were in public and someone would see me like this.

A horn startled me as it echoed all around me. The sound of children laughing and a basketball bouncing reached my ears as I walked slowly, trying not to trip over my own shadow.

"Come on, just a little further." The apprehension mixed with excitement in his voice, and I found myself getting jittery with each step.

"We have three steps to go up, but wait just a second, I need to let go of you for a moment." He dropped my hand to pull the arm away that was around my waist. For a moment, I felt isolated standing there without him next to me.

The jingle of keys caught my attention and a door opened. His footsteps came back to me, and he put his arm around my waist again.

"There are three steps in front of you. Just take them slowly," he said softly into my ear.

"You know this would be a whole lot easier if you would let me take this thing off." A timorous laugh bubbled up in me.

"Yeah, but that would ruin all the fun. I like that you have to depend on me," he whispered into my ear and kissed the side of my head.

I shuffled forward until I got to the first step. Josh was patient while I took my time climbing the three wooden steps. At the top he spoke again, "Just a couple more feet and then you can take it off."

The sound of a car engine behind me reminded me we were still outside. I blushed again, feeling silly with a blindfold on. Josh pulled me gently forward and told me to step up slightly one more time. I felt the ground under me change to something soft. It must be carpet, I thought. I heard him inhale deeply beside me.

"Okay, you can take it off," he said quietly. I reached up to take off the cloth.

I blinked a few times, allowing my eyes to adjust to the bright sunlight in the room. We appeared to be standing in the entranceway to a small older house, the living room off to our left, empty except for the beige carpet. A small hallway led back to what was probably the kitchen and dining room area because there was brown laminate floor visible from where I stood. I looked at Josh and then looked around again at the bare white walls.

"Where are we?" I stepped into the empty living room.

He stepped next to me, leaning down to kiss me. "Come on, I want to show you the rest of it." He pulled me down the hall like a child going to the toy store; I had no choice but to follow. We reached the end of the hall; my thoughts were confirmed as I stepped onto the laminate floor with the kitchen off to the right. Beige countertops and appliances filled the small space. A small window over the stainless steel sink showed a large tree out in the backyard. A bay window in the small breakfast dining area framed a mature oak.

There was another hallway off to the left. Josh paused to allow me to finish my observations of the kitchen, then quickly pulled me down the other hallway.

"Josh, where are we? Whose house is this?" I laughed as he tugged me along. He stopped at a closed door, turning around to face me, his hands on my shoulders.

Obvious excitement filled his wide eyes as he gazed down at me. "Mandy, I told you I loved you, right?" He released my shoulders, moving his hands to mine between us. I squeezed his in return.

"Yes, I know you do." I was completely puzzled by his behavior "What's going on?"

He let go of my hands. Stepping behind me and taking a deep breath, he put his hands over my eyes.

"What are you doing?" I laughed and tried to pull away, he held his hands in place.

"Reach out in front of you and open the door. The knob is to your right." He pushed me forward gently with his body. I had no choice but to reach forward and find the doorknob or be crushed against the door.

The door started to open, and the scent of roses struck my nose. I inhaled deeply, loving the fragrance. Josh pushed me forward slightly; I took a couple steps until he stopped moving. I could almost hear him counting, one, two, three, in his head before he lifted his makeshift blindfold. I gasped as I took in the beautiful room in front of me.

A huge bed commanded the center of the room, the soft cream quilt covered in red rose petals. Candles flickered from several places around the room. Deep burgundy curtains hung from the window. Two light-colored wood nightstands stood on either side of the bed, and the matching dressers completed the furnishings.

Confused, I turned to look at Josh, "What's going on?"

He took my face in his palms, kissing me gently. He picked up my hands and tugged me further into the room.

"Josh?" I asked again.

He stopped next to the bed; I felt an uneasy trepidation fill me. We had discussed this. He knew I wasn't ready to have sex. Did he think a little bit of romance was going to make me change my mind? Still holding my hands, he got down on one knee.

My mouth fell open as my heart began to thud heavily in my chest. Oh, my God! I looked into his face. He let go of one hand to reach under the bed. When his hand came out, he held a small box in his palm. I swallowed to keep the tears at bay as they threatened to ruin the perfect vision in front of me. He let go of my other hand so he could open the box, not taking his eyes from my face.

I watched him open the box slowly. Inside lay a simple perfect diamond engagement ring; the small stone in the center mirrored the light of the candles in the room, sparkling brightly in the cut facets.

"Mandy, Amanda, this place…this place is our place…or it will be our place if you say yes," he swallowed, "if you say yes you will marry me." His voice was tense, deep, and filled with emotion. "Will you marry me, Amanda?"

As much as I wanted this moment to be clear in my mind forever, tears blurred my vision.

"Yes," I whispered the reply. His smile lit up the room brighter than a spotlight. He pulled the ring out of the box, the black velvet box falling forgotten to the floor. He cradled my left hand in his and slipped the ring onto my ring finger as our gazes locked.

As the ring found its proper spot, he stood up next to me, pulling me into his arms, his kiss sweet, sensitive, and so warm that I immediately got lost in it. He gently scooped me up in his strong arms and set me on the bed, laying me over the rose petals.

He climbed slowly onto the bed, leaning over me, his face now aligned with mine, his eyes bright and shining in the candlelight like the diamond ring I wore on my finger.

"I love you, Amanda. You are mine now, forever," he whispered just as his lips met my open mouth. In that moment, a similarly-spoken sentence came up from a long-depressed memory. A thread of fear passed through me at the possessive look in his eyes—but this was Josh, not Steve.

This was Josh, and he was going to take care of me and love me forever. I pushed the unbidden thought of Steve out of my mind, giving myself over to Josh entirely for the very first time.

I would savor that feeling of being loved completely for a long time despite the fleeting fearful memory of a different time and place. I was completely won over by the dashing and loving man that held my delicate heart and spirit in his hands.

CHAPTER FOURTEEN

NICOLE

There were many days when I came to work and dealt with little incidents that had very little impact on my life. There were other days when a single call would leave such an impression, an indentation, that I would be forever changed.

"Hey, Todd! Did you remember to bring me that movie you wanted me to watch?" I yelled across the parking lot as he climbed out of his car. I was at the gas pump filling my patrol car.

"Yeah, I'll get it in a minute. I gotta go use the bathroom." I laughed while he all but ran to the garage door, unlocking it and disappearing inside. Too much coffee this afternoon, I thought to myself.

Dispatch called his unit number just as he entered the garage. I responded for him since he was a bit indisposed at the moment.

"Thirty-Seven Paul Three for Paul Two." I pulled the gas nozzle out of my tank and put it back up on the pump.

"Thirty-Seven Paul Three, ambulance and medics are being dispatched to 1324 Old Hickory Road for a fall. A nine-year-old male fell down the steps and is unconscious."

Something to understand about my job: When dispatch says both ambulance and medics in the same sentence, adrenaline picks up just a little bit because it is a more serious call. Another thing, when a child is mentioned, the adrenaline spikes fast and hard, and all thoughts of anything else are thrown by the wayside, nothing else matters—nothing.

I told them I was en route and jumped quickly into my car. Before I was even out of the parking lot, the lights were alive and pulsing, the siren screaming to all who could hear. I was moving, and moving quickly.

Todd hit me up on my Nextel as I turned quickly onto the main road, pausing only long enough to make sure the oncoming traffic took notice of me.

"Did they say a nine-year-old?" I heard the sound of the toilet flushing in the background as he spoke.

"Yeah, nine," was the only response I gave before dropping my phone into my lap so I could concentrate on the traffic of the early evening. My car sported lights across the top, lights flashing in the grill under the hood, a siren that wailed at an ungodly high volume, and yet, people couldn't seem to get out of the way.

A car slowed down in front of me, hugging the white fog line of the road, not completely stopping as it should. An oncoming car moved closer, and—the odds never failed—both vehicles came to a stop at almost the exact same place on the narrow two-lane roadway, leaving me barely enough room to squeak between them.

I held my breath as I maneuvered between the two vehicles, reen-gaging the accelerator after I passed them. The road in front of me was clear, for now. I hoped no one would decide to back out of a driveway without stopping to look first. I didn't look at my speedometer, but I knew the needle was climbing high as my foot continued to push down.

I slowed down as I approach a four-way intersection, changing the pitch of my siren to catch the attention of anyone that might be approaching from a different side. I cleared the intersection quickly, leaving behind drivers who stared at me as I flew by them.

"Thirty-Seven Paul Three, caller states the child is not breathing." My heart sank as I heard the words over my speaker; I swallowed before picking up the microphone and pressing the button.

"Thirty-Seven Paul Three, copy." There was nothing else to say.

I was almost there; the adrenaline streamed through me with each beat of my heart. I saw only what was in front of me, only what I focused on—the phenomenon called tunnel vision: the body is so attuned to what is in the direct line of sight, that you pay no attention to anything else. My mind and body were set to only one thing, getting to that child and doing it quickly.

I got ready to pull up to the residence; flipping the siren off, but not my lights. I wanted the ambulance to have no problem finding the address. With my computer screen up, I hit the F12 button to record my arrival time. Before my car stopped, I had taken my seatbelt off, and my hand had reached for the door to open it. The car bucked slightly as I threw the gear shift into park. I got out of the car running for the house as a female child around the age of six opened the door, waiting for me, her eyes wide as I ran past her into the entranceway.

My heart raced as my mind took in all the details as I entered, and I stopped cold, as if I hit a wall two steps into the house. The hardwood floor was littered with papers. A woman, I could only assume to be the mother, stood over the child staring down; tears rolling down her ashen cheeks, her hand over her mouth. She mumbled something, but the blood rushed through my ears. I could not hear her.

The child, dressed in a school uniform, khaki slacks, and a white shirt sporting the name of the local Catholic school, lay crumpled on the floor, legs twisted in an unnatural position off to the side, head turned to face me with chestnut-brown eyes looking someplace near my knees.

Can he see them shaking? I wondered as I took a step forward. I bent down to touch the child's neck, to feel for a pulse. I pressed gently, nothing. I pressed harder.

Please! Please, let there be a pulse.

Nothing.

Sitting on my knees, I stared into eyes that blindly looked at my chest. The youthful glow of life was absent from the glossy reflection. I swallowed, trying to force the bile back down my throat as I heard footsteps behind me. I slowly pulled my hand away from the cool skin of his neck. A faded bruise on his cheekbone was the only mark on the beautiful angelic face.

"Nic, what have you got?" I heard equipment dropping to the ground just before someone bent down across from me. No words came from my mouth as I looked up into the face of the EMT who reached for the child. I scrutinized his face, afraid to look back down at the floor between us. His forehead scrunched up, lines crossed the normally tight skin, and then they smoothed back out as he closed his eyes. His shoulders dropped ever so slightly, and air released from his lungs in a slow soft blow.

He slowly opened his eyes again, lifted his head to me, and in the moment we made eye contact, my eyes filled with unshed tears. I tried to blink them away. Pain was clearly written on both of our faces as we looked towards the door, hearing other rushed footsteps moving our way.

While time up to that point had rushed by, the moments ticked slowly now, the scene had been put on pause and progressed a single frame at a time. I watched as Todd crossed the threshold, others coming up behind him.

He glanced to the floor then to my face, an unspoken question in his eyes. I didn't want to face the question, and my eyelids dropped to block out the pain that would cross his features as I ever so slightly shook my head.

"No," I heard him say quietly. The others came to stand beside him, looking over his shoulder. I heard the EMT say to let only a medic in. The unbearable feeling of emotional pain hung heavy in the room; a few people sadly stepped back away from the door.

I looked to the child in front of me, his life cut short, ended in a way that no one deserved. I noticed again the papers scattered over the floor and saw that they were schoolwork. A math page lay to my right, a large C written in red on top of it.

I lifted it up, for some reason I needed to touch this paper, to hold something that had been held by his small hands while he'd lived. The paper was cold in my hands, like his body would be soon.

"I told him he could do better," a woman's voice traveled softly over the quiet room as my line of sight hit my partner's and then quickly moved to her.

"Excuse me?" I said as I stood, the paper in my hand floated slowly back to the floor.

"He should have gotten better grades. I told him he needed to get better grades. He would never listen."

Standing to my full height, I squared my shoulders, stealing a quick glance at Todd. He took a step closer to the woman. Something felt wrong here, I knew it and he did, too.

We both focused on the woman in front of us; heavy footsteps running hard on the cement walkway outside could be heard coming closer.

"What did you do?" shouted a man from behind me. Todd and I both spun around at the outburst.

The woman who had stood staring at the child looked up with dread in her eyes. Todd faced the man while I returned my attention to the woman. Fear raced across her face, her jaw opened and closed as if to speak, but no words came out.

"What the hell did you do, Beth? What did you do?" The man screamed, stepping closer to her, stopping only when Scott put his body in front of him. The man looked down at the child, tears spilling down his face; he turned to the woman again.

"I didn't mean it," she said quietly, shaking her head, her tears dried up.

"You didn't mean it? You didn't mean it?" he yelled the second question. "Like you didn't mean to break his arm last summer when he wouldn't carry his laundry upstairs? What the hell did you do to my son, Beth?"

I looked over my shoulder at his emotional outburst. His face bulged red with anger and pain, spittle flew from his mouth as he screamed. Todd stepped closer to him, putting his hands on his chest to hold him back.

"No! I didn't mean it! He brought home a C on his test! A C! I yelled at him. I didn't mean for him to fall down the stairs, but he yelled back at me and I smacked him. He fell! It wasn't my fault!" she yelled.

My attention was now riveted to her in a whole new way.

This woman, this finely-dressed beautiful woman who lived in an elegant upscale home was a cruel, evil, and sick monster.

Anger reared its evil head in me, but I controlled it and reached behind me for my cuffs. I had heard enough. Stepping towards the woman, I pulled her arm behind her back; she tried to round on me.

"What are you doing?" her voice rose higher as she shouted, trying to pull her arm out of my grasp, I held it firmly and slammed the first metal cuff hard over her wrist—not caring if it was too tight, not caring if it hurt. She tried to get away from me. I knew that as she struggled, the one cuff that was around her wrist was biting into her skin and would cause a bruise. I didn't care.

Todd quickly came to my side, pushing her up against the wall so that we could control her better. She fought us both, kicking, screaming, trying to get away, but the second cuff latched around the other wrist as Todd wrenched her arm behind her.

"What are you doing?" she screamed at us as we both took an arm, turning her towards the door.

"Ma'am, you are being detained while we investigate the death of your son." Todd spoke calmly and professionally although I knew he was as angry as I was. We started to walk her towards the door. She dug her feet down, trying to stop us. We lifted her up off the ground and started to carry her out.

"You can't do this!" she shouted, "Brian! You can't let them do this!"

I glanced in the direction of the man, assuming him to be Brian. He looked at his wife, turned his back on her, and walked to the little girl who stood off to the side with wide eyes. He scooped her up in his arms, sobbing against the little girl as we pulled the woman over the threshold and out the door. As we stepped out, I glanced one more time at the child on the ground. I didn't even know his name, but I felt such intense grief for his short life.

Beth was taken to my car and placed inside while she continued to scream at us that we couldn't do this to her. Not once did she say it was a mistake or that she was sorry. She just screamed that we couldn't do that to her.

I transported her to our local lock-up, trying to ignore her screaming as I drove. My anger mixed with grief just barely held in check. As we entered the lock-up, I led her back to the cell block. She continued to argue and yell. She didn't quiet until I removed her cuffs and pushed her into the cell.

She turned to look at me; I slammed the cell door closed, the heavy metallic sounds echoing loudly off the cement walls. I stared her down. A look of alarm crossed her face as she looked at the bars. Somewhere inside me, I felt just a little bit satisfied at the look of panic I saw.

I left the cell block without another word.

The county detectives were called in to investigate the incident. They discovered the child had fallen almost two hours before the mother called for help. The six-year-old explained that she was watching a particular show on television when the incident occurred. The husband had been called an hour later while he was at work, the mother telling him to come home because of a problem.

She was charged with a variety of things, and the husband refused to pay her bail, leaving her to sit in jail awaiting trial. I personally was proud of him for doing that.

The face of that child would stay with me for many years; I would find myself wondering why such a sweet young life could be taken so easily. I never got an answer, but I did eventually learn to deal with the grief for a child I had never known.

CHAPTER FIFTEEN

AMANDA

*S*even months later, the glass in front of me reflected back my long white dress. My hands brushed over the soft silky feel of the taffeta wrapped around my body. My dress was in the traditional style with a six-foot train, heavy full skirt, and a bodice decorated with small pearls and iridescent pieces.

My own breath hitched in my throat as I stared into the mirror. Who is this woman looking back at me?

"Don't you dare cry, Amanda! You are going to ruin your makeup." Angie stepped into the view of the mirror before me. I smiled timidly at her.

"You look beautiful, Mandy," she said softly.

I broke eye contact with her, moving back to look at myself again. "I do," I said as I took in the flawless dress, my hair hanging long and lush around my face. For the first time in my life, as I looked into the mirror, I truly felt beautiful.

"Practicing for the altar, honey?" my mother's voice filled the room. I turned to face her, her eyes grew misty.

"Oh, Amanda. You look absolutely stunning. What a lucky man Josh is to have you." My mother stood away from me, hands delicately clasped in front of her, her periwinkle dress softly flowing around her, sparkling even under the harsh yellow cast of the fluorescent lights above.

"Thanks, Mom," I said softly as we both tried to control the urge to cry.

We all turned when a small knock at the door came. My mother turned around to pull it open, and my father's voice called out from the other side. One look at him and I knew the tears would no longer stay at bay. My eyes filled quickly and I blinked rapidly to keep them from falling.

Angie pushed a tissue into my hand as my father stepped closer to me. "It's about that time, Mandy," his usual steady voice quivered lightly. I glanced around the room at my best friend Angie, my two cousins who were my bridesmaids, and my parents. All I needed now was Josh, and my happiness would be complete.

I took my father's offered arm and stepped out the door heading toward the chapel. I never thought to question anything. I never thought that this new segment that was about to begin in my life would become harsher than I could have ever dreamed, that with the excitement I felt at this moment, I would ever have anything other than a fairy tale life.

"Come on, Amanda, we're almost to the top," Josh called out from ten feet in front of me. We were honeymooning in the beautiful Smoky Mountains, spending five days in a rented cabin set high in the hills.

I looked up from the dirt path in front of me, Josh was smiling back at me. I tried to smile back, but my chest was hurting. I was in awesome shape. I worked out, I ran regularly, but trying to climb this incline was like my chest was being squeezed with a vice. I lagged behind him as he climbed upwards.

Trying to breathe slowly, I pushed on, ignoring the feeling in my chest, focusing instead on where my feet where stepping. A few minutes later, Josh let out a loud whoop. Taking my eyes from the ground, I realized I was way behind him and had another fifty feet or so to catch up. His shout gave me strength, and I pushed on.

"Come on, slow poke! This is amazing!" Josh yelled from above me. The excitement in his voice encouraged me to move faster. I cleared the tree line and stepped up next to him. My mouth dropped open at the beauty that lay in front of me.

His arms wound around me from the back, pulling me tightly to his chest. At any other time I would have welcomed his embrace, but my lungs burned and my throat was tight; his embrace made me feel trapped suddenly. I tried to pull away from him so that I didn't feel so constricted, but his hold on me was strong.

The feeling of being held against my will flashed through my mind, a flow of adrenaline quickly followed. I grabbed at his arm wrapped tightly around me and tried to pry it off. My lungs were so tight, filled with burning flames. Attempting to suck air into them was like breathing under water. I felt myself starting to teeter on the brink of passing out. Blackness was slowly moving into the corners of my mind. I fought harder as I began to panic.

"What the hell, Amanda!" he yelled as he pushed me harshly away. I fell to the ground, the gray blur still clouding my vision. When my head made contact with the rough ground, blackness surrounded me for a moment.

Stunned, I braced myself on my hands, trying to push myself up. I shook my head to clear the darkness that remained on the edge of my vision while still trying to draw air into my lungs.

"Why the hell did you push me away?" Josh's angry voice came from behind me.

I lifted my head up. My jaw fell open when I saw how close to the edge of the cliff I had fallen. Four feet in front of me, a rough stone edge fell off hundreds of feet below to the forest.

Slowly taking a few shallow breaths, I managed to push onto my knees to put more space between the edge and my body, the jagged shale an evil omen confronting me. I crawled back a few more feet, never taking my eyes off the craggy stone until I felt something run down my forehead.

I sat back on my haunches, carefully reaching up to touch my face: A small trickle of blood ran from a cut where my head had made contact with the hard earth.

"What is your problem, Amanda?" Josh's voice, rougher than I had ever heard it before, was still behind me. Why didn't he come to check on me? Say he was sorry for pushing me?

"I'm sorry, Josh," I turned to look at him. "I was just having trouble breathing, you grabbed me so tightly, and it made it harder to breathe. I panicked, I'm sorry." I panted between words.

His mouth remained set in an angry firm line; I watched his jaw tick for a moment before his face softened.

"Amanda, you're bleeding." He came to my side. Kneeling, he reached down and pulled the edge of his T-shirt up to press against my forehead.

I hissed at the contact, flinching when he touched it. A lump was already forming; I could feel it.

"It's okay, Amanda. I'm going to take care of you. It's just a little cut, no big deal; the bleeding will stop in a minute." He held my chin with one hand and pushed the material up against my head with the other. "I'll always take care of you, you know that, right? Why didn't you tell me you were having trouble breathing?"

I stared at him, wondering how he could go from anger to caring so quickly. "I didn't get a chance," I whispered.

"It's the altitude. Some people can't handle the higher elevation. Is your chest hurting?" He looked into my eyes. I relaxed as I gazed back into the softness of his. I nodded.

"Okay, let's just sit here and relax for a minute, and then we will head back down. Next time you need to tell me these things."

He placed a soft kiss on my forehead and chucked my chin gently, lifting his shirt from my head to examine the cut.

"There. It has already stopped bleeding." He sounded satisfied with himself. He adjusted his position so he was sitting behind me, pulling me into a gentle embrace. I leaned my head back on his shoulder, and I looked out over the view that stretched far and away for miles. It was breathtaking.

A haze softened the mountains in the distance and gave the view a dreamy quality. My body relaxed slowly, my lungs becoming used to the elevation. A large bird of some kind flew through the open sky, gracefully gliding and swooping in the currents above us. The feel of Josh's arms around me made me content and happy once again, even though a small throb had started in my head.

Lost in our own thoughts, we sat there for a long time relaxing with the silence of nature; every once in a while, Josh would kiss the top of my head as it leaned on his chest.

I was now twenty-one years old and happier than I had ever been. The cut on my head didn't matter. The tightness of my lungs eased, and I found myself dreaming of the future, my future with Josh.

We finally stood up, deciding it was time to head back down. I took one last glance behind me to find the beauty of the view marred by the presence of the cliff edge. A brief moment of panic hit me as I realized how close I had come to having gone over the edge.

Tamping that panic down, I turned to follow Josh. He stayed at my side, not rushing me this time, holding my hand every step of the way. The rest of our day passed quietly, relaxing in our cabin, an ice pack on my forehead as we snuggled and watched movies.

We had one more full day before we needed to head back home to our everyday lives. Our plans for a romantic dinner would end the trip nicely for us. The restaurant was a bit more extravagant than we would normally have chosen, but it was our honeymoon after all, so we treated ourselves. Josh made sure to call ahead for a reservation, having heard that the restaurant was one of the most popular ones in the area.

"Amanda, hurry up, we are going to miss our reservation."

I finished fastening my earring into my lobe and turned to walk into the bedroom wearing a simple basic black dress. Josh smiled gently. He walked over to me and put his hands on my shoulders.

"You look beautiful, Mandy," he leaned in and kissed me softly, "but you know this dress is kind of revealing, don't you think?"

I pulled back and looked up at him; the smile on my face disappeared. "I thought you liked this dress."

"Oh, I do like it, but I don't think you should wear it out in public." He smiled slightly, before turning his back on me.

I stared at his shoulders while he walked to the bedroom door. "What?"

"It shows too much cleavage, Amanda. I don't want men drooling over you."

His observation left me feeling cold. In the almost two years we had been together, Josh had never commented on any of my clothing as being inappropriate. He had always complimented me on what I wore, even this dress. His comment not only floored me but confused the hell out of me.

"Josh, I have worn this dress a bunch of times, and you never said anything before. I thought you liked it."

I glanced down, it wasn't revealing. It barely showed the slope between my breasts. Yeah, it was a bit tight, but it was not revealing.

"I told you I do like it, but it's for my eyes only. You're mine now, Mandy, you need to dress that way." He turned and walked out, leaving me speechless.

His comment echoed in my mind for a moment, I stood there not sure what to do. Was I supposed to change?

"Come on, Mandy, we are going to be late for our reservation," Josh yelled from the other room. I assumed that meant I didn't need to change. I picked up my purse, following him to the car.

The ride to the restaurant was quiet. While Josh didn't seem angry, he didn't seem exactly happy either. I kept to myself, watching the scenery pass outside the window.

The steak house we chose was busy, but our table was ready for us. Bypassing the long line of people waiting, we followed the hostess.

As she escorted us towards the back of the restaurant, I took in all the rich wood that adorned the walls and ceiling, warming the ambiance naturally. I went to sit down, facing the majority of the customers after the menus were placed on the table.

"No, I'll sit there," Josh said harshly. I furrowed my brow but didn't respond, moving to the other seat.

I picked up my menu, glancing at Josh, his jaw clenched tightly while he scanned the room. "I should never have let you wear that dress." He spoke through gritted teeth.

"What?" I really wanted to ask him what the hell his problem was, but the look on his face made me hold back, afraid to upset him further.

"Every man in here watched you wiggle your goods as you came to our table." He shook his head, picking up his menu to put it between us. I glared at the heavy plastic between us for a moment. I glanced casually over my shoulder as if to examine the structure and not the patrons. No one was looking at me.

"What are you talking about, Josh?" I whispered over the table as I pushed his menu down to see his face. The heated expression I encountered caused me to sit back.

"Amanda, just drop it. You have already ruined the evening. Just let it go. When we get home, I want you to throw that dress out. You're not wearing it anymore." He pulled the menu back up. I cocked my head to the side. Who was this man, and where did Josh go? I thought as I looked down at my menu.

How could a dress that I had worn many times suddenly ruin an evening? I went back to reading over the menu feeling a bit spiteful. What's the most expensive thing in this restaurant? Ah, yes, filet mignon. That's what I'm ordering tonight.

I set my menu down and gently folded my hands over the top of the table, my mind in a whirl on this new issue that had arisen.

I had never pictured him trying to control the clothing I wore, what else would he try to control?

CHAPTER SIXTEEN

AMANDA

*D*ays turned into weeks, and the weeks slipped quickly past to become months, then a few years flew by, four to be exact. My life was busy and, for the most part, happy. My eyes and heart had long ago left the honeymoon phase.

I frequently thought back to those words my aunt had spoken so long ago: *I'm concerned that he doesn't give you enough space.* Had she seen something that I had missed? Had I been blinded by the need to feel loved? A brief memory of Josh staring down at me on the night we'd met —a possessive look in his eyes before he'd kissed me—sent a small shudder through my mind. I pushed the memory away.

"Come on, Amanda, we haven't been out in months! Let's go see a movie on Saturday. Look, *Father of the Bride* comes out this weekend."

I wrapped the telephone cord around my finger as I lay on the couch, the cord from the kitchen phone pulled tightly around the corner to reach where I sat.

"I know we haven't been out in a while, I've been busy. I'm sorry." I wrapped the cord around my finger again, watching the tip turn purple. I continued with the cord, curling and uncurling it absentmindedly.

"A while? Come on, it has been months!" I heard Angie blow into the phone, she was smoking—a habit she had picked up recently.

"I'll ask Josh if it's okay when he gets home." I pulled my knees into my chest.

"What? Is he your father now? You have to ask his permission? Jesus! It's a freaking movie! It's not like we are going to go watch male strippers!"

I smiled. The thought of us going to a club with strippers was not something I would ever dream of doing. "No, he's not my father, Ang."

"Then, come on! It's a freaking movie!" she hissed into the phone.

I laughed, "I'll ask and give you a call back later. I need to go get dinner started, Josh will be home soon." She groaned into the phone, and then we said goodbye.

I walked back into the kitchen to set the phone back in its cradle on the wall, my hand resting lightly on it as I stood thinking about what she'd just said. Why did I always ask Josh for permission? Had I done this to myself? I wondered.

Dinner, I needed to make dinner. The old beige-colored refrigerator creaked open as I pulled on the handle. A pound of cheap ground beef sat on the shelf requesting attention; I pulled the meat out and started to brown it. We lived on a strict budget, hamburger helper was one of our staple meals, and all you needed was the beef and a box mix, cheap and easy. I absolutely hated the taste, but it was affordable and that was what counted.

I stood over the stove stirring the meat when the front door opened and closed with a bang. The vibration of the door closing so hard filled our small place, and I jumped slightly. Damn, he's obviously in a bad mood. His boots stomping on the floor confirmed my suspicions as he approached the kitchen.

I closed my eyes for a second. So much for asking about the movies, I would have to wait to bring that up. I turned, looking over my shoulder as he entered the kitchen.

"Hi, honey," I said quietly.

"What's for dinner?" he tossed his jacket over the back of a chair. His back to me, he dropped down into a chair and flipped through the mail.

"Hamburger helper, cheeseburger mac," I turned back around to stir the meat again. The sound of his hand slamming against the wooden kitchen table made me jump and spin, wooden spoon in the air whipping bits of meat and grease across the room.

"Can't you ever make anything else, anything good?" he shouted. I tried not to cringe at the explosion of his voice.

"You told me to make this when you called me this afternoon."

"Whatever," he replied in a quieter tone. I turned back to the stove, the sound of the chair scraping over the linoleum caught my attention, and I stiffened.

"Throw that shit out, or eat it, I don't care, but I'm going out."

I turned halfway around, my mouth dropped open. "Where are you going?"

"That doesn't concern you, I'm just going out." As if the door to leave was about to close shut, he hurried away. "I'll be back later."

Grease from the meat rolled down the handle of the spoon onto my hand. The door slammed, and I jumped, almost dropping the spoon.

What the hell was that? I turned around slowly, going back to the cooking meat. I sure didn't like this stuff, but I wasn't going to just throw food out, so I finished cooking it.

I sat down and began to eat slowly, blowing on the hot food in my bowl, wondering if something happened at work. Maybe I should have come to him when he walked in, rubbed his shoulders, kissed him, paid him a little attention. What if something happened at work, and he had just needed me to be there for him?

A few bites into my cheeseburger mac, I couldn't stomach another mouthful. I dumped the contents of my plate in the trash, pouring the rest into a Tupperware container and tossing it into the fridge. The dishes were few, and I finished them quickly.

Okay, now what? Dinner was over, dishes were clean, and the house was pretty much spotless because Josh expected me to keep a pristine house. I was home alone with nothing to do. I went through the few pieces of mail strewn over the table, a couple of bills and several pieces of junk mail. I put the bills in a pile for Josh; he liked to take care of that. I wasn't good with money, so it didn't bother me. I tossed the junk mail in the trash, moving to the living room.

Curling up on the couch, I wondered again about his outburst. Had I done something that I wasn't aware of? I was finding, more times than not, that I was the cause of his anger. I didn't quite understand how that worked, but he always seemed to be angry with me for one thing or another.

I fell asleep on the couch. When I woke up, the television flickered at me and the kitchen light glowed down the hallway. I looked at my watch, 3:47 A.M. Had Josh come home and not awakened me? I went to the bedroom to find it empty. I checked the other rooms, too, but there was no sign of him. Looking out the front window, I saw that his car was not there. Fear spun in my chest. Did something happen to him?

I paced. Who could I call? I didn't know his friends, and I sure didn't know their phone numbers. It was four in the morning, so would I call them even if I did? I continued to walk in circles inside the house, worried he was lying in a hospital someplace, alone and hurt.

The minutes went by slowly; eventually the sun began to rise. I turned on the news to see if they were reporting any accidents. The clock continued to move slowly and inched closer to the time I needed to leave for work. I grabbed clothes, heading into the bathroom for a shower. Halfway through washing my hair, I felt the vibration of the front door closing.

As a relieved sigh left me, the anger crept in. Where was he all night? Why couldn't he have called to say he was alright? I would ask him when I got out of the shower. In the meantime, I took my time, allowing the hot water to relax my tense and tired muscles. I pulled the door open slowly once I was dressed and walked to the bedroom; it was empty.

I tossed my dirty clothes in the hamper and walked to the kitchen: empty, too. Glancing down the hallway, I caught a sliver of the front yard, his car pulled away. I ran to the window and looked out. What was he doing? He just got home and he left again without saying anything! What was going on? I threw the towel in my hand to the floor and stomped on it like a two-year-old.

I knew he was safe now; the anger that I had just been on the verge of since waking took full force. I stomped back to the bathroom to do my hair. Jerk, I thought to myself as I picked up the blow dryer.

Every time the phone rang on my desk at work, I reached quickly for it, hoping to hear Josh's voice; I never did. I was torn between anguish and anger. I didn't understand why he had stayed out all night and left before talking to me.

Feeling like I needed to do something to make things better, I stopped by the store, splurging on some fresh fried chicken and salad fixings. Maybe while having a nice dinner he would tell me what was going on. I grabbed a fresh loaf of French bread before checking out.

I cut up the salad and cooked some instant potatoes to go with the chicken as soon as I got home. I was agitated about him coming home; keeping my hands busy helped them not to shake, so I scrubbed the already clean counter while I waited.

When the front door opened, it didn't slam shut this time. I turned around to wash the cleaner off my hands. I couldn't trust myself not to glare at him when he entered.

"Hey, babe, how was your day?" Josh spoke as soon as he walked around the corner, his voice giving away nothing.

"Fine. Yours?" My back still to him, I rinsed my hands longer than necessary; the anger crept up, my shoulders stiffened.

"Same ol' stuff, nothing too exciting. What's for dinner? Smells good." He put his hands on my hips, rubbing his body against mine provocatively.

"Fried chicken, potatoes, salad, and bread," I said gently, but my body instantly betrayed my need for anger as he slipped his hands around my waist, pulling my back up against him. I wanted to fight him, yell at him, but his hands on me melted the anger away too easily. It had been weeks since he had come to me like this.

He kissed my neck, "How about I have you and then we eat?"

I twisted my neck to the side to allow him easier access to my neck.

"Mmm," was all I could manage as his tongue slid up my neck. How could I be angry when the man I loved was touching me this way? He kissed my neck again and then stepped back quickly.

"On second thought, I'm starving. Let's eat now." He reached up to grab a plate out of the cabinet. I watched in surprise as he filled his plate quickly. Usually when he was being amorous, there was no way he would stop, but a switch had just flipped. I stared in disbelief when he walked to the table.

Absently, I took down a plate, setting some food on it slowly. By the time I reached the table, he was already halfway done. I kept my eyes on my plate, picking at the crunchy skin on the drumstick.

When I had barely eaten a quarter of my dinner, Josh stood up and put his plate in the sink without a word. I stopped chewing, watching the muscles in his back move as he walked down the hallway to the bedroom. Normally, we would sit together until we were both done. Normally, we would talk during dinner. This was so not normal.

A few moments later, Josh came out, planting a kiss on my cheek. "I'm going out, don't wait up for me."

What? He was going out again? I didn't even know where he'd gone the night before, now he was going to be late again tonight? The door closed. I dropped the drumstick, my appetite gone.

Tears burned the tissue of my eyes. I dumped the rest of my food into the trash, fighting back the tears as I put the leftovers away. What the hell was going on?

CHAPTER SEVENTEEN

NICOLE

The years moved along, and I became much more comfortable with myself and my career. I stopped second guessing my decisions, and my confidence grew. I felt equipped to not only help people, but to mediate in situations that didn't necessarily require the usual legal action.

"Thirty-Seven Paul Three," a static-filled voice came over my radio while I sat typing up a report on station about a verbal domestic I had just cleared a few minutes ago.

"Thirty-Seven Paul Three," I responded, clicking the save button on my program. I pushed away from the desk and stood up.

"Thirty-Seven Paul Three, you have a physical domestic at 104 White-hall Way. The caller states her husband just pushed her up against the wall and tried to choke her."

"Thirty-Seven Paul Three, okay, I'll be en route." Once I'd heard the words physical domestic, I had started towards my car.

"Thirty-Seven Paul Three, the caller states that her husband is intoxicated and there are guns in the house, but they are locked in the safe in the basement. Do you want another unit?"

"Paul Three, yeah, send me another unit." I flipped up my laptop once I was in the car, double checking the address. I knew the caller, Rebecca

Swift. I had been to her house a few years before for a report. The laptop clicked loudly as I pushed it closed. I put the car in gear and pulled out onto the roadway.

This was the third domestic in just my jurisdiction tonight, although the first two had only been verbal arguments. They were smart to call when they did because they would have probably turned physical if we had not shown up.

Most times, for verbal domestics we played mediator. We'd listen to the parties involved and try to help them figure out a temporary solution to get through the night peacefully.

The caller would many times apologize for bothering us, but we always told them to never apologize. We'd rather come out to help deal with an argument than come out and deal with something that had gone too far, like the call to which I was responding.

Chances were, this incident had started out as an argument and, thanks to the alcohol, had escalated into something much more. Physical domestics could get sticky, and when alcohol came into play, they were like caramel apples.

I pulled into the development of single family homes, the standard cookie cutter ones that developers threw together quickly on half-acre lots. It was obviously a newer development from the state of the landscaping, the trees just starting to grow from the saplings that had been planted. The dark streets had only a few small streetlights to brighten small circles around their bases. I slowed down as I closed in, reading the numbers on the mailboxes for the correct address.

Before I stopped, I picked up my car mic, "Thirty-Seven Paul Three, anything further?" I waited for my dispatcher to respond as I pulled my car to a stop a few houses down from the residence to which I was heading.

"Thirty-Seven Paul Three, we currently have an open line. We can hear a man yelling in the background."

"Okay, I'll be on location." I put the mic back in its clip as another car pulled up behind me. From the headlights reflecting in my rearview mirror, I recognized the vehicle as a police cruiser; my backup had arrived. We drove slowly down the roadway, turning our headlights off before we got too close to the residence, and we parked in front of the next-door neighbor's house. I never took my eyes from the front of the modern two-story Victorian house once it came into view, watching for any movement at the doors or windows on the first and second levels of the home.

As I got out of my car, I heard a car door click gently behind me, a quick glance revealed Adam walking up to me. He worked for a neighboring department. Our departments sometimes only worked with one officer on the street, so it was not unusual for us to back each other up. I tipped my head to him once quickly as I turned back to the house.

We scanned the nine windows on the front of the house and watched for movement coming from the sides as we walked quickly by cautiously. Our portable radios were on but turned down to a lower volume, not only to keep them from hearing us, but so that we could hear small movements. In situations where we had no idea what we were walking in on, we always erred on the side of caution.

We made our way up the side of the driveway, crossing in front of the beige garage door, both of us peeking in the windows as we went. At the end of the garage, we stopped, and I peered around the corner to the front of the house.

Two windows stood between us and the front door. The lights shone through onto the lawn, and there was no one visible. I stepped out from the cover, walking at a fast pace to the front door, watching the windows while I moved. Adam's tactical boots softly thudded on the limestone pavers behind me.

Stepping up the two cement steps to the front porch, I stood off to the side of the door away from the small glass window beside it. Adam moved off to the left behind me.

I glanced into the side window, and movement in the back of the house caught my attention. A man's voice could be heard yelling. I reached for the doorknob. I didn't need to knock; I received my invitation to visit them personally when the call was placed to 911. The doorknob turned easily. I pushed open the door with my left hand, my right hand on the butt of my firearm still inside my holster. Adam stepped in quickly behind me; he pushed the door mostly closed before we started toward the commotion inside.

My hand still rested on my firearm when we entered the kitchen. The bright lights of the kitchen caused me to blink for a moment as I took in the scene. The kitchen area was separated slightly from the kitchen table by a beige countertop. The smell of spoiled food and dirty water filled the air, and dishes were piled up next to the sink. My quick scan of the surfaces showed no weapons. My attention moved to the incident transpiring in front of me.

It was obvious by the way the man, facing away from us, was yelling at someone that he had no idea we were there; I was glad of that. The man stood about six foot one, his burly shoulders rounded, his arms moving up and down as he yelled, like an angry bird trying to scare away a predator. Just to the left of him, the shoulder of a smaller person could be seen.

"You are such a bitch, Rebecca!" he shouted at the person, raising his hand as if he would strike her. One hand open to strike, the other fisted at his side; I released my firearm, reaching across my body for my Taser on the left side instead. If he didn't go on verbal commands, he would listen to what fifty thousand volts of electricity had to say. When my hand connected with the Taser, I pushed the button to release it, calling out to him.

"Step away from her."

I stepped closer pulling the Taser slightly out of the holster, just enough to make for a fast and easy removal if needed.

The man spun around, shocked at my voice.

"You called the police!" he shouted, turning back to Rebecca.

In his brief movement, I saw the woman huddled up against the wall, the side of her face red. There was a hole in the wall just to the right of where she stood, fist sized. Anger seared me as my vision went back to him.

"Step away from her—now." I took a single step closer to him. Almost simultaneously, Adam did the same beside me. Mr. Swift looked between both of us, frustration evident in his eyes while he stepped back from his wife, his hands up in the air.

We walked to him immediately, "Turn around and put your hands behind your back," I directed while I approached him. His hesitation to do what I told him was noticeable, but he eventually turned. He obviously did not want to listen to a woman. Oh, well, sucks to be him, I thought.

When he had his back to us, we each grabbed an arm; I slipped my other hand behind my back, grabbing my cuffs from the leather clip that held them to my duty belt.

"What did I do?" he yelled, trying to pull away from us. The odor of alcohol wafted towards us with his words. I saw eyes bloodshot and glassy when he looked over his shoulder at me.

"You're under arrest for assaulting your wife," I responded as the ratcheting of my cuff filled the room around one meaty wrist.

"I didn't touch her!" he bellowed, resisting us more. Adam had a tight grasp on his other arm, wrenching it up behind his back enough to put the guy on tiptoe. I pulled his other arm up, securing the second wrist. His struggling continued for a moment before he turned and spat on me.

Oh, yeah, so not a good idea.

Adam watched the man spit on me and immediately reacted. The man promptly found his face pressed tightly against the light oak kitchen cabinet, the beige Formica counter digging into his oversized gut.

Adam's voice was tense and assertive as he spoke, "Add resisting arrest and assaulting an officer to the charges. You want to keep it up? We could keep going, see how many more charges we could add to it." His forearm pressed firmly on the back of Swift's neck to hold his face tightly to the wooden cabinet door.

I turned my head to search for Rebecca. She stood silently watching us, huddled against the wall, her arms wrapped around her body tightly, as if she were cold. The red mark that had begun to appear on her face stood out against the white wall behind her.

I glanced over the counter top, finding a roll of paper towels just behind me. I pulled one off and wiped the offending body fluid off the shoulder of my uniform shirt and then tossed the towel onto the counter.

"Are you done?" Adam asked Swift as he leaned into him and spoke directly into his ear.

"Yeah," Swift responded.

Adam eased back, ready to lay into him again if he tried to fight.

Swift hung his head as Adam released him from the imprisonment of his arms, the fight in him now gone.

"Thirty-Seven Paul Three, Thirteen Paul Five, your status?" our radios keyed up in stereo.

"Thirty-Seven Paul Three, status is fine, one in custody," I responded while taking the man's arm. He would wait in the car for now.

He looked at his wife when we started to walk past her, "Baby, I didn't mean it. Tell them I didn't mean it," he pleaded with his wife.

Liar, I thought to myself. I'd heard that before, it was always a lie.

After slipping him into the rear compartment of my car, I grabbed my clipboard from my gear bag in the front passenger seat, heading back to the house for the wife's statement. Adam stayed out with the prisoner.

I found Rebecca sitting at the kitchen table; I sat down quietly beside her, waiting patiently for her to look up at me.

"Rebecca, are you injured, would you like an ambulance to check you out?" I spoke softly to her.

Her head shook before she answered, "No, it's just a headache." She went back to inspecting her hands that lay on the table.

"Tell me what happened," I continued speaking gently to her.

Her shoulders drooped slightly while she thought about her words. "It was my fault." I watched her inhale and exhale before she continued. "Jason got home from work and he was in a bad mood. I left him alone mostly, but I'd asked him to fix the kitchen sink, the drain was stopped up." She made eye contact, so this was truth. "He said he would, so I left him alone and went to my office to do some work."

She paused, I waited. These things took time and patience. Mentally, she was walking through the whole incident trying to decide what she wanted to share. I reached out, resting my hand over her forearm, "What happened next, Rebecca?"

She looked at my hand, then at me before closing her eyes and slowly shaking her head. She wasn't telling me no, she was trying to tell herself that it hadn't happened.

"I came back into the kitchen about two hours later; he was sitting on the couch watching television. The sink wasn't fixed, so I asked him about it." Her face came up quickly to mine. "He just flipped out then. He jumped up off the couch, started screaming at me, and then pushed me up against the wall." The cadence of her voice rose as she spoke.

"Did he hit you then?" My hand still rested on her arm, giving her a small comfort.

"Yeah, but it wasn't hard." She looked away.

"It was hard enough to leave a mark on your face." I pulled my hand back. She was starting to transition into denial. As my hand moved away, she lifted her hand up, touching her still-red and now slightly-swollen cheek.

"Did he hit you with his fist or an open hand?"

"I don't know, maybe his fist," she said quietly, her gaze locked on the grain of the oak table.

"Is this the first time he has hit you?"

She shook her head but didn't speak. I nodded absently, I'd figured as much.

"Are you really taking him to jail?" she reached for a napkin in front of her, the first tear eased down her inflamed cheek.

"Yes, he is going to jail tonight. I need you to give me a written statement about what happened."

"Am I going to have to testify against him?" Horror crossed her features.

"Yes," I nodded, "Rebecca, yes, you will be called into court to testify to what happened here tonight."

She already began shaking her head before I finished. "I can't."

"Rebecca, you have to—not because I am going to subpoena you, but because you have to put a stop to this. If you don't do something now, it's not going to get better. It's only going to get worse."

"But I can't," she cried out. "I testified against him before and it only made things worse. He was good for a while but then held it over my head. He kept blaming me for having to go to counseling and pay the fines. I know it was my fault, so I can't go through that again."

It was the same old broken record. I'd heard this way too many times in my life.

"Then why are you staying in this relationship?" I tried to keep the frustration out of my tone.

"I have nowhere else to go. He won't let me work, so I don't have any money," exasperation filled her voice.

"Do you have any family or friends that could help you out?" I cocked my head as I asked, careful to keep my voice soft and not threatening.

"No. My family all lives out west, and the only friends I have are friends of his." A deep sadness crept into her words.

"You do know there are organizations that help women like you, right?"

She shook her head. "I don't need their help. I'll figure something out; it's really not that bad."

I couldn't count the number of times I'd heard those words. "Not that bad? Rebecca, your husband struck you. You say it's not the first time he has done it, and I can guarantee it won't be the last time either. Men like him don't get better, they just get worse—especially when they see they have control, and you won't fight them back. "Rebecca, there are a lot of resources to help women who are in abusive relationships. You don't have to be afraid to contact them."

"I'm not afraid. I just don't need their help." She twisted the paper towel in her hands.

"From where I am sitting, I think you do." I thought for a moment. "Rebecca, if you think that things are going to get better, they aren't. Your husband has a problem. You need to face that. You need to get out of this relationship before something really bad happens. If you don't do something now, it will only progress."

"You don't know that," she said without conviction.

"Yeah, actually I do know that. I know that people who are abusive start out by being verbally abusive, and then they get mentally abusive before they finally turn physical. I know that sometimes that progression can take years, sometimes just days. The one thing that I absolutely know for certain is it does not get better on its own. They need to be punished for what they do to people. You can't allow him to keep doing it to you. You have to stop it, and if that means testifying and putting him in jail for a little while and finding a way out of this, then that is what you need to do!"

I let my words sink in a few moments. "Rebecca, at least do me a favor and contact the Domestic Violence Hotline. They can help you. They can help you get a Protection from Abuse order against him so he can't touch you again. If he does while you have one, then he goes immediately back to jail on an indirect criminal contempt charge."

She continued twisting the napkin in her hands, mulling over my words. Finally, she relented, "Okay, I'll give them a call."

"Good. That's good, that's the first step." I reached for her arm, squeezing it gently. "Now, I need you to give me your written statement for what happened tonight, while you are doing that I'll get you the phone number." I smiled gently; making sure it touched my eyes when she looked up. I wanted her to know that it was the right thing to do, and that I was happy she was doing it. I pulled the paperwork out of my clipboard, sliding it across the wooden table along with a pen.

Victims were like children, they needed careful handling. Many times it was necessary to reward them with a smile or small gesture like a pat or a gentle squeeze on the hand to urge them to do what needed to be done.

I sat back in my seat, waiting patiently while she wrote. Deep inside, I knew that she might make that phone call, but I had no idea if she would take it any further. Most women said they'd call, but once we closed the door and left, they never did. Until they decided to leave and take control of their lives, we would be coming back, again and again.

CHAPTER EIGHTTEEN

AMANDA

*J*osh didn't come home that night, or the next, or the next. Each night, I lay in bed staring at the ceiling, listening for his car, hoping he would come home. Anger burned in my body over his actions. Pain lanced my heart from not comprehending them.

What had I done to make him do this? I spent hours dwelling on that question, no answer ever coming to mind.

During the day, my focus scattered. I worried about his safety. I buried myself in my work, cleaned the house like there was no tomorrow, and skipped eating. No food could fill the void inside me. Each time the phone rang, my heart would skip a beat, my hands would shake. Was it him, or was it a hospital calling to tell me he was dead?

I would raise the phone to my ear, the blood rushing through my veins making it hard to listen; I would find myself disappointed to find it was neither. Not that I wanted him dead, but any word would have been better than nothing. When my friends called, I found excuses to get off the phone quickly. I spent hours staring out the window into the darkness that mimicked my heart.

I woke on Saturday from a brief and restless sleep; rolling out of bed, I looked over at his side. Something must have happened to him, he hadn't even been home to get clothes. I just didn't get it.

I put coffee on and sat at the table, once again staring out the window. A cardinal landed on a tree branch outside, I wished that I could be like him and fly away. Did a cardinal feel pain? Did it have emotions? The cardinal opened its wings; stretching its throat, it called out. A female cardinal landed on a branch nearby, a mate perhaps. They sang together for a few moments and then flitted away.

A sigh from deep within me escaped. I poured my coffee and sat back down. Even though it was not cold inside the house, my body felt frozen, I wrapped my hands around the mug, the warmth of which barely touched the muscles in my hands, definitely not reaching the most important one, my heart.

The sound of the front door caused me to jerk. Hot liquid spilled over the side of my cup, burning the top of my right hand slightly. The door closed, my heart thudded erratically in my chest. He's alive, I thought; adrenaline and fear coursed through my body, my hands shook. I wrapped them more tightly around my mug to steady them, ignoring the small burn on my hand.

Afraid to move, almost afraid to breathe, I sat and waited.

His footsteps slowed as he entered the kitchen.

"Hey, Amanda," he said quietly.

Did I hear embarrassment in there? I didn't trust my voice to speak; I turned my head, looked at him briefly, then went back to my very interesting coffee before me.

"Glad you got coffee on, I could use some." He walked past me. My body jangled with nervous energy, the anger rising. I clenched my jaw.

He pulled out the chair next to me and set his full coffee mug on the table. I stared at the white knuckles of my hands, prayed I didn't break my mug with the tension in my fingers.

"How are you?"

My eyelids flickered quickly a few times while I absorbed his words as I looked into the depth of my coffee mug.

Really? Did he really just ask me how I was doing? I looked at him. His face was cleanly shaven, a T-shirt I had not seen before on his body. No apparent injuries and—would you look at that?—he actually looked rested. Glad someone was. I took in his face a moment longer, lingering on his green eyes slightly before putting my attention back to my captivating mug. My hands relaxed slightly, I lifted the mug up to my lips, sipping lightly.

"What, you're not going to talk to me?" his voice was full of disbelief, or was that arrogance?

I took another sip, glanced at him again, and then stood up. I walked out of the room. I was so angry, even more so now that he was acting like nothing happened. I would need to seriously calm down before I attempted to speak with him.

Standing next to the bed, I closed my eyes, counting to ten. I got to seven before he walked into the room and stood behind me.

"Why did you walk away?"

My God, was he that dense? How could he not know that I would be upset when he stayed away for days without even a phone call?

"Where have you been?" I asked quietly, my voice shaky to my own ears.

"I was out." I could almost hear the shrug that went with the attitude. I nodded to myself.

"You were out. Nice." Inhaling deeply, I started to count to myself again, but stopped at five this time when he put his hand on my shoulder.

"Come on, Mandy girl, I just needed some space." He tried to turn me around, but I refused, jerking out of his grasp.

I took two steps forward, whirling around on him when the anger exploded through me, "Space! You needed space!" I screamed. "You come home one night then walk out in the middle of dinner with no words! Then you come home three days later and say you needed space!" The anger and fear shook through my body as I let out the verbal assault.

He ran his hand through his hair. "Yeah, I guess I didn't handle that very well."

"Ya think?" I laughed angrily and crossed my arms over my chest. "What was there to handle, Josh?" I yelled back. Still unable to get a grip on my anger, my eyes filled with tears.

He turned his back on me. "Look, I just needed some space. I have a lot going on, and I just needed some time to think."

The tears spilled out of my eyes and ran down my cold cheeks. My hair swung about my head as I shook it. I didn't understand this. I wanted so badly for him to pull me into his arms and tell me he was sorry, to tell me that everything was alright.

"Talk to me, please, Josh." The words barely got out of my mouth. I stared into his back. I wanted to beg him to talk to me, but I couldn't.

His shoulders went up in a big shrug. "There is nothing to talk about, Amanda."

My shoulders dropped. Deflated by his words, I turned, sobbing into my hands.

While I cried, I hoped that he might attempt to console me, yet at the same time I didn't want it. I wanted to be angry. I finally wiped my face with the backs of my hands. He sat on the bed, elbows on his knees, his head hung low staring at the floor.

I pulled open a drawer on my dresser, blindly taking out underwear and socks. In the closet, I grabbed a pair of jeans and a shirt. I needed to get away from him before I completely broke down. The shower would at least hide the tears I knew would break through again.

"Where are you going?" Josh asked as I walked out of the room. My answer was the sound of the bathroom door slamming.

With the shower turned as hot as I could stand, I climbed in, allowing the water to shelter me and absorb the tears that instantly fell again. Why does someone need space from his wife?

Afraid to find out if he was still there or if he had left again, I took my time drying my hair to delay learning the answer. Sadly enough, part of me wanted him to be gone, which didn't make much sense. A larger part wanted him there to make things better, to explain why this was happening.

I walked slowly to the bedroom, it was empty. My heart beat rapidly inside my chest while I dropped my clothes in the hamper. In the kitchen, I found him standing at the sink, looking out the small window above it, his hands resting lightly on the counter. I didn't approach him but leaned back against the wall.

He turned his head to look at me over his shoulder. He took a deep breath and turned around. He crossed his strong arms over his chest and leaned against the counter, the heel of one foot resting on the tip of the other.

"Look, Mandy, I have some things going on. I can't explain them to you, I'm sorry, but I promise I won't do it again." There was pain in his eyes as he spoke.

Could he actually be sorry? What if I wasn't ready to forgive him yet? "Where were you?" I took up the same position next to him.

"It doesn't matter," he spoke softly, his face pointing to the floor.

"It does matter, Josh. You left three days ago, and you never called me to tell me where you were or that you were alright. I was worried about you. Did you not even think about that?" I watched him while he continued to stare at his feet.

"Yeah, I thought about it, but you knew I was fine." He rolled his shoulders back, lifting his chin from his chest. "I promise; I won't do it again, okay?" His eyebrows rose while he turned to me.

Would I just let it go and not expect answers? Should I press him and tell him it was important? Voices warred inside my head. I wanted so badly to forgive him and just let it go. That was the side of me that eventually won, "Fine."

He reached for me, pulling me into his arms, right where I wanted to be. I wished for the last few days to disappear. I just wanted us to go back to the way things used to be with us.

I clung to him tightly, resting my face on his chest. He pulled back, smiling gently down at me, "Hey, how about we go out for a little while, one of the guys I work with is having a party. Let's go out and have some fun."

I couldn't resist smiling back. Fun…that sounded nice. It had been a while since we had done anything like that. "That sounds good."

He leaned forward, kissing me quickly before he let go and walked away. While part of me felt better, felt that we could put this behind us, the other part of me continued to be frustrated that he would not tell me where he had been. I decided I needed to let it go for now so we could enjoy the day.

The ride to the party was quiet. I wasn't sure what to talk about, and he didn't seem inclined to start a conversation. I passed the time by looking out the window, trying to relax.

When we arrived, I found myself sitting alone, Josh walked away to talk to his friends. I barely knew any of the people here. A few kids ran here and there, their antics kept me occupied for a time.

Watching the young smiles and hearing the sounds of their laughter brought back a long-forgotten memory. My child would have been close in age to these little ones. How different my life would have been. Yet, if things had gone along another route, I wouldn't be where I was now. Where exactly was I now?

I scanned the room and found Josh sitting outside with a beer in his hands, laughing. Getting off the sofa, I went to join him. I made my way to the cooler and pulled out a soda.

I planted myself beside Josh; laying my hand down on his shoulder. He stiffened, laughed at a joke someone said, and then moved away from me. My eyes roamed the group of people, but I didn't believe anyone had noticed. A sliver of pain pierced my heart; I wrapped both my hands around my soda, looking down at the ground.

Josh never spoke much about work, so listening to them joke about what they did was interesting to hear. I stayed quiet, standing beside his chair, feeling out of place, but not willing to give up hearing the little bits and pieces they let fall.

Food was served soon after, Josh piled his plate full then walked away to sit someplace where there was no seat beside him. I found a single seat on the corner of the patio away from the group. Feeling like an outsider, alone even in this group of people, I kept to myself and ate in silence. Why had he wanted me to come if he didn't want to even talk to me?

Many of the wives joined in on the conversations from time to time, but few spoke to me. Some gave me shy smiles while they passed by. I was already not an overly social person, and the vibes I got off Josh and the problems we were having kept me off balance and even more quiet than normal.

The sun began to set when I found myself in the kitchen making small talk with a few women, helping get things cleaned up. The conversation soon turned over to children, a topic I knew nothing about, and I made my way back outside.

On the back porch, I stopped and looked around: Josh was nowhere to be seen.

"He went out to get more beer," one of the guys responded to my questions quickly when I asked him Josh's whereabouts. I nodded slightly, walking away to sit in the chair by the edge of the porch again, more uncomfortable than before now that I was alone. The guys would glance my way once in a while, the darkness helped to hide my embarrassment and pain.

Time moved slowly, a few people started saying their goodbyes. It had now been two hours since Josh had left. Where the hell was he? I wondered what the people were thinking each time they turned to look at me.

Embarrassed and angry, I made my way to the bathroom. Why would he go off and leave me here? I leaned back against the closed door. The anger I had tried to tamp down earlier hit me with a vengeance.

With my shoulders held high, I opened the bathroom door; I slipped out, quietly walking out the front door without saying a word to anyone. I wasn't going to wait any longer, I would walk home. I felt mortified that he had left me for hours with people I did not know. I wrapped my arms around myself and walked down the dark street.

My head hung down, my eyes trained on the sidewalk with my mind a million miles away; I didn't look up as I heard a car coming down the road.

Josh's voice broke me out of my painful thoughts as he yelled out the window, "What the hell are you doing, Mandy?" The car stopped, but I refused to.

"Mandy, get in the car!" he yelled at me again. I kept walking, my eyes still on the cement in front of me.

The car door opened and closed, anger and sadness mixed in my head, and I wanted to run from him. He ran to me, the grip he had on my arm as he spun me around shocked me.

"I asked you a question! Where are you going?" He clenched my arm tightly enough to make me flinch.

"Let go of me, Josh," my voice came out in a heated whisper. He pulled my arm up, causing me to go up on my tiptoes and lean forward towards him. His breath raced over my face; I gagged at the intense odor of alcohol that rolled over me.

"Get in the car, Mandy," he seethed at me before he pulled me towards the car.

"Let go of me, Josh, you're drunk! I'm not getting in the car with you!" my voice was now loud in the dark night. I had no choice but to be dragged to the car when I could not pull my arm out of his grasp.

"Josh, I said let me go!" Tears blurred my vision, pain radiated up my arm and into my shoulder the harder he tugged on me. At the car, he yanked the passenger door open.

"Josh, I'm not getting in the car with you!" I shouted at him.

He jerked my arm so hard, I thought he had dislocated my shoulder. Using his body, he pinned me to the side of the car. He was breathing hard, his face red, his eyes bloodshot and glassy.

"Shut up, Mandy. You embarrass me! Jesus, you embarrass me! Just get in the fucking car." He yanked open the door and pushed me inside.

I fell into the seat as he pushed me. The look of anger on his face and the intensity of the way he yelled at me shocked me profoundly. Memories of a time long ago with Steve surfaced, chilling me to the bone. Josh got into the driver's seat, throwing the car into drive immediately. I reached for the seatbelt, but he accelerated so quickly that the belt locked back.

"Josh, slow down!" I screamed from the passenger seat.

"Shut up, Amanda, I don't want to hear another word come out of your mouth!" he shouted back.

I braced myself against the dashboard and door with my arms. My eyes wide, my heart racing, everything sped by me. What could I say to calm him down?

Alcohol and anger did not mix; he drove like a lunatic. He skidded around one corner and raced down the dark residential streets.

"What is your problem, Josh? Slow down!" I screamed. I wanted to look at him, but my eyes were locked on the road. I never saw the hand that snaked out and grabbed my hair, yanking me close to him.

"I told you to shut the hell up!" I closed my eyes tightly from the pain and fear. Spittle flew into my face as he yelled, throwing me away from him with such force that my head struck the passenger window. Shock and pain registered first in my mind. Surprise that the window did not shatter came next.

My hands went to my face as I started sobbing. What was going on? What did I do now? He had left *me* at the party, he left *me* there! Why was he angry at me? What the hell did I do?

I couldn't control the sobs as they racked my body. I knew Josh was yelling at me, but I couldn't make out his words over the sound of my own tears.

What I did hear next was the sickening sound of tires locking up, the clashing of metal against metal, and the tinkling of glass and other small pieces falling around us. My body was picked up with such astronomical force that I flew through the windshield onto the hood of the car.

For a few seconds, the silence around me was deafening. I could barely make out the tick, tick, ticking of the hot engine under my ear along with a hissing noise from someplace in front of me. No other sounds registered in those first few seconds. Once the agony started, even those sounds faded away.

My palms and face were hot against the hood, I tried to push myself up, but the movement caused a bolt of pain to streak through my stomach, the sound of my own voice screaming vibrated around my skull. I fell back to the hot metal, the discomfort became overbearing in intensity to the point that I very quickly disappeared into the darkness of my mind.

CHAPTER NINETEEN

AMANDA

Slowly, awareness dawned. I heard odd noises off in the distance that made no sense to my cloudy mind. I tried to move, but I felt too heavy, buried under a thick layer of mud. My mind felt fragmented and distant while my mouth felt as if someone had shoved cotton in it. I tried to lick my lips, but my tongue wouldn't seem to move.

The noises grew louder, the constant beeps and a steady humming vibrated in my ears. A dry coldness blew into my nose. I wanted the cold air away from me, but I didn't have the energy to move it.

Where was I? What were all these sounds? I felt a hand squeeze mine gently, a voice drifted to me through the haze in my mind.

"Amanda? Amanda, open your eyes." I knew that voice, it was Angie. Why was she in my bedroom while I was sleeping? I was sleeping, right?

I tried to do as she asked, my lids fluttering slightly, but they failed me. All at once, I felt so tired that I willingly retreated back into the darkness.

When my mind came around again, I picked up on the same noises faster as I tried to open my eyes. They slowly flickered open. The room was bright white, and a beige curtain hung next to me. A machine beside my bed beeped regularly, keeping time with my pulse. I was in a hospital. Why?

"Amanda...there you are." Angie's face came into view when she bent, she squeezed my hand again. "Glad to have you back."

I tried to swallow, but there wasn't much to swallow, my mouth was so dry. She picked up a cup, holding a straw to my lips. I sucked gently, never so thankful for the taste of plain water as at that moment.

With my mouth wet, I looked back to her. "What happened?" I asked, my voice deep and hoarse to my own ears.

Angie reached forward, pushing hair off my face, "You were in an accident, a car accident. Do you remember any of it?"

I stared at her, trying to remember, but I couldn't. I slowly shook my head once. Her lips tightened.

"Josh was driving, he struck another car." She was watching me carefully for a response. I remained silent.

Josh...the car...the screeching of tires and the twisting of metal. We had been fighting, he had been mad at me, I had been sobbing, and he'd grabbed my hair and yelled at me, throwing me against the car door. I remembered the heat of the metal hood under me, the sound of the scream.

"He crashed because of me," I said hoarsely.

"What? No! He crashed the car because he was drunk, Mandy!" Her anger was visible; I flinched at the venom in her tone. "He was twice the legal limit; he went through a stop sign and struck another vehicle. You were tossed out the front windshield. It wasn't your fault." She shook her head adamantly, squeezing my hand to the point that it almost hurt.

"It was my fault. He was angry at me, we were fighting," I said quietly.

"No! Amanda, it doesn't matter if you were fighting or not. Josh should not have been driving that car. Why did you even get in the car with him, and why weren't you wearing your seatbelt?"

I knew the blame for the accident lay with me. I looked away from her. Josh had been angry and driving that way because of me. Angie wouldn't understand.

"I didn't have a chance to put it on," I said quietly looking at the curtain. "Where is he?"

"He's in jail where he belongs! They not only charged him with driving under the influence, but they might charge him with attempted vehicular homicide. You almost died, Amanda." her voice softened as she spoke.

My eyes closed. I didn't want to think about Josh being in jail. I deserved what had happened to me, but he didn't deserve to be in jail.

"I called your parents; they should be here later this afternoon. They took the first flight that they could get."

I nodded with my eyes closed. "I'm tired." I didn't want to think about what my parents would say to me. I just wanted to lose myself in the dark hole in which I had been hiding.

"Go back to sleep, I'll be here when you wake back up. I'm not going to leave you until your parents get here."

I nodded slightly but was already sliding back into the much-needed darkness. Maybe it would have been better if I had died, I thought as I slipped back into a dreamless sleep.

The next time I woke, I felt a little bit more coherent. The numbness in my mind seemed to have receded quite a bit, making it easier to come to the surface. I opened my eyes, my mother and father stood near the window looking out, their backs to me.

"Mom," I spoke hesitantly.

She immediately turned as did my dad, both moving to my side. "Oh, honey…how are you feeling?" My mother's hand felt so good in mine.

"Tired…a little hungry…how long have I been here?"

"Two days, honey." She patted my arm while she squeezed my hand.

"Two days? What happened to me?" As the words escaped my mouth, I felt the pain in my body for the first time. My muscles felt sore in my arms and shoulders, my back seemed stiff, tender. My stomach, right leg, and hips throbbed intensely with each beat of my heart.

My mother glanced at my father before looking back at me, sitting carefully on the side of the bed. She pulled my hand into her lap, holding it with both hands. My father walked to the other side of the bed, stopping near my face, resting his hand on the top of my head to smooth back my hair. Their response, so unexpected, instantly made me fearful.

"What? What's wrong with me?" I looked back and forth between them.

Tears came to my mother's eyes and she did nothing to hide them as they slid down her cheeks, leaving soft shimmery water trails on her skin.

"Amanda, honey, you were hurt pretty badly in the accident. You flew out the window when you crashed. They didn't know if you were going to make it. They rushed you into surgery as soon as you got to the hospital."

"What was wrong with me, Mom?" my voice sounded frail, and fear gnawed at the back of my brain.

She needed a moment to compose herself before she began, "When you went through the window, the glass cut deeply into your stomach. You had a perforated bowel and some other damage." She looked down with the last words.

"What other damage?" When she wouldn't look at me, I spoke more loudly, "Mom, what other damage?" My father's hand smoothed along my head more intently, obviously trying to calm me as he had when I'd been little.

"Honey," my father spoke, I traded his face for my mother's, "your uterus was damaged." His eyes looked pained, but I wasn't sure why.

"I'm alive, so they must have fixed everything, right?" I said, looking back to my mother. She sobbed slightly and stood up.

"Daddy?" I asked as I looked at my mother's back.

"Honey, they fixed your bowel, and they set your leg, you broke that, too, but they weren't able to fix your uterus." There were tears in his eyes as he spoke. I didn't understand why they were so upset, but then it hit me.

"I'll never be able to have children?" I said just above a whisper. My father's eyes shut, a single tear eased down his cheek.

A memory of long ago came to mind; a time when I had once held a child inside of me. I had never allowed myself to think of that time, always believing that someday, things would be different and I would have a child with the man I loved.

I felt not only sorrow but anger travel through me; an anger that I had not felt in so many years. All over again I remembered what I had been forced to endure, anger at the odds of my life. I wanted to laugh…the odds of my life! What odds? My odds were oddities!

"Honey, it will be alright," my father spoke as he stroked my hair. The soft sounds of my mother crying at the window were the last sounds I heard before I fell back into the nothingness of sleep.

The final time I woke that day, I didn't want to open my eyes. I lay there quietly, thinking about what I knew. Josh had been drunk and very angry with me when we had gotten into the accident. I had been thrown from the car. The injuries were severe enough to take away any chance of having a child, and Josh was in jail.

It was all my fault.

I just couldn't understand what I had done to make him so angry. He was the one that wanted me to go to the party with him. We were going to have fun, yet when we got there, he had ignored me. He left me there for hours alone, with no one to talk to, so I had left feeling mortified.

Was the damage to my body punishment for what I had done to upset Josh? Was God looking down at me and telling me I was worthless and I should not have lived? If that was it, why didn't He just let me die? God probably didn't think I was good enough for heaven. Even He didn't want me.

Was there a way I could make it up to Josh; a way to fix our marriage? The sound of a sniffle got my attention, I opened my eyes. Josh sat in a chair in the corner of the room, head held in his hands while his elbows rested on his knees.

"Josh."

His head rose quickly, his eyes bloodshot. He wiped his cheeks with the backs of his hands and stood. He slowly walked towards me.

"Amanda," his voice cracked with emotion as new tears slid down his cheeks. "I'm so sorry." He stopped at the edge of the bed, obviously leery of coming any closer.

My heart broke at seeing the pain he was in, tears spilled from my own eyes. I reached for his hand, "It's okay, Josh."

He reached for my hand while he bent to his knees next to the bed, cupping my palm on his cheek, "I'm so sorry. I never meant for you to get hurt. I really didn't. Can you ever forgive me?"

My heart soared! He was worried about me, worried I would not forgive him. Here, I thought I might have upset him so much that he wouldn't want me back. "Of course, I forgive you, Josh, but can you forgive me?"

His head came up and he looked at me questioningly, "Forgive you?"

"If you weren't angry with me, none of this would have happened. I'm so sorry I made you angry."

He cocked his head; I looked into the face of the man I loved, praying he would forgive me.

"Of course I forgive you, Amanda. I know you didn't mean to fight with me. I love you, baby." He stood up, leaning forward to kiss me gently. Nothing else mattered at that moment, not the past, not the future, only this moment. He loved me and he forgave me. We could figure out the rest later, except his endearment raised a question, "Josh, you know I won't ever be able to have kids now, right?"

I watched his brow furrow, "Yeah, I'm sorry about that, but we don't need kids. As long as we have us, we don't need anything else, right?"

I smiled gently while my heart did a little flip, "Right... we only need us." He kissed me again and I closed my eyes, once again tired, drifting back to sleep content to know that Josh still loved me and everything would be alright.

The naiveté I had would threaten me more than any physical deed could. Accepting his simple apology and not realizing he had turned the tables on the blame would cost me dearly in the future.

CHAPTER TWENTY

NICOLE

"Sure, if we find your dog, or anyone calls, we will let you know." They thanked me again and I hung up the phone. I ripped the note off the pad of paper I had written it on and pulled a thumb-tack out of the drawer beside me. Turning to the wall where our huge corkboard hung, I pushed the pin into the paper where the other notes about missing dogs and cats hung.

My Nextel chirped. I unclipped it from my belt. "What's up, my man?" I replied when I saw it was Colton on the phone.

"Hey, honey, how's your shift going?"

I leaned back in the gray swivel chair, kicking my feet up on the wooden desk in front of me. "Pretty quiet, what about you? Oh, damn, did I just say that?" I laughed as I released the side button. I realized that I had used the taboo word of "quiet" out loud. Every cop knew if you used that particular word, you usually got slammed with calls.

"Yes, you did," he was laughing, too. "I meant to ask you earlier today where you wanted to go for dinner for our anniversary tomorrow night. Any place special you might want to go?" Our anniversary, five years married now and as peaceful and relaxing as the day it had begun. Thank you, God!

I leaned my head back on the top of the chair and stared up at the white ceiling above me. I watched a spider crawl over the eggshell paint above me and held back a shiver—ugh.

"How about Mexican? We haven't been down to our favorite place in a while. You want to invite Tom and Suzanne to go with us? We can make a little party out of it." I straightened up while I answered, unnerved at the slow speed of the spider above me. The soles of my boots planted on the wooden floor under me pulled me closer to the laminate desk so I could rest my elbows on it.

"It has been a while since we went there, great idea. I'll give Tom a call and see if they want to come." While he was finishing up his sentence, I heard my dispatcher call me. I answered her before I hit Colton back up and told him to hold on.

I got up, walking through the locker room to the back door of the station where our patrol cars were parked. "Hey, I gotta go, honey. I just got dispatched to a suicidal teenager, I'll call you later, be safe." I waited for his response, told him I loved him quickly, and put aside our conversation as I climbed into my car.

Suicidal teens—they were always a tough situation to deal with; they were so fragile. Luckily, I did well with teens and could usually talk to them at their level. It amazed me since I was an only child and had no kids of my own. How I was able to relate to them I didn't know; I just knew that I could and I would use that to my advantage.

I pulled up to the house in another one of our cookie cutter developments and saw a man standing at the door, ready to open it as I approached. I cut across his freshly-mowed lawn instead of walking around to the driveway. "Evening, Officer, thank you for coming."

Nodding, I stepped into the foyer. The chandelier of the standard two-story suburban home threw odd shadows on the wall around us creating a mysterious backdrop with two of the six bulbs burned out.

"What's going on?" I glanced around, taking in the formal living room on one side and formal dining room on the other side of the foyer, both clean and neat. I listened for unusual sounds from within the home, but only heard the voice of the newscaster from the eleven o'clock news coming from down the hall talking about a recent development overseas.

"My daughter Lucy has locked herself in her bedroom. I guess she got in a fight with her boyfriend today and now she says she wants to kill herself. She locked her door and won't let me in."

"How old is Lucy?" My attention remained on him, even though I continued to listen for sounds around me.

"She is about to turn sixteen. Her mom is out of town and normally she deals with this stuff." He shook his head and held his hands out to me, "I have no clue what to do, I called her mom, and she told me to call you guys."

I smiled slightly at him, "Alright, where is her room?"

He pointed up the beige carpet-lined stairs and started heading that way with me right behind him.

The stairs led up to a hallway with four doors, three were open so the odds were good which one was Lucy's room.

"Thirty-Seven Paul Three, status," my dispatcher checked on me. Generally, one minute after we put ourselves on location, our dispatchers would check our status. Most of the time, we advised them that we were okay. Sometimes we would tell them we were okay for now and they would check back with us a few minutes later.

"Thirty-Seven Paul Three, my status is fine, you can have EMS proceed in, but have them stage outside until I advise." I called over my mic clipped on the front of my uniform shirt, the cord running over my right shoulder and down my back to the radio on my belt.

They acknowledged my transmission while I stepped up to the door. Her father pointed at it like I wouldn't know it was the correct room. I knocked on the white painted wood.

"Lucy?" I called out, but received no reply as I waited a few more seconds.

I knocked louder in case she had headphones on. "Lucy, this is Officer Nolan. I need you to open the door." Still no response. I tried the door-knob, it was locked.

"Sir, how long has it been since you have spoken with her or heard any movement in the room?" My voice was soft, trying to keep the conversation between us.

He shrugged, "Thirty, maybe forty minutes ago."

I banged on the door harder, yelling for her to open the door. No response. My adrenaline kicked in as I wondered if she was alive on the other side of the door. I stepped back taking the call to the next level. Using my karate training, I kicked the door near the knob. The door frame splintered as the lock was forced in. The door started to bounce back at me, but I stopped it with my palm and moved into the dark room rapidly.

My flashlight came off my belt in one swift movement. I turned it on and scanned the room. A twin bed divided the room in two, the covers twisted at the bottom of the bed and clothes and papers scattered over the top. I looked over the bed to the other side of the room, in the corner lay a small female on her side in the fetal position. I climbed hurriedly over a mass of clothing piled on the floor and went to her side.

"Thirty-Seven Paul Three, I need EMS inside now!" I dropped to my knees, feeling her neck for a pulse. There was a soft beat under my fingertips, but it was slower than it should have been. I rolled her onto her back, pulling her out from the corner to lay her flat in what little open space I could find. Her body was heavy from the deep sleep she was in. I grabbed a pile of books and threw them up to the bed, then pushed an array of cosmetics, papers, and shoes across her gray carpet to be hidden under her desk so there was room to work.

"Lucy, Lucy! Can you hear me?" I called out loudly to her, using the knuckles of my left hand to rub her sternum hard—no response. The floor was covered with clothing and makeup, I needed to figure out if she had taken something; I kept scanning as I tried to wake her. Just under the edge of the bed, I found what I was looking for; a soda can on its side next to a prescription bottle. I grabbed the bottle and read it. Damn!

"Thirty-Seven Paul Three, I need medics dispatched for a fifteen-year-old unconscious, possible overdose with Hydrocodone." I was sure they acknowledged me, but I wasn't listening.

On general medical calls, an ambulance was dispatched with EMTs. They were trained to do basic life support and injury, but when someone's life hung in the balance, we called out a medic. They were actually nurses who could administer medicine and make medical decisions that the rest of us could not. This had quickly become a matter of life or death, and their assistance was needed immediately.

"Sir, is your wife Barbara?" I glanced at him while keeping my hand on Lucy's chest to make sure she was still breathing.

"Yeah," he was standing by the door, shock on his face as he watched me on my knees. "Those pills were from about two months ago when my wife had surgery."

"Sir, how many were left in the bottle?" I looked back to his daughter, taking the knuckles of my right hand and digging them into her sternum to get a response, nothing. I heard the door open downstairs, a voice called up.

He shrugged, "I don't know…maybe fifteen or twenty. The doctor gave her more than she needed."

Two EMTs pushed into the room, I told them what I knew. I helped them get an oxygen mask on her and watched as they started taking her vitals.

A third EMT entered the room with a portable stretcher and we moved Lucy onto it, strapping her down. We were putting her into the ambulance when the medics pulled up. I ran over to their vehicle, helping them pull their medical equipment out of their vehicle and carrying it to the waiting ambulance, while telling them all I knew about the girl, the family, and what might have been taken.

Minutes later, with everyone loaded up, the ambulance took off, lights and sirens blaring. I stood on the side of the road next to my car looking up at the house. The windows were all lit from the inside. The look of fright on the girl's father's face as he pulled the door closed behind us to jump into the ambulance with his daughter imprinted on my memory.

I shook my head and opened my car door. How little teenagers think of themselves, feeling like there is no one else in this world for them. I remembered as a young adult wanting to end my life over something that now seemed so silly. Back then, it had seemed as if life would be so much better if I weren't part of it, but I had grown to know better.

Climbing into my patrol car, I cleared myself from the call, still thinking about Lucy as I drove around. If she survived, she would be forced into counseling. She would most likely be held in a program for a few days to figure out if she was still a threat to herself. A plan of action would be developed to help her deal with her self-esteem issues, and hopefully she would learn that no one person should have that effect on her young life.

As I weaved in and out of the quiet neighborhoods, patrolling, I thought of my own life as a young adult. How many times had I wished I were dead? Five or six maybe? I knew that I had dealt with some major depression. I had learned to fight it, well, actually learned to conquer it. There was no one more important in this world to me than me, and I would not allow anyone to change the love I had for myself. Never again, I said to myself.

My computer beeped at me, I lifted the lid to find I was being dispatched to a suspicious condition. The caller said he'd heard a motorcycle in his yard and now it was lying in the back. He didn't see anyone around it.

I put myself en route to the call and considered the most direct route before I turned my car around in a dark driveway. Most likely a stolen motorcycle, who else would be riding one at midnight in someone's backyard?

The location of the incident was in the rear of a large development, where the house backed up to the woods. The closer I got to the house, the more the stolen motorcycle idea made sense.

As I pulled up in front of the two-story colonial at the far end of a cul de sac, a man walked out of the front door, heading my way. "Evening, Officer. Sorry to call you out here so late."

Chuckling, I answered him, "Sir, it's not late to me, I'm here all night. What's going on?"

He explained that he'd been watching television in bed and heard a motorcycle rev its engine. When he looked out the window he saw it lying on the ground at the bottom of his hill, but there was no one around it.

After a few more questions, I sent him back inside. Making my way down his long driveway, I stopped where the blacktop met the grass of his backyard. Surprise struck me as I noticed a twenty-foot sapling lying flat on the ground with tire marks next to it. Damn, that must've hurt, I thought. The backyard had a serious slope down about fifty to sixty feet, the beam of my flashlight followed the embankment.

I stood up straighter as the light beam struck something.

"What the hell is that?" my voice whispered into the night. I kept staring but couldn't figure out what I was looking at. It sure wasn't a motorcycle. The beam of my flashlight moved along the bottom of the hill. I could see scattered debris strewn everywhere. What was all the debris from and where was the motorcycle?

I looked behind me over the length of the driveway, then back down the hill. Usually, when people tell us that they saw or heard something, we tend to find pretty close to what they were describing, but I was at a loss here. I focused my light on the ground in front of me, making my way down the hill. I drew closer to the object, my eyes opening wide as I finally made out what it was. "Wow...seriously?"

At the bottom of the lawn lay a mangled trailer and, flipped upside down, a small fishing boat. A boat? I looked back up the hill to the driveway. Did I have a runaway boat? From where?

I walked closer to the boat, realizing the debris scattered about were the cushions and gear normally stored inside. I stopped near the mangled wreckage and looked around. How could this sound like a motorcycle?

Shining my flashlight around the area in a wider pattern, I walked up an embankment on the back side of the yard, my light beam moved back and forth. Baffled, I turned back around to the boat.

A sound behind me caused me to turn quickly and reach for my firearm in my holster. The crunching of branches could be heard in the woods; I lifted my gun and pointed it in the direction of the noise. I took two steps to the left and I stopped when my light hit something on the other side of a tree, a man, and not just a man, but an old man and a car.

"Hey! What are you doing?" I called out as the man stood with his back to me. I kept my gun trained on him as he turned around. He lost his balance and fell against his vehicle.

"Umm." I heard him mumble as he tried to stand up straight again. I wasn't sure if it was his age, the fact that he was standing on an incline, or that he was drunk, but for whatever reason, he lost his balance and fell back again.

"My television fell and hit the gears of my car and it just accelerated."

I chuckled to myself; I had my answer. "Sir, we need to get you out of the woods. Are you alright?" I holstered my gun, walking over the dense brush towards him.

"I'm fine. Just a little scared, that's all." He didn't look up at me, but I knew that my flashlight was pretty bright and most people did not try to look up through it.

The sticky bushes snagged at my pants and jacket as I got closer to him. About eight feet away, one of my hypotheses was confirmed when he spoke once again. The intense odor of alcohol wafted through the heavy night air. Whew! I blew out my nose to clear the scent.

"Come on, sir, we need to get you out of here." I helped him out of the thick brush, trying to keep him from being smacked in the face by branches. Once out, I had him sit down on the ground and get his bearings.

"Sir, do you know where you are?"

He looked around the area and I followed his eyes, not much to see but the outline of two-story houses in the distance. It was really dark back here.

"Kind of," he looked at the ground.

"Sir, how much have you had to drink tonight?" I stood over him.

"Probably about four beers," he replied hesitantly and hung his head.

Well I knew that when someone said they had "about four," they really had "about eight." It's just one of those things you learn being a cop. I eventually got him up to the front yard and out to my car where he submitted to a field sobriety test and failed. Surprise, surprise. He was taken into custody without incident and would spend the night in jail.

In my opinion, he deserved more than one night in jail, especially since he had admitted to having had several DUI arrests in the past. My tolerance for drunk driving was very low. Anyone who would jeopardize someone else's life by getting into a car after they had been drinking deserved a much greater punishment.

I did find out from the homeowner that the boat actually belonged to him and had been parked at the end of his driveway. The motorist thought the driveway was a continuation of the roadway, and he'd just cruised right on down, never seeing the obstacle until it was too late.

In my eight years on the job, I had seen way too many accidents with drivers under the influence of drugs and alcohol. The worst part of it was they almost always walked away uninjured, while the others suffered injury or death just because of the drunk drivers' bad judgment. Not wanting to dwell on it or the anger it caused, I shook my head and made my way back to the station.

CHAPTER TWENTY-ONE

AMANDA

For months after I got out of the hospital, Josh catered to my every whim with breakfasts in bed, back massages and foot rubs, staying home from work some days when I wasn't doing well, and sitting up with me at night when I couldn't sleep.

With him beside me, the healing was easier, inside and out. This was the happiest I had been in a long time. I cherished every moment together and hung on his every word.

We never spoke about the accident. I knew he had gone to court for his DUI charges, but he told me he got probation, some community service, and had to go to some classes. As far as I was concerned, we never had to speak of it again, it was water under the bridge.

Even with the happiness I felt, I soon started to see him withdraw from me again. At first I didn't mind, thinking he needed some time to himself after doing so much for me, but the day came when I started wondering. Was I being too needy? Was I not there for him enough?

Nine months after the accident, I lay on the couch, waiting for him to come home. I found myself bored, with nothing to do to fix that. Josh and Angie did not get along at all now, and Josh refused to let me go hang out with her. Trying to keep the peace, I allowed the friendship I'd had with Angie to slowly slip away.

After we got married, I dropped out of my college courses, we just didn't have enough money at the time. I quickly lost touch with the few friends I had made there.

I stopped going to the gym years ago. Like my schooling, Josh said we couldn't afford it. I had often wondered if there was more to it than that. He had commented a few times about how he didn't like the other men looking at me while I lifted and made me change from my normal workout gear to T-shirts and baggy sweats. At the time, I didn't think much about his requests, finding his jealousy rather endearing.

These days, I left the house to go to work at my secretarial job and to run household errands. There was nothing else to fill my days, and I would sometimes think back on that one conversation I'd had with my aunt about always being with Josh. So much had changed in six years.

I no longer found his jealousy endearing, instead I found it irritating. Why he thought I would cheat on him was beyond me. Since the day we were married, I had never looked at a man twice for any reason.

As late night television came on, I sighed and looked at the window. The darkness behind the glass reflected in, I watched the television images ripple in the darkened glass. I looked at my watch, 11:47.

Turning the television off, I went into the bathroom to brush my teeth and get ready for bed. I wasn't going to sit up and wait. He would come home when he came home. After fluffing my pillows, I quickly slid off to dreamland.

Something woke me with a start. I sat up in bed. My eyes wide, my heart pounding against my chest, I listened carefully. Something hit the wall in the hallway. I gripped the sheets tightly to my chest. Another thump and then I heard something fall. A loud *oomph*! followed the sounds of the fall; I recognized the sound of that voice. Throwing the cover back, I jumped out.

The bedroom door was closed, and I hesitated just a moment before pulling it open. Josh was on his knees trying to stand up, his hand against the wall to balance himself. The hallway reeked of alcohol. I put my hand onto his arm to help him, but he pushed it away mumbling something.

He finally made it to his feet, but after one step lost his balance again. I reached out instinctively to stop his fall.

"Josh, let me help you."

"Leave me the hell alone. I don't need your help," he slurred and tried to push me away again, but this time I held on.

"I said leave me alone." He jerked his arm up faster than I expected, striking me in the face. With my back against the wall, I slid to the floor as pain overwhelmed me. Tears welled in my eyes as I held my nose, unable to talk or breathe until the agony cascading through my body started to recede. Blood flowed onto my hands.

Josh stumbled to the bed and fell face first on the mattress, feet hanging off the side. He passed out as soon as his head hit the sheets, or maybe before, I didn't know or care.

I closed my eyes, trying to contain the pain. Once the stabbing in my sinuses stopped, I pushed myself off the floor, moving towards the bathroom. The light shining in the room showed the horror in the mirror. Blood dripped down my chin onto my nightgown and the beige Formica of the countertop. A washcloth sat next to the sink. I held it under my nose, careful not to squeeze too hard. Obviously, my nose was broken thanks to Josh's elbow.

The swelling had already started when I pulled the washcloth away, the area over my nose and under my eyes an angry red. Pain continued to pound in my face with the steady rhythm of my heartbeat. I refused to allow myself to sob, no matter how much I wanted to.

In the kitchen, I removed a cold pack from the freezer, wrapped it in a cloth with one hand, while the other hand continued to contain the dripping blood.

Gingerly, I made my way to the living room. Each step vibrated up my body right into my nose. Sharp pinpoints of pain moved towards my brain, an ice pick stabbing me repeatedly. Once at the couch, I lay back, putting the ice pack gently on the bridge of my nose, and pulled the washcloth off. My nose continued to bleed.

The ice finally started to work, numbing the skin and swollen cartilage. Sure, I knew this was an accident, but I was angry at him for it. He had come home drunk. My thoughts froze as I was suddenly seized by the awful realization that maybe he had driven himself home. I pulled the ice pack off my face and stood up slowly. The blood that pooled in my nose moved with gravity, I held the washcloth under it tightly to catch it.

The window loomed in front of me; I felt my hand shake as I reached it. Josh's car sat partially on the driveway, with the majority of it in the front yard. I wanted to scream. I felt the need to shake him awake and yell at him. Was he absolutely nuts to get into the car and drive while he was drunk? Especially when he was this drunk! Didn't he learn the first time?

My head throbbed, or more correctly, my face. I moved back to the couch, anger seethed in me, raising my blood pressure, the pounding worsened. I put the ice back in place on my nose. Eventually, the bleeding stopped and I found some pain medicine left over from my accident. I swallowed one, climbed back onto the couch, and tried to fall asleep. Eventually, the pain medicine did its magic, taking the pain and my consciousness away.

The pounding in my face woke me as the sun started to enter the living room window. Just moving slightly hurt, and I tried not to move my face at all, breathing out of my mouth. The house lay still; I assumed Josh was still passed out.

Too afraid to see the damage to my face, I didn't turn the light on in the bathroom. I looked into the bedroom; he lay in the middle of the bed, still fully dressed, shoes and all. I shook my head, wincing at the pain. Pulling the door shut, I went to the kitchen to make coffee.

While the coffee brewed, I sat staring out the window into the backyard. There were so many things that angered me that I didn't know where to start. Maybe I should start with the most serious: the fact that he drove home when he couldn't even walk straight; or maybe why he didn't bother to call and say he'd be late; or should I start with the fact that he broke my nose?

My coffee ready, I sat at the table trying to drink it without bumping the mug on my nose. When I heard movement down the hall, I glanced at the clock, it was just after eight, he was up sooner than I'd expected. I continued to stare out the window, the cadence of my heartbeat picked up with the thought of confronting him. The sounds of shuffling into the bathroom were telltale signs he was probably half asleep and very much hungover. I sat up straighter in my chair.

The water ran for a while in the bathroom, then I heard only silence. When the door opened, I listened to his footsteps as they came closer, hesitating at the entrance to the kitchen. I picked up my mug, holding it between my two hands.

"Morning, Amanda," his voice was husky as he walked to the cabinet to get a mug. He poured his coffee. "What, not going to talk to me because I stayed out late?" His voice held a defensive tone that I recognized. I stayed quiet, not trusting my voice as my heart raced against the inside of my chest, causing my nose to throb.

"Get off your high horse, Mandy." He walked closer to me raising his voice. "Don't be such a bitch. I was out with friends."

I nodded slightly, out with friends, nice. Wish I had friends to go out with, I thought to myself. A novel thought since he'd chased away the only good friend I had.

"What? Nothing to say?" he stood behind me, I continued to stay quiet. "Fine! Be that way!" His coffee mug came down hard on the counter causing me to flinch, a slight splash of warm liquid running over the edge. He walked out of the room towards the bedroom and the door slammed.

A few moments later the door opened and the bathroom door closed. I heard the shower go on, I sat stiffly in my chair, not doing anything but listening to the noise from the bathroom.

My coffee was bitter cold when he finally exited the bathroom. He stood behind me, "You got anything to say?"

The sounds of his footsteps were blocked out by the blood pumping through my ears. "Not even going to look at me?"

Taking a slow deep breath through my mouth I turned to look at him. The eyes that had once been so full of life and love were now hard and bloodshot.

"What happened to your face?" he asked harshly, and I turned away.

"You hit me in the face last night with your elbow when I was trying to help you," my voice was quiet and void of emotion.

"I didn't do that!" A nasty hollow laugh came from behind me, "Don't go around telling people I did that! No one would ever believe you anyway. You're so clumsy you probably walked into a wall."

I didn't feel the need to answer him, as I had no intention of telling anyone. Obviously, he had been too drunk to remember anything from the night before.

I could feel his eyes burning into the back of my head. He laughed again, "You are worthless. You know that? Why did I ever marry you? I have no clue." He turned while speaking, walking out of the room and slamming the front door.

He slammed more than just the door; I felt a piece of me closing as the wood clicked into place. Outside, the car started and tires squealed as he pulled away quickly.

My legs were numb from sitting so long. I got up slowly. I placed both mugs in the sink and went to get dressed.

The swelling of my nose didn't look as horrible as it felt. I also had light circles under my eyes, but nothing awful. Eventually, the swelling would go down; I would just need to keep ice on it.

The words he'd spoken before he walked out rang in my ears. Was I really worthless? Where was my life going? Over the last year, my marriage seemed to have fallen apart. Things had seemed better after the accident, but as I looked around the room, I wondered if things would ever really get better or if this was what my life would be forever.

Confusion clouded my mind while I recalled the laughter, jokes, and just kicking back together that we used to do. Was the time he took care of me after the crash just his way to apologize for what had happened?

He once again had grown distant, worked later, and went out with friends more often, never bothering to call me during the day. The wedge from a year ago was coming back, now deeper than ever.

His words had hurt me, but most of the things he did caused me pain. Maybe he was right, maybe I was worthless. I didn't have any friends, worked in a simple office job doing menial tasks. I had no goals for my future, no thoughts of what I wanted for myself. I seemed to have failed at everything, including my marriage. Would I now become just a statistic? Another marriage gone bad?

If I got divorced, where would I go? My parents had moved to Pennsylvania just before the car accident. I didn't know anyone, so would I go there? Would I stay here? Hell, I didn't even know anyone here!

I leaned my head back on the couch cushion with a fresh ice pack on my nose. I needed to figure out what was going on in my marriage first. Maybe we could fix it, go to some counseling—although I doubted Josh would be willing to do that. He didn't want to talk to me, so why would he talk to a stranger? Could we fix what was wrong? Could I get Josh to love me again like he used to?

Saturday morning passed slowly as memories of my past haunted me. Would I forever be in relationships where pain and fear were a constant? Would I ever feel like someone would love me enough to die for me? Those so-called fairy tale happy endings didn't seem to be part of my life.

Somewhere inside of me, I knew that I was worthy of being loved and that I deserved it. I just didn't know where or how to find that love.

Maybe I could call Angie, but she probably wouldn't want to talk to me. It had been so long since I'd returned one of her calls that she had finally stopped calling.

Guilt sat on my shoulders like a lead weight. I really wanted to talk to someone, but I was alone. Even if I had someone, would I say anything? That might mean acknowledging the fact that my marriage was falling apart. No, I couldn't tell anyone, it would just prove what Josh had said: I was worthless.

Besides, the only person I could talk to was Angie. She didn't like Josh, so telling her these things would only make her angry and hate him more. I didn't want to hate him, I wanted to love him. Loving him used to be easy; getting his love in return proved to be the hard part.

CHAPTER TWENTY-TWO

AMANDA

*T*he day dragged by interminably. I flipped from channel to channel trying to find something to fill the time. The medicine kept the physical pain away, but not the emotional pain that crushed me like a weight, pulling me under so I drifted in and out of sleep amongst the soft cushions of the couch.

A quiet knock at the door got the blood moving when I got off the couch. Not thinking, I pulled open the door without looking through the peephole. Angie stood on the front step. I straightened up taller and tried to smile, wincing slightly as the pain moved over my face.

"What the hell happened to your face?" Angie stepped closer and pushed the door open without an invitation.

"Nothing," I said as she stood in front of me. I took great care in turning to close the door, trying to think of what to say to explain my injury.

"Don't tell me nothing!" Angie yelled from behind me. She looked mad as hell when I finally got up the nerve to face her again.

Walking past her, I went back to the couch, "Really, Angie, it's nothing. I walked into the wall." Josh's excuse sounded like a good one.

"Somehow, I don't believe that, Amanda. You don't just walk into a wall and come away with a swollen face." She shook her head and sat on the other side of the couch. "Did Josh do that to you?"

"No!" I answered too quickly, her eyes tightened at my response. "No, Josh wasn't even home." Physically maybe, but not mentally, I thought to myself. My tone was calmer when I continued. "Seriously, I was walking, tripped, and hit the wall. No big deal." Shrugging, I looked away from her, pretending to be interested in the television.

The lie was almost too easy to say. Why was I lying to Angie anyway? Earlier I had wanted someone to talk to, maybe now was the time. She was my best friend, and even though she didn't like Josh, maybe if I told her my problems she might know what I should do. The temptation to share with her was great, yet I felt that because she didn't like him, she would not be able to give me sound advice on how to make things better. Her advice would be to get away from him as fast as I could, and that was not something I could do. I loved him, and I knew he loved me too. I knew we would make it work.

Wanting to move the subject away from the incident, I asked, "What are you doing here?"

She smiled, "I missed you! You never answer the phone or return my calls. I was in the area, thought I would stop by and check on you."

"I'm sorry," I responded with my eyes cast downward, and I really was. I felt awful for ignoring her, but it was just easier to avoid her when Josh was around. "We have been so busy lately." Another lie, but I wasn't about to admit I was home alone every night wondering if and when Josh would return.

"Where's Josh? I saw his car was gone; it was the deciding factor for stopping. I was hoping you would be home alone."

"Um, he's out with friends. I didn't want to go looking like this, so he went alone." I stood up, "Do you want a drink? I was actually thinking of putting a movie in. You have time to watch one with me? I could put popcorn on."

"I'd love nothing more than to chill with you, I have all afternoon!" She jumped up and we headed into the kitchen to prepare movie-watching snacks. With the flavorful bowl of popcorn sitting between us, we settled down and put in a VHS movie from my collection.

Having her beside me reminded me of all the fun we used to have. I found myself missing that old life, the one where I laughed all the time and got out of the house more often than just to go to work or to run errands.

With the popcorn long gone and the movie finished, Angie looked at me. Obviously she had something on her mind. I was afraid to encourage her to talk and avoided her eyes.

Angie reached out and touched my arm just as I went to stand. "Amanda, I need to talk to you about something."

I sat back down, resting the bowl on the coffee table. "What's up? Is everything alright with you?"

She smiled, "Yeah, things are great with me." She looked down at her hands. "It's actually about Josh."

Crap. Here it goes, I thought. This is the reason I had not spoken to her, because she didn't like him and she was now going to tell me just how much.

"What about Josh?" I asked hesitantly as I watched her look around nervously. Her chest expanded as she filled it with air and then she blew it out in a steady stream before looking at me.

"Look, Amanda, I know you love Josh and all, but there is something I need to tell you." The nervousness spread out around her, and I wondered if I should stand up and walk away or send her home before she spoke.

When I didn't respond, she continued, "Amanda, I know you aren't out with him at night, and I know this because I see him quite often. Do you know where he goes?"

Her eyes held mine intently. I wanted to answer yes, but I could only shake my head ever so slightly.

"I didn't think so." She looked down at her hands clasped together, appearing to gather strength from them before she went on. "He hangs out at the bar around the corner from where I work."

The fact that he was out drinking wasn't news to me, where he was hanging out was. "Okay, why is that such a big deal?"

"It's a big deal because he is not there alone. I have seen him more than once walking in with another woman." The stress she put on the word woman did not go unnoticed.

I shrugged, "So, it's probably just someone from work he hangs out with." I wasn't going to make this a big deal, so he was out drinking with friends; at least one of them was a woman.

"Does he hold hands with the people he works with?"

I closed my eyes, wanting to block out what she was trying to tell me. If I closed my eyes tightly enough, it would go away, right?

"Does he kiss the people he works with?"

My eyes opened of their own accord as my back straightened. She stared at me, waiting.

"What do you mean kiss them?" my voice whispered into the quiet room.

Her glance encompassed the whole room before it came back to me. "Yesterday, I got off work a little late. I was stopped at the light right next to the bar, I saw his car and standing against the car was Josh. He had his arms wrapped around another woman and they were kissing, pretty passionately."

"That had to have been someone else, Angie, Josh wouldn't do that." Would he?

She was shaking her head, "Sorry, Mandy, but I know what Josh looks like, and he was only like twenty feet away. I saw him. I'm sorry."

"Who was the girl?"

She shook her head, "I don't know. I've never seen her before, well, except with him."

"How many times have you seen her with him?" As much as I didn't want to admit it, I needed to know more.

"I see his car at the bar almost every night after work. I guess I have seen him with her maybe five or six times over the last few weeks." She reached out and took my hand. "Did you have any idea?"

"No." Did I? Did I not know that things were different, that we had drifted apart? Had I ever considered the possibility that there was someone else? Not really.

"Talk to me, Amanda. Tell me what's going on." She squeezed my hand as she spoke. The pressure of her fingers was like the popping of a water balloon, all the emotions and anger burst forth. I leaned into my hands and sobbed, not caring about the pain in my nose.

Angie moved closer, wrapping her arms around me, trying to soothe me with her touch. She didn't speak but let me cry until I finally got a hold of myself.

"I don't know, Ang, I just don't know what's going on." I got up off the couch to get a tissue, blowing my nose as gently as I could, bringing the box back with me. Angie sat patiently waiting for me to pull myself together. I sat with my feet tucked tightly under me, and I considered how much to tell her.

"Before the accident, Josh and I were going through a rough time. I don't even know what was going on. He would blow up at me for no reason and then leave and not come home for days. I never knew what kind of mood he was going to be in when he came home. It was like walking on pins and needles when he was here."

"Did things change after the accident?"

I looked up at her as she snuggled back into the couch cushion, pulling her own feet up under her. "I never told you this, but the accident was my fault." I waited to see what she would say.

"Actually, when you were in the hospital, you said it was your fault, but it wasn't, Mandy. Josh was drunk; he is the one who caused the accident, not you."

"He was angry with me." I took a second to think before I continued, "We had been at a party, and he left me there to go get more beer or something." Shaking my head, I looked down at my hands and absently picked at my fingernail as I continued. "I waited for like two hours before I finally was so embarrassed I left and started walking home. He found me walking and made me get in the car. We were arguing and I was crying, it distracted him and it caused the accident." I tore the tissue I was holding in half, twisting it around my finger.

"Amanda, did you know that he was going over fifty miles per hour when he struck that car. You were on a residential street where the speed limit was only twenty-five. Yeah, you guys might have been arguing, and you might have been crying, but *he* is the one that was driving at that speed! He is the one that went through the stop sign! He is the one to blame, not you." She sat up closer and reached for my knee. "That accident was not your fault. It was his. Your only fault was getting into the car in the first place."

"Yeah, well I didn't really have a choice." I muttered, looking down at my lap again.

"What do you mean, you didn't have a choice?"

I wondered as I started to speak why I was telling her all of this. I already knew she didn't like Josh, and hearing these things was not going to make it better, but a dam opened, I just couldn't hold back the words. "He dragged me to the car and pushed me in. I didn't have a choice."

"He dragged you to the car? As in held your hand and led you or as in grabbed your arm and physically dragged you."

"No, he actually dragged me there. When I got in the car, I was telling him to slow down, and I never got to put my seatbelt on because he was driving so crazy I was holding on. I started yelling and crying, and he grabbed me by the hair and threw me against the window." I stopped talking as I thought back on the incident, seeing it in my mind as if it had just happened yesterday, I shuddered. "That's when the accident happened. If I had just stopped crying and been quiet, he wouldn't have gotten distracted."

"Are you crazy?" Angie grabbed my calf with both hands and I jumped slightly. "This is *not* your fault! Did you force him to drink? Did you get into that car willingly? Did you cause the car to crash? No! You didn't! I can't believe he forced you into the car in the first place. If I had known that I would have told the police! He should have been charged with attempted homicide!"

"Angie, no!"

"Don't tell me no! Listen to yourself, Amanda. You need to stop saying no and start seeing what is around you. You never call me, you never go out anymore. You dropped out of school over halfway to getting your business degree. You stopped going to the gym to work out. Why? Because he doesn't want you to do those things? He almost kills you while he is driving drunk and then you defend him! He did that to your face, didn't he?"

I looked away from her. "It wasn't on purpose."

"Wasn't on purpose," she parroted. "What did he do, push you into the wall?" The disgust in her voice was apparent.

I shook my head, tears spreading down my cheeks again, "No, he came home drunk and fell. I tried to help him up, and he accidentally hit me in the face with his elbow."

"What did he say about that?"

"Nothing, he was too drunk to remember it, and when he got up this morning and saw it, he denied doing it." Pulling a new tissue out, I dropped the old one on the floor and wiped my eyes. "Then he told me I was worthless and he had no idea why he married me." The tears turned to sobs as I finished my sentence, and Angie pulled me into a tight hug, holding me as I let out the sadness and confusion.

"Oh, Mandy." She rubbed my back as I held onto her and let out all the pain. I knew I should not have told her all of this, but I felt as if a weight had lifted from my shoulders now that I wasn't holding on to it alone.

All at once, the pain I had stuffed deep inside of me for eight years, since I was nineteen, came crashing down, the tears just kept falling. Snippets of my life flashed through my mind's eye as I remembered Steve and Mark, how I had destroyed the one child I had ever carried in my body, and how the man I now loved was cheating on me with another woman.

The depression that sat so heavily on my mind and body constantly reminded me of what I had allowed to happen in my life, and as I began to see this, I still felt powerless to stop the pattern.

CHAPTER TWENTY-THREE

NICOLE

*A*nother season had come and gone, I stood outside watching the leaves blow across the ground. I had never been a fan of the winter; signs of it heading our way already made me gloomy. The thought of the blustery cold winds and icy conditions made me long for the return of summer even though it had just barely ended.

My booted foot rested on the front crash bar of my patrol car. I watched a lone car pass by on the road, my paper coffee cup steaming in my hand. As I stood there, I began to wonder how many cars I had watched pass by me in my eight years on the force—too many to count.

"You start your Christmas shopping yet, Nicole?" Adam asked me just before he put his cup to his mouth.

I chuckled. "Dude, it's only September!" shaking my head, I put my foot back to the ground and took another sip of my sweet coffee. "Don't tell me you already started."

Todd laughed beside me, "I started."

We both turned to face my partner. A mischievous smile played over his handsome features, lifting the side of his mouth in a crooked grin.

"You did not!" I threw out at him. "You wait till two days before and do it all in two hours." I glanced back to the road when another car passed by, seeing the brake lights flash briefly as they slowed, I could see both the driver and passenger turn their heads in our direction. People always turned to look at us no matter where we were or what we were doing.

"No, really, I did! I bought Cindy a bracelet."

"Wow! She must really be the one if you're shopping for her four months before the actual holiday." Adam's comment had me laughing as my attention came back to them.

Todd was about to respond to his quip when the radio came to life, calling both our unit numbers. Todd keyed up and responded while Adam and I listened carefully to our call. Inside my car, I heard my computer beeping as the call came down. I took another sip of my coffee, knowing that I was about to ditch the rest.

"Thirty-Seven units, you have a 911 hang-up at 104 Whitehall Way. On the initial call it sounded like there was a struggle going on. We got an answering machine on call back." I tossed my coffee cup in the direction of the trash can, not caring about the litter when someone's life was in jeopardy. We all moved quickly to our cars.

"Hey, Nicole," Adam called out, "isn't that the same house I went with you where the guy spat on you."

I yelled over my shoulder as I opened the door, "Sure is."

Pulling out of the driveway in a flashing procession, we made quick time to the other side of the township. As usual, we all killed our lights and positioned our cars in different locations, moving quickly towards the house because the dispatchers had lost contact with the caller.

Todd was in front of me, and Adam went off to the left as I stayed on the right. We each took peeks in the windows and then moved to the front door. A woman's scream from inside put my nerves on edge, and I watched Todd try the doorknob, it must have been locked, he stepped back and looked at me. I nodded, knowing what he was about to do.

Using much more force than I could have, he kicked the front door open, a snap and tearing sound gained my attention as the door frame splintered. We all rushed into the house and moved in different directions, guns drawn.

The woman screamed again, and we entered into the kitchen area to find Mr. Swift kicking Rebecca while she lay on the ground. Droplets of blood were smeared along the beige tile floor. Oh, how I wanted to shoot the guy at that very moment, but, as always, I resisted the urge.

Todd holstered his weapon as did Adam, and they both moved in to tackle the guy. I heard a grunt of pain as they landed on the floor, and I hoped it came from Jason Swift and not my partners. As I saw Adam and Todd take control of Jason, I holstered my firearm and moved to Rebecca.

"Thirty-Seven Paul Three, we need an ambulance at this location. Our status will be fine," I glanced over at Todd and saw him sit back, Jason's hands were cuffed behind him, "and we will have one in custody." Todd nodded and I went down on one knee next to the sobbing woman.

"Rebecca, it's okay. It's over now. It's going to be alright." She opened her eyes, the fear and pain written so clearly in them. I gently rubbed her arm as I spoke, "Hold on, the ambulance is on its way, just stay still till they get here."

A dish towel sat on the counter; I grabbed it, put it on the floor next to me, and pulled out a pair of nitrile medical gloves. I used the towel to staunch the flow of blood from the laceration on Rebecca's head.

"What happened tonight, Rebecca?" I turned to watch Todd and Adam yank her husband up off the floor. None of us had any tolerance for men who beat their wives.

I watched Rebecca as her wide eyes followed the three men leaving the room. Her haunted eyes came back to mine. I shivered.

"He was drinking again and wanted me to make him something to eat. I was working in the office and he came up yelling at me. I came down and was going to warm up some leftovers for him when he threw a glass at me, telling me he didn't want them. It hit me in the head, and I screamed and grabbed the phone. He tried to get it out of my hands, but I managed to dial 911 before he did. Then he threw me around, and I fell to the ground. He stood over me, yelling and kicking at me. I think he broke a rib or something. It hurts to breathe."

"Alright, just lie still. The ambulance is on its way. We are going to get you to the hospital, and we will get you fixed up."

The front door opened, a voice called out. I directed the EMS workers to our location. The EMTs did their thing; I stayed by Rebecca's side, holding her hand to keep her calm.

She was taken out by stretcher and put into the ambulance. "Rebecca, I will be up to the hospital in a few minutes. We have some things to finish up."

She nodded slowly, our eyes trained on each other until the doors were closed. A deep and soulful sigh escaped me. Todd stood beside his car talking to the husband; I locked my jaw down, grinding my teeth slowly.

Todd appeared to be adjusting the handcuffs when I stepped beside him. When he unlocked the right cuff, Todd's heavy leather gloves lost grip on the cuff as it released and fell loose. Jason Swift immediately pulled his arm up.

Todd attempted to gain control of the other arm, but Swift was already moving in momentum, his elbow now coming back to connect with Todd's head. I saw what was about to happen. If I had been a few inches closer, I could have stopped him. I lunged for Jason's elbow just as it struck Todd's cheek with a thud.

Todd's head snapped to the side, causing him to lose balance and fall into the open patrol car door. Todd let go of the other side of the cuffs without even realizing it, and Jason started to move away from him.

I reached for my Taser. Just as Jason stepped past Todd, I flipped the safety lever, aimed the red laser beam on his back and pulled the trigger. The power raced into the firing mechanism, sending the metal probes out to find purchase in the guy's back muscles. Fifty thousand volts crackled in the air around us as I watched the power of the tool drop him to the ground like a lead brick.

As he hit the ground, I landed on his back with my knee, careful to avoid the probes that were still firing the electrical charge. When it ended, I kept one hand around the Taser while grabbing his cuffed arm behind his back. My knee dug in deep, and I heard him groan.

"Hurts, doesn't it?" I leaned over him so my voice wouldn't get lost. "Now you know what it feels like! Next time you want to beat up a woman, why don't you find one that will fight back." Adam grabbed Jason's other arm and pulled it back, securing it in the stainless steel cuffs. I made sure to put all my weight on my knee before I stood up.

Todd came over to me, nodding before he bent down to help Adam get the guy off the ground. They stood him up and turned him. I looked into the eyes of an angry beast.

"You bitch! I'll get you for that." He tried to spit on me again, but Todd saw the action coming and jerked Jason at the same time Jason launched the body fluid towards me. I moved, too, and watched the offending spittle land on the ground next to me.

After forcing Jason up against the trunk of the car, I photographed his back where the probes had made contact, then yanked them clear. He yelled. What a wuss, I thought. They didn't hurt that much to be pulled out. The door to the patrol car was closed on him. A muffled string of obscenities reached us through the window, nonetheless.

"You alright, Todd?" We moved to the back of the car away from the door.

"Yeah, that was unexpected." He put his hand up to his jaw moving it around to make sure it was working. "Gonna be sore as hell, but I don't think he broke anything."

"You sure you don't want to get checked out? You could go take Rebecca's statement and have it looked at."

"No, I'm good, Nicky. Besides, you are much better with the victims than I am." He winked and walked back to his car.

We all drove from the scene, Todd took Jason Swift to the lock-up, and I made my way to the hospital to get the pictures and statements.

As I walked into the emergency room, the bright lights and sterile environment gave me the chills. I was frequently in and out of the hospital with people I'd arrested or with victims from incidents. Normally, it was no big deal. Raw emotions gnawed at me while I located Rebecca's room; I couldn't get the image of Rebecca lying on the floor, injured, out of my thoughts.

I peeked around Rebecca's curtain. A nurse was examining her head injury; I nodded to the nurse as I stepped inside and then gave Rebecca a small reassuring smile.

Quietly waiting for the nurse to finish, I sat down in the only chair in the curtained room. Once the nurse stepped out, I set my clipboard where I had been seated and stepped closer to the bed.

"How are you doing?"

Her eyes filled with tears which spilled down her cheeks. She shook her head and closed her eyes.

"Rebecca, do you remember the last time I was at your house?" She nodded slightly, not opening her eyes. "I told you this was going to happen."

"I know…I know you did." She raised the hand that wasn't attached to an IV and covered half her face, trying to hide herself from me, or the pain, or the embarrassment—who knew.

"The last time, you refused to testify and he got what, some probation and had to go to some classes?" I watched her carefully hiding behind her hand. "Are you going to testify this time?"

After thirty seconds, she hadn't responded.

"Rebecca, listen to me." I reached over and put my hand on her arm gently with just enough pressure for her to know I was there. "You have to testify. Next time he might kill you. He has a problem, and you need to understand it's not your problem; it is his. He assaulted an officer tonight, so no matter what, he is going to be in big trouble for tonight."

She lifted her hand to shield her eyes from the bright lights and looked at me. "Did he hurt you?"

I smiled at the concern in her voice, "No, no, I'm fine. He hit my partner."

Relief washed over her face, I squeezed her arm gently. She put her hand back over her eyes.

"I thought he was going to kill me." Her hand came away from her face and fluttered softly to the bed beside her.

"He might the next time," my voice was soft, barely rising above the beeps and whooshing of the noises in the emergency room.

"No, there won't be a next time. I'll testify against him." Her eyes were strong as she looked into mine, a spark of determination shining in the depths of them. I picked up my clipboard and pulled out a statement form.

"Did you call the Domestic Violence Hotline the last time?" I clipped the statement to the front of my clipboard and pulled a pen out of my pocket.

"No, I didn't. I know it was stupid; I should have taken your advice. I will though. This time, I promise I will."

I handed over the clipboard, asking for her to write out her statement. When I walked out of the emergency room an hour later, I replayed the phone call she had made using my cell phone in my mind. The domestic violence group was already working on a protection order for her and would have it ready as soon as she was released from the hospital. She had taken the next step.

As I drove back to my jurisdiction, I was proud of myself. I might have helped to save a woman's life. Maybe I made a difference in her life. Maybe someday she would find happiness.

CHAPTER TWENTY-FOUR

AMANDA

*H*ours later I was much calmer when Angie left. Taking a hot shower finished calming me down, then I climbed in bed to fall asleep, exhausted from my hours of tears and the release of all my secrets. I had shared everything with Angie, everything. She now knew why I had moved to live with my aunt and everything I had gone through before with Steve and Mark. She knew about the child I had conceived, and she knew the hidden pain I carried inside knowing what I had done and that I would never again nurture a life inside my body.

She held me, cried with me, and listened for hours, never once judging me or telling me I had done something wrong—even though, in my mind, I still felt to blame for everything. There had to be something wrong with me for these things to happen to me over and over again.

I awoke to see the sun just cresting the horizon, and I stayed where I was. I watched the sun climb higher; having forgotten to pull the shades closed the night before. It was a new day, but what this day would bring, I had no clue.

I turned to look over my shoulder; the other side of the bed was empty. How long would Josh stay away this time?

I continued lying there until the sun had risen over the tops of the houses. I didn't have the energy to get out of bed and I had nothing that needed to be done. It was just any other Sunday, and I was home alone with a sore nose and a heavy heart.

The phone ringing beside me caused my heart to skip a beat. I lifted the receiver, pulling it to my ear slowly. "Hello," I said quietly.

"Get out of bed, girl! I'm coming to pick you up and we are going shopping!" I smiled at the enthusiasm in Angie's voice.

"I can't, Angie, I have things to do." I sat up in bed, holding the phone in the crook of my neck while I adjusted the pillow behind me. I tried to think of an excuse.

"Yeah, like what? Sitting around and waiting for your lame-ass husband to come home?" As funny as that might have sounded, it upset me to hear her say that.

"Angie, please don't talk about him that way." I put my hand on the phone, straightening my neck and resting it back against a pillow.

"Please...he is a lame ass. No...he is a lame-ass cheating prick!" She laughed after she spoke, and I found myself chuckling slightly. "I'm on my way over, so get out of bed and get dressed." I could hear water running, she was probably in her bathroom putting on makeup.

"Seriously, Angie, I can't go out. My face is still swollen. I don't want anyone to see it." I crossed my arm over my chest like it would protect me.

"So we will drive over to Twelve Oaks Mall, no one will know you there. Who cares what people think? I'm getting you out of the house today. You can't say no. I'm on my way." The phone clicked in my ear, and I smiled.

She was a good friend, and I still felt awful for how I had treated her, although she said she understood. I threw back the covers and got up, grabbing jeans and a T-shirt to change into after a shower.

I was just putting on the last of my makeup when Angie arrived. My face was still sore and my nose ached, but not as bad as it had the day before. The swelling had gone down, and I was still surprised that I did not swell or bruise as badly as I could have. I knew people who had gotten complete black eyes when they broke their noses. As long as I didn't try to move my face too much, the pain was manageable.

The day out did me good. I felt wonderful laughing and just having fun. How I had missed hanging out with her. We stayed away from any conversation of Josh and my past, although at one point she saw me looking wistfully at a mother and her three children. She squeezed my shoulder to let me know she understood.

It wasn't until we were on our way home that we broached the subject of my marriage again. Angie brought up a question that had been hovering around in the back of my mind most of the day.

"What are you going to say to Josh?" she asked me quietly as we drove along the highway. I gazed out the window beside me, watching the scenery flash past quickly, reminding me of the memories that had crossed my mind the night before, a rapid succession of images that began to blur together if I didn't blink.

"I'm not sure," I answered the window as I continued to view the passing world outside. "I'll figure it out when the time comes."

Turning up the volume on the radio, Angie let it go at that. We sang to the music for the rest of the ride home. As we turned onto the street, my heart stopped when I saw his car in the driveway next to mine. "Damn," I muttered under my breath.

"You want me to go in with you?" Angie said as she pulled over in front of the house. "I can if you want me to."

I smiled, "No, that's alright." I thanked her for a great afternoon and for being there for me. I promised not to push her away again and stepped out of the car. I picked up the bag with the single item I had purchased in it and made my way to the front door.

I didn't take my keys out as I stepped up, figuring Josh would have left the door open when he got home. I glanced back at Angie, waved, then reached for the doorknob as she pulled away.

The door swung quickly open, and I lost my balance, stumbling into the foyer. I hadn't even recovered my balance when I felt hands push me against the wall. The door slammed shut. I cringed as the door vibrated the wall next to me.

"Where the hell have you been?" Josh yelled.

I turned so my back was to the wall. I could smell alcohol coming off of him and his eyes looked aggressive and glassy.

"I was out shopping with Angie," I responded meekly to his question.

"Bullshit! Who were you with?" He got in my face and my knees started shaking.

"I was with Angie," I repeated quietly.

His forearm immediately came to my throat, forcing my head back to the wall. I tried to turn my head to release the pressure, but he held me too tightly against the drywall.

"You better not be cheating on me! Who were you with?" Spit landed on my face as he shouted. A buzzing grew in my ears as the oxygen was denied to my lungs. My heart slammed against my chest and I tried to push him away from me, but didn't have the strength to compete with his alcohol-induced anger.

"Who were you with, Amanda?" He pressed harder on my neck and I felt things moving around inside. Breathing became even more difficult.

"Angie," I squeaked out.

Suddenly, he released my throat, punching a hole in the wall beside me. I cringed away from him as far as I could get, sucking air into my hot lungs, the sound of bees still in my ears. I didn't move any further until he turned and walked away. My shoulders slumped, and I bit my lip to keep the tears back.

"Where have you been?" He flopped down on the sofa and put his feet out on the coffee table. Dirt fell off his boot on to the wood. My head felt foggy, I couldn't remember what he'd just asked me.

"What?" I licked my bottom lip, tasting my own blood from biting down so hard.

His boots came back to the floor, and he stood up in a swift movement. I froze for just a second as he turned to look at me, I felt like a deer in the headlights of an approaching Mack truck. He started to move, and I decided I didn't need to be against the wall anymore. I tried to walk towards the kitchen to get away from him.

He was too fast. He grabbed me by my long blond hair, yanking me to a stop. I reached up to try and release the tension he had on me. He yanked me back to him, and I smashed into his chest, almost knocking us both over.

"Where the hell have you been?" he screamed at me as he twisted my hair down. I fell to my knees to ease the pressure.

"We were at the mall. Josh, let go, you're hurting me!" The pain in my head was like someone had sliced me with a knife. He twisted the long hair around his hand and yanked. I screamed and he flung me away from him. I fell to the floor and lay there, one hand touching the soft carpet under me and the other touching my head where the hair had been pulled. If I hadn't been touching it, I would have sworn the hair had been pulled out, but the soft locks were still at my fingertips.

I not only heard the sound of his boots on the floor, but I felt the vibration of them as he got closer. My body trembled. He put one knee into my back and pushed my neck down with his hand, forcing my face into the carpet.

"You ever, and I mean ever, cheat on me, Amanda, and I will kill you. You got that? I swear to God if I ever see you with another man, I will kill him and then I will kill you," his cold voice slithered over me. I had never heard such venom come from him. The carpet fibers dug into my cheek, my cheekbone sharing the pain with my nose. Moisture ran down my cheek as my nose began to bleed again.

"You got that?" he shouted one last time and pushed down on me with his knee and hand before standing back up.

I didn't speak, only nodded my head slightly into the carpet.

"Stupid bitch," he muttered before he kicked me in the hip. It hurt, but it was obvious that he hadn't used all of his strength. With his boots, he could have really done some damage.

"Stay away from Angie, too. She's more of a worthless bitch than you are." He turned around, walked to the front door, yanked it open then whipped it closed behind him a second later. I didn't try to move until I heard his car start and his tires peel away on the pavement.

I slowly curled up on my side in a fetal position wrapping my arms around my stomach, sobbing like I had never cried before. My body shook with each sob, over and over as I realized how bad the situation around me had gotten.

What had gone wrong? Where had the Josh I had fallen in love with vanished to? When did all the drinking start? The cheating? Where had this evil, nasty, and physical man come from? Did he really just threaten my life? Would he really try to kill me?

The answer to my question chilled me to the bone, the tears stopped falling immediately. Yes, he would kill me. If I did something he did not like, if I spoke to the wrong person, if he didn't believe me when I told him the truth, yes, he would kill me. I had no doubt. The threat—the fear of death—it was another way to control me.

I wiped at my face, blood smeared on the back of my hand. I stood up slowly, my hip hurt more standing up than it had lying down. My throat was sore and my head throbbed. I walked to the bathroom and looked at the mirror.

The person staring back at me was a stranger. Who was this young woman? How had she gotten into this situation, yet again? There were no answers looking back at me, no comments other than the painful words echoing in my head: "Worthless bitch." Was that all I was? Was that all I would ever be?

I turned on the faucet and, using a fresh washcloth, wiped the smeared blood from my face. My deadpan eyes watched carefully in the mirror, the sparkling life that normally appeared in them flat and absent.

Maybe Josh was right, maybe Steve was right. Maybe I was nothing but someone to bully around. I had no real career, no children, and no friends except Angela. I was worthless; I saw it now as I looked in the mirror. I saw what they all saw now. I saw a nobody.

Rinsing out the washcloth, I tossed it into the hamper, then walked to the bedroom and undressed, dropping my clothes into a pile on the floor. Josh would be upset if he saw it, but I didn't think he would be home tonight. There was no doubt in my mind that he had run to that other woman.

The thought of his being with another woman swelled angrily deep inside of me. How dare he accuse me of being with someone when he was the one who was cheating on me! I picked up my clothes and threw them across the room in frustration. I wanted to hit a wall, wanted to kick something, scream at someone. Yet, I did nothing more. I pulled on a T-shirt, crawled into bed. I wanted to fall asleep forever.

My eyes closed, and I thought about how easy it would be to swallow the rest of the pain pills, maybe mix them with some other things from the medicine cabinet. How nice it would be to just fall asleep and never wake up, never have to deal with the pain again. While the thoughts spun around in my mind, I pictured myself walking to the kitchen for a tall glass of water. I saw myself walk to the bathroom and take out the orange bottles. I could feel myself pouring them out and dropping them onto my tongue. I tasted the bitterness of them as they flowed down my throat, and yet I continued to lie there on the bed and do nothing but picture the possibility.

Some little voice inside my head, just a tiny little voice that could barely be heard over the rushing of the blood in my ears and the pounding of the pain in my mind, said to me, "You might not think you are worth it, but I do."

I fell asleep trying to hold onto that little voice, trying to figure out who it was and where it had come from. I didn't figure it out that night, but I did fall asleep feeling just a tiny bit of peace.

CHAPTER TWENTY-FIVE

AMANDA

*M*orning arrived; the sleep ebbed from my brain. There was no way I would have the energy to go to work. Sadness like I had never known settled over me during the night, the thought of even getting out of bed was too much to contemplate. I closed my eyes and went back to sleep.

The ringing phone woke me, and I reached for it absently. "Amanda? Are you alright?" I recognized Dee's concerned voice.

"No, I'm sick. Sorry, I woke up feeling terrible. I guess I fell back asleep, I meant to call."

"That's okay. I was worried about you. You usually do call. You go back to sleep, feel better." I hung up the phone after we shared a few more words and pulled the covers up to my chin, burrowing down into my pillow, falling quickly asleep.

The deep growling of my stomach woke me not much later, and I crawled out of bed and sluggishly made my way to the bathroom. Picking up my toothbrush, I opened the medicine cabinet to get the paste; I stood staring at the contents of the cabinet. The label on the pain medicine bottle stared back at me, beckoning like flashing neon lights.

I reached for the paste and brushed my teeth slowly as I continued to stare at the bottle. How easy it would be to take them and the muscle relaxers next to them. I spat out the toothpaste and rinsed the brush.

I pushed the cabinet door closed slowly and came face to face with my image. The reflection showed someone I no longer knew: deep circles under my eyes, swelling over the bridge of my nose and cheek bones. I looked at my throat; there were no marks there, thankfully. I walked into the kitchen to make coffee.

The smell of the coffee turned my stomach and, as much as my stomach growled, the thought of eating made me want to vomit. I settled on the couch with my coffee mug and turned on the television, all thoughts of food forgotten.

The phone rang twice that morning, but both times I ignored it. I found an old romance novel that I had picked up somewhere along the way sitting on a shelf. I climbed back in bed, the phone beside me unplugged. I didn't want to talk to anyone, Angie included.

Still in my pajamas at six that night, I heard someone knocking on the door. I stayed in bed. Eventually the knocking stopped. I read late into the night, finishing the book. How wonderful it was to fall into someone else's life and forget all about mine for a time.

The next morning arrived and I forced myself out of bed. The circles under my eyes gave some truth to my story of not feeling well. I kept to myself when I got to work, typing the documents I needed to in solitude.

At lunchtime while everyone went out, I stayed at my desk catching up on what I had missed the day before. The last thing I felt like doing was eating.

On my way home, I stopped at the library. Picking out a few romance novels, I found my way to the checkout line and opened up an account. Since my life was nothing to think about, I would live the lives of the characters on paper. I could pretend to be one of them, if only for a little while.

I arrived home to a silent house, my stomach growled as I entered the kitchen. My lack of energy and want of food had me pulling out a piece of white bread. I ate it while I walked to the bedroom. Kicking off my shoes, I changed into my pajamas, climbed into bed, and opened up a book.

In this way, I began the new trend in my life.

Friday arrived without a word from Josh. Angie called me at work. I told her I had been sick in bed, but that I was fine. Somehow I managed to convince her that all was well. I guess my acting skills were getting better.

Like I had every night since Tuesday, I ate a piece of bread and climbed into bed to read. My stomach no longer growled, and every time I smelled food, it made me nauseous. Who needed food when I had intimate couples that loved one another to the bitter end to read about? It was food for me and I ate up every loving minute, wishing intensely that some noble caring man would come to rescue me.

Saturday morning, a soft touch on my cheek woke me, my eyes opened instantly. Josh stood over me looking down, his jaw tight as a muscle ticked in the side.

"Hi," he said awkwardly.

I pulled the covers over me while I sat up against the headboard. "Hello."

"I just put coffee on, you want some breakfast?" he asked as he stood looking at me.

Really, he was asking me if I wanted breakfast? He threatened to kill me, stayed away all week, and came home to be Betty Crocker. I shook my head slightly, watching his reaction.

He shrugged and looked around the room. "Okay, well I'm going to go make something to eat." He walked out of the room without another word, leaving me staring after him, confused.

The sounds of him moving around the kitchen were foreign to my ears. I climbed out of bed, pulling on sweatpants and a sweatshirt over my T-shirt.

When I entered the kitchen, I watched him break two eggs into a bowl and stir them. "What are you doing here?"

He laughed as he stirred his eggs, "I live here, Amanda, or did you forget?"

"I didn't forget, but I thought you had." I leaned against the wall and crossed my arms over my chest.

"Ouch." He looked over his shoulder and smiled. It was a smile that I had craved to see, and my heart fluttered in my chest.

"Where have you been, Josh?" My hands were clammy as I spoke, knowing that I might be saying the wrong thing and this quiet Saturday morning could be blown all to pieces.

He shrugged, pouring his eggs into the pan. "I was staying with friends."

Friends, huh. I walked over to the cabinet, pulled out a mug, and poured myself coffee.

Sitting at the table, I wanted to ask so many things, but I was so afraid to say what was on my mind.

Josh finished cooking and brought his plate to the table. He smiled as he sat down, my heart leapt in my chest. My lips curved up slightly as I watched him sit.

We didn't speak while he ate. I watched his every move, wanting so much to ask him questions or just hear his voice. The silence around me was cut only by the sound of his fork scraping the plate.

"Not much in the fridge to eat, why haven't you gone to the store?" he sat back in his chair, his plate now empty.

"No reason to shop for groceries when I don't know when you will be here or not." I said a bit more bitterly than I had meant to say.

He threw his head back and laughed. Confusion rolled over me, and I shook my head, resting my elbows on the table and crossing my arms to lean on them.

"Josh, where have you been?" I wasn't sure what had gotten into me, but I felt that I needed to start asking questions.

He stopped laughing and looked at me, "I already told you that. I have been staying with friends."

I looked him in the eye, fearing the next thing I would ask, but knowing I had to. "What's her name?"

"Whatever, Amanda." He pushed back from the table, picked up his plate, and walked to the sink.

"Don't whatever me, Josh. I know you are seeing someone. Who is she?" I stayed in my seat, afraid that my shaking legs wouldn't hold me up.

He rinsed off his plate and set it in the sink. Turning around to look at me, he crossed his arms and leaned back against the counter.

"What makes you think I'm seeing someone?" I had expected his voice to be angry, but it wasn't.

"Because someone saw you with a woman, and you were kissing her."

I stared him down, expecting him to get angry. His jaw tightened and I braced myself for the attack I knew was coming.

"Doesn't matter who she is," he stated and started to walk away.

I was flabbergasted. He had not tried to deny it, not only that, he didn't seem angry that I asked. I watched him walk away, my mouth hanging partially open.

Anger burned through my veins. I stood up, following him quickly. I found him in the bedroom looking in one of his drawers.

"What the hell do you mean, it doesn't matter who she is? It does matter. I'm your wife, Josh, or did you forget that?" I stood at the door, fisted hands clenched tightly by my side.

"No, I didn't forget that." He kept his back to me while he spoke, still pushing things around in his drawer.

"Then would you mind telling me what the hell is going on? Because I don't understand this! I don't understand how you can do this!" Without meaning to do it, the emotions started welling up and tears came to my eyes.

"Oh, grow up, Amanda! Don't start freaking crying." He slammed his drawer shut and pulled open another one.

"Grow up? You want me to grow up? Why don't you grow up and start telling me what the hell is going on instead of running away and never talking to me?" I couldn't help the tears as they fell. I had no control over them.

He spun around. I stepped back slightly. "You want to know what I'm doing?" he shouted at me. "I'm getting the hell away from you and your boring life!" His words smacked me in the face, and I recoiled at them. "I can't stand being around you. You're boring and you never have anything to say. You sit around and just watch television. I want more out of my life."

"Josh, I'm only doing that because you don't let me do anything else. You never wanted to do anything else, you always wanted to stay home and relax. I don't understand." I wiped at the tears as they hung off my chin like raindrops on a tree branch in a storm.

"Yeah, well that's not what I want anymore, Amanda." He turned back to his dresser, opened the drawer, and started pulling things out.

"What do you mean, that's not what you want anymore?" I stepped closer, watching him throw things on the bed. His clothes piled higher on the bedspread.

Fear gripped me as he removed more from his dresser. "It's not what I want. You're not what I want." He spoke quietly as he pulled out his jeans and put them next to his shirts.

"I'm not what you want? Josh, I'm your wife! Doesn't it matter what I want? Let's talk about this, please!" I stepped close to him and grabbed his arm.

He spun on me, "Don't touch me, Mandy. I hate when you touch me."

The words punched me in the stomach, the air sucked out of me, and my head began to spin. "You hate when I touch you," I whispered.

"Yeah, I hate when you touch me, I hate having sex with you. You suck at it. It's just another thing you can't do right." He turned his back on me and walked to the closet, grabbing a duffle bag and returning to the bed to fill it with his clothes.

His words spun around in my mind like a twister in the darkness. He hated me touching him and I sucked at sex. I wanted to die. Right at that second, I just wanted to be struck down by lightning and die.

Unable to move or speak, I watched him throw his things in the bags.

He walked to the closet, pulling out some hangers, taking the shirts off of them, and pushing them one by one into the bag as I continued to stand there dumbfounded.

"What are you doing?" I asked stupidly.

"What's it look like I'm doing? I'm leaving, Amanda." He dropped the last hanger and shoved the last of the shirts in, the sound of the zipper a haunting tune as it closed.

"Leaving? Why? Josh, please! Let's talk about this. We can fix this, I know we can." I stood in his path, trying to block him from leaving the bedroom, our bedroom.

"Move out of the way before I move you, Amanda." His voice was stern as he stared over my head, not meeting my begging eyes.

"Josh, please! Please talk to me about this!" My hands were on his chest, forgetting that he told me not to touch him. I needed him to stop, to look at me, to see the way he was hurting me, and how much I loved him.

Without looking at me, he pushed me to the side and brushed past me as I regained my balance. I ran after him as he made his way to the front door.

"Wait! Josh! Please!" My voice was calling after him as he moved quickly in front of me.

"Jesus, Amanda," he whirled on me, dropping his bag and looking at me, a mixture of anger and pain in his eyes. "Just stop! I'm leaving you, Amanda, I need some time."

"Where are you going?" We stood in the hallway, he looked down at the carpet. I knew my answer. "You're going to her, aren't you?"

He didn't speak for a moment, and then looked at me, "Yeah. I don't want to be here, I don't want to be with you. She makes me feel good. She cares, and the sex is awesome." He snickered to himself as he spoke those words. My heart split in half.

"I care about you too, Josh. Doesn't that matter? I'm your wife. Don't you care about me?" the quiver in my voice made me sound like I was whining while I was only trying to speak coherently.

I stood under his heated gaze for several moments, before he bent down and curled his hands around the straps of his bag.

"No." He made eye contact again. "No, actually I don't care about you."

Stunned at his final words, I watched him turn and walk around the corner towards the front door. The sound of the door closing sounded like the final note in a scary movie, echoing through my heart. My eyes closed slowly over the constant flow of tears that ran from them, my body falling back to the wall, sliding down to the ground as I curled up into a ball. The anguish that rocked my mind and body tore through me in wretched torrents as I lay there.

No matter the amount of anger or the pain I had felt for what Josh had done to me, I could not accept the words he said. As much as he had hurt me over and over, I had always innocently believed we would make it work, that we would fix the problems that we had. To beg him to stay, as degrading as it felt, had been my last chance to try to hold on to what I had known. No matter how bad our relationship, it was all I had in my life. Sadly enough, I felt that he was all I had in my life.

CHAPTER TWENTY-SIX

NICOLE

"Officer, can you please state your name, rank, and department for the record," the attorney stood in front of the witness stand waiting for my reply.

"Officer Nicole Nolan of the Englewood Township Police Department." The chair I sat in faced the courtroom where other defendants, victims, and officers waited for their turn on that stand with their cases. It wasn't a big room, not like the county courtrooms. This local courthouse held our traffic hearings and preliminary hearings. At this particular hearing, the Commonwealth needed to prove to the judge that we had enough evidence to charge the suspect, Mr. Swift, with the crimes filed against him for assaulting his wife and my partner.

The hearings were generally short and to the point because only the Commonwealth testified. The questions were basic, as to when, where, and how the call was received, and what had transpired. Since Todd had been assaulted at the call, I became the affiant of the criminal complaint and took the stand first, spelling out the facts of the incident.

As the affiant, I had to give reason to believe that a crime had occurred. I had to give true and correct facts of what knowledge I had of the crime. I listed the charges, gave specific details to explain each one, and then signed and swore to the document that it was "true and correct to the best of my knowledge" before the court.

I was questioned on what we had observed upon our arrival and all the details until the police car was closed to take Swift to jail. I stated the facts and nothing more.

Todd was called to the stand after me, and proceeded to repeat much of what I had testified, too, talking in more detail as to what had occurred directly towards him once Mr. Swift was in custody. At this hearing, it wasn't necessary for Adam, the other responding officer to speak, so the victim was called to the stand after Todd was finished.

Rebecca waited in a small room across the hall; one of the court constables led her into the courtroom. She looked pale and scared to death as she entered, slowly making her way to the witness stand. I knew the fear she felt at not only testifying, but testifying against her husband while he sat at the defendant's table with his attorney.

She raised her right hand and put her left on the Bible, swearing to tell the truth and nothing but the truth. She then took her seat facing us. Her eyes found mine immediately, and I gently smiled to reassure her. The attorney next to me began with general questions, her identity and where she lived.

He asked her what had transpired on the night of the incident, and Rebecca hesitantly started to talk, retelling the story that she had once told me, the same one she had written on paper in her statement.

She was tense when the questions first started, giving only brief answers. Ever so slowly she started to relax, her talk became more fluid, and the details emerged.

I wouldn't say that she ever completely relaxed—how could you when you were testifying against someone you had loved?—however, she did calm down considerably and looked more confident as the time went by.

"Mrs. Swift, do you know the difference between baseball and soft-ball?" the attorney asked her.

"Yes." Her face was a mask of confusion at the question. I looked to my right and up at the attorney who was standing, having no idea where his line of questioning was going.

"Can you explain the difference to the court?" The attorney smiled at me before refocusing on Rebecca.

"Well, softball is normally played by women with a larger ball. The pitcher tosses it underhand. Baseball is played by men, and they pitch the ball overhand." Rebecca sounded perplexed while she replied. Once she answered, I knew what the next question was going to be, the corner of my mouth hitching up slightly.

"Can you tell me, Mrs. Swift, the night of the incident, did your husband throw the glass at you like he was pitching for the softball team or the baseball team?"

The puzzlement melted from her face, she sat up straighter. "He threw the glass like he was a pitcher in the World Series."

I couldn't help that both sides of my mouth rose in a Cheshire smile; I put my elbow on the arm of the chair, resting my hand over the side of my face to hide it from the defendant's table. It really wasn't nice to laugh at these kinds of things.

The rest of the hearing went smoothly, and Rebecca descended from the stand looking stronger and more confident than ever. The judge found enough evidence to hold all the charges over to the Court of Common Pleas.

The judge ordered Jason Swift to have no contact with his wife, and the attorney explained to the judge that a protection order was already in place. The judge spoke sternly to Mr. Swift, making sure he understood that if he violated that order in any way, he would immediately be taken to jail. Swift told her he understood, and the courtroom was cleared for the next case.

Rebecca was waiting for me outside the courtroom, and I led her to the waiting room, giving Mr. Swift time to leave the building. I explained to her that the next step would take place at the county courts and that she would be contacted by them to go over her statement. Additional questions would be asked, including what she wanted to see as punishment.

"I get to decide his punishment?" This startled her so much that she sat down.

"Well, no, not exactly. The court sets his sentencing if he is found guilty. They will ask you more along the lines of how you feel about such things. Some victims want the defendant to serve maximum time, and if the assistant district attorneys think there is enough evidence to substantiate that, then they will push for it."

After a few more questions, I escorted her to her car, making sure she was safely inside. She drove away after a small wave, and I turned, heading to my own car.

As I approached it, I looked over the roof, Jason Swift stood staring me down from four cars over. I held eye contact for quite a few seconds before I pulled open my car door and slipped inside. I wanted to see that guy get the harshest punishment that he could. He deserved it. All men-or women for that matter—that thought they could assault or abuse another person should be thrown in jail.

Todd met up with me for lunch after the hearing. After ordering from the menu, Todd sat back and looked at me. "You think she'll stay away from him now?"

A small bubble of laughter escaped me as I picked up my straw wrapper, twisting it around my finger. "Who knows? They always say they aren't going back, but you know as well as I do that almost eight times out of ten they do."

"Yeah, I know." Todd picked up his drink, sipping from the plastic straw. "Maybe you got through to her though, who knows."

Shrugging, I changed the conversation, not wanting to think about domestic violence anymore. It didn't matter the kind of house the victims lived in or the amount of money they made at work. Anyone could be a victim.

In my years on the force, I had seen children abused, teenagers assaulted, lovers fight, and spouses trying to destroy one another. People never thought it could happen to them, and when it did, they went into denial, believing it was a one-time thing. It took strength and courage to walk away from those kinds of conditions, and so many people thought they had no other options. The mentality of "I made my bed and now I have to lie in it" was strong to many of these victims. I hated it, but I understood it.

With lunch over, I left Todd and started home. Although I had been to court, it was my day off, and I intended to spend the rest of it with Colton.

He was sitting at the computer in the living room when I walked in. I kissed him on the cheek, went into the bedroom, and took off the slacks and blouse I had worn to court.

"How did it go?" Colton asked as he walked into the room.

"She testified. All the charges were held over." I smiled as I draped my pants on a purple plastic hanger and walked into the closet to hang them back up and grab some jeans.

When I turned around, Colton was standing behind me, looking at me with a passion in his eyes that I could appreciate. A playful smile spread over my face as I forgot about the jeans and walked to him, sliding my hands up over his chest.

His kiss was perfect, and we slowly made our way back to the bed, lying down and making love like it should be made: slowly, gently, lovingly.

I snuggled up next to him. I couldn't help but think about Rebecca again and wonder if she would ever find happiness.

"Why are you sighing?" Colton wrapped his arm around me tighter. "Was it that bad?"

I laughed, slapping playfully at his arm, "No, that was awesome as it always is. I was just thinking about Rebecca again."

"It was awesome, wasn't it?" He kissed my neck slowly. "You need to let it go, Nicky." Resting the side of his face on my head and speaking softly in my ear, "You know you can't help everyone, only the ones that want to be helped."

"I know." I turned, and he lowered his face to allow us to come nose to nose. "It's just so frustrating. I feel like sometimes I just want to scream at them, shake them, and try to make them see what is real."

His thumb rubbed the side of my cheek, "I know you do, but you can't control them, honey."

"You're right, I can't; however, I can control you." I put my hands on his shoulders, quickly pushing him back so I was over him now.

"Oh, I love it when you control me." We both laughed, and I kissed him long and leisurely.

I stopped kissing him and I smiled, "I do too. I like being in control," and I showed him just how much I liked it as the afternoon gave way to a beautiful sunset, turning the room soft and colorful as the day ended, and I lay beside the man I loved like no other in my life.

CHAPTER TWENTY-SEVEN

AMANDA

Somehow I made it through the next several weeks on auto pilot. Each morning the sun rose, I got out of bed. It was the hardest part of my day to put my feet on the floor and stand up. Each night as I stared at the ceiling, I wished for God to come and take me away in my sleep.

As often as I thought about suicide, I just didn't have the strength to do it, another weakness of mine, obviously. Josh would probably make fun of me for that too if he knew. He'd probably urge me on to do it so I would be out of his life for good.

The longer he was gone, the harder it was. I would force myself to dress and go to work. I barely ate, only spoke when someone spoke to me, and never answered the phone at home. I told people at work not to put any personal calls through to me. I didn't have the energy to talk to Angie or even my parents.

What would I say to them? How could I pretend that all was well? My mother would know right away that there was a problem. What would I tell her? My husband left me because I sucked in bed and didn't make him feel good?

I left work on a Wednesday, twenty-eight days after Josh had left me, driving straight home like I had all the other twenty-seven days. With the car in park, I started to get out. A sign in the front lawn caused me to stop and stare. My jaw dropped as I looked at it. He'd put the house up for sale! He didn't even bother to tell me! What was I supposed to do? Where was I supposed to go?

I walked to the front door, numb from head to foot. There were no emotions left in me, no tears to cry, no pain to feel. I had been left out in the bitter cold for too long, and my body had stopped feeling anything.

I opened the front door and stepped inside the foyer to find the pictures removed from the walls. Only one picture remained, me with my parents. The walls looked at me wistfully, somehow reminding me of two lawn chairs I had left on my balcony years ago, except this time, a few nails stood out from the drywall, tiny daggers in my heart.

All thoughts of closing the door forgotten, I walked deeper into the house. Wherever I looked, I found things missing, not things that would be stolen as if I was burglarized, just personal possessions. I made my way slowly to the bedroom, stopping to stand at the threshold. Some of the drawers of his dresser hung slightly open, I could see they were empty from where I stood.

The six steps it took to reach the closet were some of the slowest I had ever taken. The side that once held his clothes now gaped completely empty. Not even a hanger hung from the silver metal pipe that ran across the top of the wall. It was barren, like my mind and body.

I dropped to my knees at the door to the closet, staring into the depths of the small walk-in closet. The left side full of life and color, the right side now void of anything but the shadows from the light bulb.

A sound behind me made me slowly turn my head, and Angie stood there with a question written over her face.

"He left me, Angie," my voice broke. She rushed forward to sit on the floor with me, wrapping an arm around my back. My head lay gently on her shoulder as I stared into the empty area.

"You deserve better, Mandy. You deserve so much better," she whispered into my ear.

When my neck started to cramp from leaning on her shoulder, I sat up and sighed. I looked around the room again, remembering the moment he'd proposed to me, all the nights we'd made love in the bed. "I'm not sure what I am supposed to do."

Angela stood up next to me, "When did he leave?"

"Twenty-eight days ago," I walked past her out of the room. I had to get away from the memories.

"Twenty-eight days ago, and you didn't call me? Why?" She followed behind me into the kitchen, the only room that didn't look like it had fallen victim to his packing. I could be wrong though, I hadn't looked inside the cabinets yet.

Pulling out a chair, I sat down heavily. "Wasn't your problem. Besides, I didn't want to talk to anyone."

"Why did he leave?" She sat beside me, pulling the chair closer to the end where I sat.

I shrugged and scraped my fingernail across the table. "He didn't want me anymore."

"What the hell do you mean, he didn't want you?" She reached out for the hand that was pushing imaginary things off the tabletop and held it.

"He said he didn't care about me, and he went to live with her." A sad laugh escaped my lips, "Said he didn't like my touch, hated having sex with me, and that he didn't want me around." My voice was so blasé about it I could have been talking about cleaning the toilet.

"He did not!" The anguish in her voice caused me to pull my hand away from her.

"Yep, he did." I put my hands in my lap.

"When did the house go on the market?"

I laughed again. "Your guess is as good as mine, but I am assuming today. The sign wasn't there this morning when I left for work."

"What are you going to do?" she asked me quietly.

I shook my head. "I have no idea, Angie. I never saw this coming. I don't know what to do."

The room grew quiet for a few moments as we both got lost in thought. "Look, why don't you come stay at my house tonight. Let's get you out of here and give you a change of scenery. We can talk about it over a bottle of wine on my couch."

I smiled and was about to tell her no, but then thought about the alternative: sleeping in a half-empty house. I decided to go with her.

We spoke for a few more minutes before I walked into the bedroom to grab a change of clothes, changing out of my work stuff, taking out jeans and a T-shirt to put on. As I dropped my shirt to the bed, I heard a sharp intake of breath from the door. I looked up quickly.

"When is the last time you ate? My God, Amanda, you are nothing but skin and bones!" Her eyes widened as she took me in.

"I lost a few pounds, no big deal." I reached over for my T-shirt while she walked closer to me.

"Have you looked at yourself lately?" her voice took on a gentle tone, even though it sounded angry.

I shrugged, "No, not really."

She stood behind me, putting her hands on my shoulders, guiding me to the mirror in front of the dresser. When she stopped, her hands remained on the tops of my shoulders, and I saw how they curled around the bones there. For the first time, I noticed how far they stuck out.

I allowed my eyes to roam slowly down to my stomach, my ribs stood out sharply against my pale skin. My stomach was sunken in and the black belt that held my slacks up was hiding a section of bunched up fabric, my pants now too big for my already-thin frame. My eyes slowly moved back up. I took in the individual lines of each rib under my breasts and the indentation between them. She was right.

My God! I had allowed myself to waste away, the stress of everything had taken away my will to survive. How had I allowed myself to get this way? A shiver ran up my spine.

"When is the last time you ate?" she asked as our eyes met in the reflection. Ever so slightly I shook my head, not knowing the answer.

"Well, put your shirt on because the first thing we are going to do is get some food in you." The thought of eating made me queasy, but seeing myself in the mirror made me realize she was right.

That night, we sat up late and talked about everything that had happened in the last few weeks. I told her about the day we went to the mall, and exactly what Josh had told me the day he'd left. She cried from the other end of the couch as I talked, silent tears shed because she was so upset that she had not been there to help me.

She talked me into calling my parents the next morning and sat beside me as I explained to them that Josh and I had separated. I didn't want to say we were getting divorced, because I didn't know if that was true or not, but I asked them if I could come home, and they said they would fly out and help me get packed up. We could rent a U-Haul and bring my stuff back. They didn't even hesitate.

That day, I stopped into work and turned in my notice, explaining that I needed to take the day off to deal with personal things and that I would be moving in two weeks. They understood when I explained the few things I needed to do and said they would be happy to give me a recommendation to find a new job once I moved to Pennsylvania and got settled.

This was going to be a whole new start. Maybe I would be able to get my life in order, finally.

Unlocking the door to the house, I dreaded stepping inside, knowing how empty it would feel. Strangely enough, it wasn't until his things were gone that it had felt like it was over. I walked the rooms, looking at everything and stopping to gently touch things as a memory came to mind.

The sound of the door closing gently startled me. I turned from the closet to the window, knowing it would be Josh. His car was parked on the side of the road; I froze in place, my entire body trembling.

"What are you doing here?" he said quietly behind me.

"I could ask you the same question." My response was directed at the glass in front of me.

"Why aren't you at work?" He stepped into the room, coming to stop someplace near the edge of the bed.

I looked over my shoulder at him, and emotions tore through me when my eyes landed on him. Pain, anger, hurt, and love all flooded through me. "I had things to get done since obviously I need to move out." I looked back to the window.

"Sorry about not telling you about the house, I was going to stop by and tell you the other day, but I got busy." Was that embarrassment I heard in his voice? I doubted it.

I shrugged. "Whatever."

"What are you going to do now?"

I wanted to turn and scream at him that it was none of his business, but as hurt and angry as I was, I couldn't bring myself to do that. "I'm moving to my parents'." I stepped away from the window and turned to walk past him to the kitchen. I didn't want to stand in our bedroom and have this discussion.

"Why there?" he asked as I passed him.

"Why not? I have nothing here." I walked into the kitchen, pulling a glass from the cabinet, filling it with water, not because I was thirsty, I just needed to have something to occupy my hands.

"You have a job, and I'm here." He walked up behind me. I choked on the water I was drinking.

"I quit my job, and last I looked, you moved out." I took another sip, careful to allow it to go down the right pipe this time.

His body heat was radiating onto my back. The thudding of my heart was loud, and I wondered if he could hear it.

"What if I was wrong, Mandy girl?" he slipped his hands onto my hips and stepped closer so his chest was against my back. "What if I don't want you to go?" He slid his arms around my waist, I wanted to melt into his arms, but I remained stiff against him.

There was no way I could have spoken, even if I had wanted to. I had dreamt of this moment, dreamt of feeling his arms around me again. How many times had I wished he would tell me he had been wrong? That this was all a mistake and it was me he wanted.

"Are you saying that you want us to work things out?" my voice was uneven as I spoke.

He moved his hands back to my hips, stepping back slightly. "I don't know."

I turned around, he dropped his arms. "You don't know? What do you want from me, Josh? Do you want me to drop to my knees and beg you again?"

He backed away from me, "Don't be stupid." He crossed his arms over his chest and leaned against the counter.

"Then what the hell do you want? You come here one day and tell me you hate my touch, and that you don't want me, and then you move out without telling me and put the house on the market. Then you come back and tell me you're not sure if that is what you really want. What the hell do you want, Josh?" I screamed at him as I stood there, all the anger, frustration, and pain from the last weeks pouring out.

His jaw tightened, the muscle ticking in his cheek on both sides. I imagined him grinding his teeth as he stood there trying to figure out how to respond.

"What, Josh? What do you want?" I yelled at him again.

He threw his hands up in the air, "You know what? Nothing, I don't want anything from you. I'm done." He turned to walk away.

"Just like that? Just like that you are going to throw away over five years of marriage and walk away?" I yelled, and he spun around, anger blazing in his eyes.

"Yeah, that's what I'm going to do because you are so not worth it. When are you leaving?" The muscles in his body were coiled tightly. I was afraid to keep up with my yelling, afraid that he would snap on me.

My voice softened as I spoke, "In two weeks."

Emotions flicked over his face, his jaw continued to tick. "Fine, I'll be back to get the house keys from you then." He turned, but didn't move further as I started to speak.

"So that's it? This is how this is going to end? Is that what you really want, Josh?" I wanted him to come back, wrap me in his arms, kiss me, tell me he loved me. At least that is what I thought I wanted.

His shoulders deflated, his head hung for a moment before he turned. Sadness filled his eyes for just a moment, "Yeah, that's it. Goodbye, Amanda." His eyes bore into my mine one final time before he turned and walked out, the soft click of the front door sounded more final than the slams I had gotten used to.

My shoulders rounded forward, I held my face in my hands, but for the first time, I did not cry. All of the numbness that I had felt when he was around helped to keep the feeling at bay; I walked to the bathroom to take a shower, wanting to wash away his final touch.

CHAPTER TWENTY-EIGHT

AMANDA

The two weeks went quickly, and there was not a word from Josh. The day my parents arrived, my mother pulled me into a strong embrace and cried. My arms encircled her, but I felt nothing. None of the words she spoke about getting back on my feet, or helping to find a job stirred any emotion in me. I was Novocain numb.

With the last of the items loaded in the U-Haul, my father closed the back door. A car pulled up behind the orange and white truck, Josh sat behind the wheel. For the first time all day, I felt something. My heart fluttered slightly as we looked through the glass at each other.

He got out of his car slowly, looking at the ground and not my parents as he made his way over to me. How tall and handsome he was. Even after all he had done to me, I wanted to pull him into my arms, tell him I loved him and that we could work things out. I wanted to say I could be a better wife, that I would do everything I could to please him, but instead, a new part of me made me hold my tongue. I stood there watching him.

My mother came to stand by my side, wrapping her arm around my waist, while my father stood behind me. I was thankful for their presence, but nervous that Josh would say something they would question me about later.

He nodded to my father, and then looked at me. "Can I talk to you for a minute?" My hands were sweating; I wiped them on my jeans, turning to go towards the house. I nodded briefly to the question in my mother's eyes before I stepped forward.

He followed me to the kitchen where I leaned against the counter, crossing my arms; I looked down at the dirty linoleum floor, waiting for him to speak.

"So…it looks like you are almost done." I nodded at the floor, still not speaking. "When are you leaving?"

"We're staying at a hotel tonight, we'll leave in the morning." My eyes focused on the tips of my shoes now, the scuffed white leather worn like my heart.

He was quiet for a few moments before finally saying, "Well, be careful driving."

That was it, huh? That was all he was going to say? *Be careful driving.* My heart thudded in my chest sadly even as my body gently trembled. I reached into my jeans and pulled out the house key. My intention had been to leave it on the counter when I left.

I held the key out to him. He reached out and took my hand, holding it gently before he picked it up. The touch brought tears to my eyes, but I blinked them back.

"So are you going to file for divorce?" I cleared my throat, emotion thick in my voice.

He shrugged, "Not right now."

"Why not?" Confusion mixed with the other emotions I felt. If he didn't want anything to do with me, why wouldn't he file?

"Because I don't want to right now; I don't know, Mandy," he ran his hand through his hair. "I get confused; sometimes I don't know what I am doing. Maybe this is just a separation. Part of me knows we'll get back together."

My mouth opened slightly as I stared at him, flabbergasted. How could he do all that he did, and then go shack up with another woman, put our house on the market, make me move out, and then tell me that someday we would be back together? I shook my head, feeling totally baffled.

"Why are you shaking your head?"

The dumbfounded feeling I had crossed over his features, causing me to laugh. "I don't get you. You say all these horrible things to hurt me, yet you stand there and say, 'Hey we'll be back together again.' You just don't make any sense."

"I didn't do anything to hurt you."

"Are you serious?" Closing my eyes, I shook my head again. "Whatever, Josh. Take care of yourself. You got what you wanted. I'm out of your life now." I started to walk past him, he grabbed my arm.

"It's not over, Amanda."

My voice was calm while inside I was scared to death that he would do something else to hurt me with my parents right outside. "Please, don't."

His eyes bore into mine for a few more seconds before his hand opened, and I pulled my arm free. I walked out without looking back at him. For once, I was the one leaving him—and it hurt like hell-but I did it, wiping the tears away as I moved to the driveway. I walked straight over to my car and got in. My parents were standing by the U-Haul. They climbed in and followed me out of the subdivision.

His last words kept playing over and over again. Would he be able to keep this hold over me from a thousand miles away, I wondered.

Two months later, I had a good job as a secretary, and I was saving money so I could get my own place soon. My parents were incredibly helpful with me, allowing me to keep to myself as much as I needed to and never asking too many questions. They were there if I needed them, but they never tried to hang over me.

After my first week in Pennsylvania, I stopped crying every night. My thoughts still went back to Josh and the early years of our relationship. I tried not to think about what he had done, physically and mentally, to me. It was hard to look in the mirror some days and not see the woman he had believed me to be, the poor pathetic lost soul that no one would want around.

I spoke with Angie every few weeks, and the last time we spoke, she told me that I sounded better than I had in a long time. I wasn't sure if I was better or not, but I hoped that it was a sign of healing.

The phone rang just as I finished washing the dinner dishes; I slung the dishtowel over my shoulder and picked up the phone.

"Hey, Amanda."

I froze, having not heard that voice in eight weeks, it was like traveling back in time to our house. For a brief moment, a small feather of fear brushed through my body and I swallowed.

Gripping the phone with my left hand, I closed my eyes, my voice weak when I responded, "Hello, Josh."

"How have you been?" I heard a lot of noise behind him and wondered where he was.

"I'm fine." I could have been nice and asked him the same question, but I was afraid he would say he was great and his life was wonderful.

"Did you get a job?" I heard music starting in the distance behind him.

"Yeah, I did. Did the house sell yet?" I twisted the phone cord around my finger, leaning on the wall. I looked through my reflection on the sliding glass doors into the dark night outside.

"Well, about that…um," he stopped. The muffled scratchy noise of a hand over the phone was rough in my ear. I heard him speaking to someone before he removed his hand and responded. "I decided to take it off the market."

"You what? Why?" I stopped twirling the cord.

"Well, I decided to move back in." He covered the phone again, but not completely. I could just hear him say, "Yeah, I'm going to tell her. Just wait."

"Why?" I was trying to listen hard to see if I could tell whom he was talking to.

"Well, yeah, so Sherry is pregnant, and she is going to move in with me." Never had his physical touch hurt as much as those words. A wave of dizziness washed over me, I grabbed the countertop.

"Mandy, you still there?" laughter came over the phone line, a harsh female giggle. I wondered if it was directed at me.

"Yes," I managed to get out. I heard her tell him to get off the phone.

"Hey, I gotta go, I just wanted to tell you about the house. Bye, Amanda." The call ended with a loud click.

I held the phone to my ear, the sound of the dial tone almost as loud as the blood pulsing in my ears. Slowly, I put the receiver down in the cradle and dropped the dishcloth on the counter. I walked upstairs, I closed the bathroom door. Dropping to my knees, I retched all of my dinner.

Josh was going to be a father. As my stomach cramped and the last of my meal was purged, I lay on the cold tile floor and allowed the coldness to seep into my body.

Not only was Josh going to be a father, but they were going to live in our house. This woman whom I didn't even know was living my life and loving the man I loved.

I crawled up off the floor and rinsed my mouth out, avoiding the mirror; I made it back to my bedroom, collapsing face first into my pillow. It was as I screamed into my pillow that the tears I had not shed the last seven weeks came forth and soaked my pillow.

How did I move forward when I had been beaten down so low? How could I find the strength to move on when the person I loved treated me like trash and made me believe I was nothing? How could I let go of anger and the frustration at having been used and abused by someone I had trusted? Who would want me now that I was nothing, just a shell?

The questions went around and around, but no answers formed, just more questions, more pain, more confusion. Thoughts of falling asleep and never waking up entered my mind again.

God, why are you doing this to me? The sobs wracked my body as the words filled my mind. I can't take anymore! Please stop it! Please! I begged, pleaded for his mercy that night, wanting the pain to go away once and for all.

When my alarm sounded the next morning, and I opened my swollen eyes to see the time, I realized that God had not answered my plea, I was still here. Groaning, I climbed out of bed and got ready for work.

My day was pretty much like all the rest. I got up and dressed, poured coffee into my large mug, and sat at the small wooden kitchen table making idle chatter with my father while he ate breakfast.

The sun shone brightly onto the peach walls of the kitchen, it should have helped lift my mood, but it didn't. Dad and I talked about some recent news in the paper and then I kissed him on the cheek before leaving for work.

I made it my job to stay as busy as I could. On this particular day, my goal was to do twice the amount of work that I normally would. I needed to keep the nauseating thoughts of Josh out of my mind.

I sat at my desk typing up the notes from a meeting and a few letters that needed to be faxed out. My eyes never strayed from my old metal desk or the computer screen in front of me. When someone spoke, I answered without looking at him or her and kept right on working.

The engineering department I worked in was busy, people constantly coming and going, but I quickly got used to all the activity and threw myself into my job.

Lunchtime rolled around, and I sat down at the sun-bleached picnic table outside. The sun warmed my skin, while the breeze tickled the hair on my arms. I unwrapped my sandwich and took a bite of the soft bread. While I had been getting my appetite back, today my sandwich tasted like cardboard instead of ham and cheese. I swallowed it with difficulty, trying not to gag. I heard laughter behind me as I put my fist to my mouth, hoping to keep the food down. I turned to face the sound.

Zach, one of the engineers who worked in my department, looked down smiling. "Sandwich not very good? You don't mind, do you?" He sat down across from me, not waiting for my answer, setting his newspaper and lunch bag on the knotted wooden table.

"I guess I'm just not feeling too well today." I put my sandwich back into the clear baggie and set it back in my lunch bag.

"You do look tired." His smile took the sting out of the negative statement. I found myself smiling back for a moment before I looked at the book in front of me.

"Yeah, I guess I didn't sleep all that well." I leaned down on my elbows and started reading. His newspaper corners were flapping gently in the breeze, distracting me from the page I was on. I looked away from my book and closed my eyes, tipping my head back to let the sun warm my face. Maybe if it warmed it enough, it would reach inside me and warm that too, I thought.

The smell of fresh-cut grass tickled my nose; I inhaled it deeply, listening to the sounds around me as I soaked up the warm rays. A car with a bad muffler drove by; I tried to picture what type of car it might be. As it was almost past, I opened my eyes to find a small foreign car. As my eyes moved back in front of me, Zach was staring at me. I raised my eyebrows at him. A light blush crept over his face; he looked back down to his paper.

In those two seconds he looked at me, I saw something I had not seen in a long time. I saw someone looking at me as if I were a person and not a loser. I smiled and found myself looking him over. His dark brown hair feathered and blew in the wind around his head. His long eyelashes were low over his eyes while he read his paper. I found myself staring at his lips while he chewed his sandwich.

He looked up when he took another bite. It was my turn to look away and blush, but not before I saw a small smile on his face. Interestingly enough, in the next few minutes that we sat there in silence, I felt like we communicated in a way I never had before: soft smiles, quick glances, and silence.

Glancing down at my watch, I saw it was about time to head back in to work. I sighed, not wanting to leave the fresh air for a stuffy building. I wished I could work in a job where I was outside all the time.

"Big sigh for a little woman." He folded up his paper.

Laughing softly, "Yeah, it's so beautiful, I don't want to go back to the desk."

"I know what you mean. Hey, have you ever been to Peter's Village?" He picked up his paper and lunch bag as I gathered my stuff.

"No, what is that?" I stood up.

"It's a place I like to go to just relax outside. There are these hiking paths through the woods and a big stream where you can climb on all these rocks. I take my camera, a picnic lunch, and find a big rock to relax on."

"That sounds like a great place. Are you a photographer?" We walked back toward the building. "I always wanted to learn to take pictures, I love looking at nature shots."

"I only take pictures for myself, but that's what I like to take photos of, too. I could show you how to do it; I have an extra camera I could let you borrow if you want."

"Seriously, you'd let me borrow it?" I smiled, watching the ground as we walked. I noticed as I looked at him again that he was about five inches taller than I. His profile displayed a nice strong jawline.

"Sure! What are you doing Saturday morning? It is supposed to be an awesome week weather-wise. I could take you out to Peter's Village and show you a few things."

Conflicting emotions warred within me. I was about to turn him down, knowing that Josh would not be happy with me spending time with another man—but Josh was having a child with another woman! If he had moved on, why shouldn't I?

"What time on Saturday would you like me to meet you?" I stopped and waited while he pulled open the glass door to the building.

"I could pick you up, if you would like me to." He held it for me as I entered into the lobby.

"Actually, Zach, if you don't mind, I'd prefer to drive myself." I wasn't sure how he would take that. I was embarrassed to look him in the face, but I did.

His smile relaxed me when he agreed. We planned to have lunch again the next day so he could give me directions and give me my first lesson on cameras.

I walked back to my desk, smiling from the inside out, something I had not done in a long time. For once, I looked forward to the next day.

I was proud that I told him I would meet him. I wanted to control my life, and just making that small decision told me I was starting to figure it out. No longer would I allow someone to make decisions for me or control what I did. I would do what I wanted and how I wanted.

It didn't matter how I had felt for Josh or that it still caused me so much pain to think about him. He had hurt me in ways Steve and Mark never had. He had made me feel like I was nothing, and today, someone not only looked at me like I was someone, but talked to me that way, too.

As I typed the password into my computer, a moment of worry gave me pause; I wondered if Zach was looking for a relationship. I closed my eyes. If he acted like he was, then I would have to tell him I just wasn't ready. I could do this. I could control my own life.

CHAPTER TWENTY-NINE

NICOLE

"Gentlemen, can I see you both over here, please?" I stood next to my patrol car, tearing off pages from the accident report.

"Mr. Garver, this is your copy of the report. Mr. Summons, this is yours." I handed one a pink copy and the other a yellow one. They took them without comment, I pointed out the department phone number and the incident number explaining to them that they needed to call their insurance companies and give them that information.

After both of them nodded their understanding, I turned around and opened my clipboard, pulling out three citations. "Mr. Garver, here is your citation."

"What the hell did I get a citation for? He's the one that hit me!"

I squared my shoulders and looked him in the eye, "It's not for the accident. It's a disorderly conduct citation for getting into a physical confrontation with Mr. Summons in the middle of the street."

Mr. Summons laughed. I looked at him sternly, "Don't laugh, you got one, too." I handed him his copy; the smile vanished from his face. He looked down at the paper with disgust but took it from my hands.

"Mr. Summons, you also get another citation for not stopping at the stop sign, here is that one." I held it out; he shook his head and reached for it. Mr. Garver started to laugh but stopped when I glared at him.

"Gentlemen, both of you get back in your cars and leave. Do not say another word to each other and please allow your insurance companies to deal with this. It is very obvious you can't discuss this like adults."

"He's the jerk that started it," Mr. Summons raised his voice.

Not wanting to allow the other guy to get the last word in, Garver yelled back, "If you had stopped at the stop sign, I wouldn't have had to punch your lights out!"

This was going to escalate quickly if I didn't take action. I stepped between them, putting my hands on both their chests pushing them away from each other. "If you do *not* stop right this second, I will physically arrest you both and take you both to jail."

Turning my neck back and forth, I waited till I had their attention. "Go get in your cars right this second and get out of my Township before I change my mind."

As both men grumbled, I watched them turn and move towards their respective vehicles. Mr. Garver just couldn't let it go and flipped the guy the middle finger before glancing at me. He climbed in his car quickly when he saw my angry expression.

I shivered and turned the heat up in my car when I got inside. The temperature dropped as the sun began to set, and I thought again about how much I hated the cold. I cleared the call and went back to the station to finish the paperwork for the accident. It was an easy report, just a little blotter entry with the vehicle and driver information along with a narrative explaining why they both got cited for disorderly conduct.

I sat at the desk, typing at the computer when the outside buzzer went off and I reached up to release the door. Rebecca Swift walked in, "Officer Nolan, I'm so glad that you are on duty."

"Rebecca, hello, how are you?" I stood up to shake her hand when she got close enough.

"I was doing really well until Jason started texting me." She rested her hands on the counter in front of her. I saw them shaking as she gripped the edge.

"When did he start texting you?" I sat back down in my chair looking up at her.

"Yesterday, he sent me a message, and I ignored it. Then today I got six more from him, each one getting angrier because I wouldn't respond."

"How did he get your phone number? I thought you changed it." I pulled myself up to the desk, reaching for a notepad and a pen from the cup that held them.

"I have no idea, although I think maybe his sister might have given it to him."

"How did she have it?" I tapped the end of the pen on the paper twice.

"I gave it to her." I raised my eyebrows at her. "I know, I know. I see now that I shouldn't have. She promised me she wouldn't give it to him."

"Let me see the text messages." She pulled her cell phone out of her purse and found the messages I needed to see. Reaching out, I took it from her and scrolled through them.

"Bitch...answer me or ur gonna die!!!!"

Okay, that was enough. I set the phone down and walked into the other room, picking up the camera.

Standing over the phone, I touched the screen to bring it back to life and snapped a few pictures of the screen showing the threats he was making.

I turned off the camera, setting it down next to my computer. I would load the pictures and include them with the criminal complaint. Handing the phone back to her, I saw her hands still shaking.

"It's alright, Rebecca. I'm going to type up the charges for Indirect Criminal Contempt right now, and I will get them in front of a judge later tonight. We will have a warrant issued for him and we'll get him picked up."

She nodded to me, "What if he comes to the house?"

"If he shows up, you pick up the phone and dial 911 immediately. We will be there as soon as we can, and we will take him into custody. Lock yourself in a room upstairs and wait for us."

"I was thinking about buying a gun. Do you think I should do that?"

I stood up. "Rebecca, I can't answer that. Only you know if you should do that. It's a bit more than just buying a gun. You need to know how to use it and use it safely."

"I just don't know what to do. I'm putting the house on the market, I talked to a realtor today, and as soon as it sells I am moving back west."

"Good for you, I'm proud of you for that. You know I was worried you were going to go back to him."

Her brown curls bounced around her face as she shook her head furiously. "There is no way in hell I would ever go back to him. You helped open my eyes the last time. I can't thank you enough, although I wish I had listened to you earlier."

"I'm glad to hear that, I wish you had too, but you had to make the decision yourself. It wasn't an easy one, I know, but it was the right one."

She agreed, and we spoke a little longer before she left. I flipped on the television for background noise; I rolled over to the computer and plugged in the camera to download the pictures of the cell phone screen.

A word on the television got my attention, and I growled to myself. The weather map displayed snow heading our way. It was only the beginning of December, and they were talking about a snowstorm. What would Colton think about doing a lateral transfer to someplace warm? I'd need to ask him.

Printing out the pictures and typing up the complaint didn't take long; I faxed them over to the court on call for the night. I would have to go swear to the complaint in front of the judge and wait for the arrest warrant, but the night court was not open yet. At least the paperwork was ready for them.

When I stepped outside, the wind blew angrily against me, winter was moving in quickly. I pulled my coat more tightly and climbed into my car, glad that I had left the heat turned up.

Time for some patrol before I had to respond to court. I stopped a few cars for traffic violations and issued each of them citations. Twilight had settled over the township, and I drove around the darkened streets. I pulled into our township park, noticing a car in the back of the lot. I drove up to it and hit my lights. The red and blue lit up the whole area.

The car started bouncing around in front of me. The windows were fogged up, a telltale sign that something intimate was probably happening inside the car. I took my time getting to it, hoping the occupants would be dressed when I finally approached.

I watched a male figure climb into the front seat from the back. I tapped on the window with the back of my flashlight. The window came down, a flustered male sat in the seat, embarrassed as he looked up at me.

"What are you doing?" I asked him.

"Um, my girlfriend and I were just hanging out."

"Roll down the back window, please." I waited as he did so, shining my light into the back seat. The driver looked to be about nineteen or twenty, but the girl in the back looked like she was twelve.

"How old are you?" The girl's brown eyes were like saucers in her face, her lower lip trembling.

"I'm fourteen." Her soft fearful voice spoke from the other side of the car. I looked her over; her shirt was buttoned incorrectly. Her hair was mussed up, and her lips looked swollen.

"Do your parents know you are here?" I glanced at the driver who now had his head resting back against the seat.

"No," the young girl replied. She looked away from me, crossing her arms over her chest.

"Sir, can I see your license and vehicle information, please." I stood next to his door again, shining my light into the seat. I waited while he gathered the items and handed them to me.

"Both of you stay in the car." I looked into the back again, "What's your name?"

"Melissa Thompson." She wiped a tear from her cheek. "Are you going to call my parents?"

"You hold tight, and I'll be right back and then we will talk about that." Making my way back to my car, I went over the radio to say my status was alright and asked for another unit to head my way. When dealing with juveniles, it was always better to have two officers present at the scene, just in case.

When Adam rolled up next to me, I smiled at him through the window. We both put the glass down at the same time. "What have you got?" he asked.

"Well, I thought I just had a couple of lovebirds, but as it turns out I have a fourteen–year-old female and a nineteen–year-old male."

"Nice," he said sarcastically. "What would you like me to do?" He was looking towards the car, taking in the scene.

"I'm going to take her out of the car and talk to her. Do me a favor and talk to the guy, see what he has to say." He pulled away from my car so he could open his door, and we both approached the vehicle.

"Ryan," I had gotten his name, Ryan McDermott, from his license, "I need you to talk to this officer for a few minutes, please." I walked to the other side of the car and opened the back passenger door. "Melissa, grab your jacket and climb out, we need to talk."

The loud adolescent huffing could easily be heard from inside the car, and Adam smiled at me over the roof. I managed to hold it in, but just barely.

I walked Melissa over to my car, turning her so her back was to Ryan's car, this way I could watch Adam and Ryan talking.

"Melissa, you do know how old he is, right?"

"Yeah, he's nineteen, so what's the big deal?"

I crossed my arms, not trying to be condescending, but needing to keep warm against the wind, "The big deal is that you are a minor, and he is not. Melissa I need to ask you a few questions, and you need to be honest with me."

She nodded, wiping tears off her cheeks.

"Were you having sex with Ryan?" I bent my neck to the side trying to see past the curtain of brown hair into her face.

"I didn't want to," she whispered.

"You didn't want to have sex with him? Was he making you have sex?" I put my hand out onto her arm to show her some compassion while speaking softly to her.

She nodded. "He told me if I didn't have sex with him then he was going to tell everyone I was a slut. I thought if I did, he wouldn't say anything. At first I wanted to, but then when we started I got scared and told him to stop."

"Did he stop?"

"No, he held my hands above my head with one hand and did it." She covered her face with both hands.

"He did what, Melissa? I know it's hard to say these things, but you need to tell me exactly what he did." I let her cry for a few moments, before I squeezed her arm again, "Melissa, what did he do?"

"He pushed it into me." She cried louder now.

"By it, do you mean his penis?"

She nodded as her cries turned to sobs.

Adam heard the sobbing and turned to look at us. I nodded at him and took both my arms and crossed them gently at the wrists. He nodded in return, and I watched as he reached for the door handle and pulled it up.

Telling Melissa to stay where she was, I walked over to Adam as Ryan was stepping out of the car. Pulling my handcuffs from my belt, I stepped immediately up to him and took his arm, while Adam held his other arm, so he couldn't move away.

"What are you doing?" Ryan tried to turn and look at me.

"You're under arrest, Ryan." I wanted to kick this kid's ass, but instead, I put the cuffs on gently and spoke confidently and professionally.

"What? She wanted it! You can't arrest me if she wanted it!" He bucked against us as we started to push him towards Adam's car.

"Get in the car, Ryan. You have enough charges against you right now, you don't need resisting arrest." He calmed down and walked to the car, climbing in before he spoke again.

"How can you arrest me if she wanted it?"

I leaned down with one arm on the roof of the car and the other on the passenger door. "I can arrest you because you are nineteen and she is fourteen. It's called statutory rape, and it's against the law." I closed the door on his next words, not caring what he had to say.

Adam took Ryan to lock-up, while I took Melissa to the hospital for a rape kit. Sitting at the hospital, we waited for her parents to arrive, and then I explained what had happened. The nurse who had examined her stated that there was vaginal tearing, which went along with her story about being forced. Signs of bruising were already showing up on her wrist.

Melissa spoke with her parents for a few moments in private before she told me she wanted to proceed as quickly as possible with prosecution.

I left the hospital, hoping the girl would heal both inside and out and without issue. I stopped next to my car, looking up into the dark sky as the first of the snowflakes started to fall.

CHAPTER THIRTY

AMANDA

*Z*ach and I pulled into the dirt parking lot at one of the state parks, bouncing over the potholes in his truck as we drove. He pulled to a stop under a shade tree, and we both climbed out, grabbing our camera bags from the back seat.

For the last four weeks, we'd gone out every Saturday morning to walk and take pictures of nature. I found a passion I never knew existed when I looked through the lens of the camera. Zach said I had such a great ability to capture the beauty through photography that I put his pictures to shame. I laughed at his flattery.

We each had a camera strapped around our necks, and he carried a larger bag with more lenses in it, while I carried a small backpack with our lunches and water. We made our way towards a trail; I stopped next to him when he spotted a hawk flying above us. Putting my hand over my eyes to shield the sun, I looked between the hawk and Zach. Our friendship had grown quickly, and I felt comfortable being out with him.

He knew I was separated and that my breakup had been bad, but I never told him what I had gone through, and while I knew he obviously wanted to ask more, he graciously didn't.

He had been married and his divorce was finalized a few months earlier. His daughter lived with his former wife. The relationship he shared with his ex-wife was friendly for the most part, and I had even gotten to meet his daughter when she joined us one Saturday morning.

Our time together was relaxing. He taught me how to use the camera in the manual mode and how to change things to make adjustments to lighting and the speed of the lens. I picked it up quickly, excited to learn.

For the first time in a very long time, I felt comfortable and almost happy. A small piece of me still held onto the sadness of my past. The memories of Josh haunted me late at night when I was alone, but for the most part, my days were filled with good things.

As we entered the wooded area, Zach reached down and took my hand for the first time. My lips curved up as I looked in front of me, enjoying the gentle feel of his hand in mine. We walked, taking turns stopping to take pictures of things we saw, always returning to hold hands as we continued with our expedition.

A few hours later, I heard his stomach growl. "You are always hungry!" I laughed as we found a fallen tree and sat down.

"It's all the working out I do. With the day job and the night job, I'm always active." He set his camera down next to him.

"That's right. I forget you work another job. What is it again that you do?" I unzipped the backpack, pulling out a bag of crackers and two sandwiches.

"I teach karate, so I work out for hours after work each night, teaching kids and adults, and then I do training for myself."

I laughed, "You don't look like a ninja man."

"Hey, what's that supposed to mean?" he laughed while he reached for a sandwich.

"I don't know, but I would have never guessed you did karate." Taking a bit of my roast beef sandwich, I set it down next to me and cracked open a bottle of water.

"You should try it. I bet you would like it. We have an adult beginning class starting soon. I could get you signed up for it." He took the bottle of water I passed to him.

"I'm not so sure about that." I shook my head, "I don't think I would be very good. Besides, I can't picture myself being a ninja girl."

He laughed out loud, covering his mouth with his hand to keep the food from falling out. "Why don't you come watch me teach a class?

There are a lot of women there. Many of them are a lot older than you. Some do it for exercise; some for self-defense."

"That stuff doesn't really work as self-defense, does it?" I chewed another bite.

"Of course it does," he scoffed at me. "Sometimes it's not about the moves; it's about the way it makes you feel. When you are confident in your abilities and you have strong self-esteem, you don't project a victim attitude."

I looked away from him as he finished his sentence. How nice it would have been to have known self-defense before when I'd been with Josh or Steve. Maybe they wouldn't have hurt me the way they had. "Maybe I will come watch a class sometime."

I changed the subject after my comment, and we enjoyed the rest of our walk. With another hundred pictures in my camera, we exited the woods, making our way back to his truck, still holding hands and laughing as we walked. Zach unlocked the passenger door. I went to step past him and glanced up to his face. The look in his eye stopped me from climbing into the cab; I smiled into his hazel eyes.

His lips came down, hesitating just slightly before touching mine. It was a brief, gentle kiss, testing the waters. I wasn't sure that either of us was ready for anything more. I knew I wasn't, but it was nice to feel that gentle touch and see affection in someone's face. I grinned shyly at him and clambered up into the seat.

As we drove out of the parking lot, neither of us noticed the person behind the wheel of the car parked at the end of the lot opposite us.

Zach dropped me off at home and talked me into watching his adult karate class on Monday. It was a holiday, and we were off from work.

The week before, I'd found an apartment, just a few miles away from my job and my parents' house. It wasn't much, but it was mine and I could afford it with the paycheck I earned. I unlocked the metal mailbox door in our community mail center and pulled out the few pieces I found inside.

I read a piece of junk mail while I made my way to my door, absently pulling my keys out of my bag. As I turned the key in the door, I heard a footstep behind me. I figured it was my neighbor and didn't think twice about it. Pulling out the key, I turned the knob and glanced over my shoulder.

The keys fell from my hand at the look in Josh's eyes. My knees weakened at the purposeful gait he used while moving toward me. I gasped at the murderous look that distorted his face. I pushed at my door, trying to get inside before he could get to me. Dropping my bag as I entered, I pushed against the door trying to close it before he reached it. I felt him shove against the outside of the door. I was thrown back by the force. The door bounced off the stopper and he pushed it out of his way as he entered. He forcefully pushed the door closed behind him and locked it.

"What are you doing here, Josh?" I managed to mumble from my spot on the floor. Flashbacks of when Steve had entered my apartment like this so many years ago roared through my mind. I wasn't as quick to stand up as I had been back then.

"I told you if you fucking cheated on me, I'd kill you!" He reached down, grabbed me by the arm, and pulled me up in front of him. His right hand released my arm as I came to my full height. He slapped me so hard I saw blackness on the edge of my vision.

"I'm not cheating on you, Josh," I cried as I tried to move away from him. "Please, don't," I begged him when he raised his hand again.

"Don't lie to me! I saw you! I saw you kiss that guy!" He shoved me back against the wall. The pictures rattled, threatening to fall to the ground. How had he seen me? Was he following me? Why was he even here in Pennsylvania?

"I swear that was the first time he kissed me, and it was no big deal. Josh, I swear I'm not cheating on you!"

"I saw it with my own eyes! You were holding hands with that asshole and then you kissed him! He must not have slept with you yet, or he wouldn't still be around!"

The force of his words stung almost as much as his hand hitting my face. The second slap spun me around and knocked me to the ground.

I landed on my elbows. Remembering what he had done to me the last time I'd been in this position, I pushed off the carpet, trying to get away from him. I managed to make it to my feet.

"Why are you here?" I yelled at him, trying to put distance between us.

"I came here to bring you back, to tell you I wanted you to come home," he yelled while I cringed at the anger in his voice. "I can't believe I came all this way to tell you I wanted you back, and here you are with some other guy! You are such a slut!" he yelled.

He stalked me, holding me still with the menace in his eyes. Each step closer caused my heart to pound and my knees to shake more. I knew without a doubt he was about to hurt me.

The third time he hit me, a fist to the face, I fell to the ground, my head spinning, my jaw aching. "Josh, please," I begged, and I tried to crabwalk away from him. He kicked my legs out from under me. I managed to get them back under me and tried to scramble away. He was faster on his feet than I was crawling. He grabbed me by the hair, yanking me to my knees, a second punch in the face caused stars to fly through my vision. I tried to move away, but he held my hair in a vice grip.

I screamed as he punched me a third time, "Please, Josh, stop!" I tasted blood on my tongue and couldn't tell if I had bitten it or if my mouth was bleeding. I fought to get away from him, kicking and wriggling to move away. I managed to get away and started to crawl, but he jumped on my back, tackling me to the floor with his weight.

A screech left my lips as he lifted my head up off the floor and slammed it into the carpet, not once, but twice. The room was growing dark around me when suddenly the weight on my back was lifted. Shouting around me caused me to roll to my side away from the commotion. I opened my eyes to see two men sitting over Josh, both of them with dark clothing. I lost consciousness but vaguely remember the sound of metal clicking shut.

I woke up a few hours later with a pounding head and a sore face. My body ached all over, but my face felt like it had been stomped on by an elephant. I opened my eyes, or tried to. One of them was swollen shut.

I felt my mother's hand squeeze mine. I turned my head to see the most heartbreaking look in her eyes. "Hi there, sweetheart," she said softly.

By the smells and sounds around me, I knew I was in the hospital. "Hi," I could barely whisper. "How did I get here?"

"A neighbor saw Josh push his way into your apartment and heard you scream. He called the police. You dropped your keys outside, so the police were able to get into your place when they got there. Although one officer told me he heard your screams. He said they would have kicked the door down if your keys had not been there."

"What happened to me?" My face was throbbing and my throat felt raw.

"You are going to be alright. The doctor said you have a concussion, and your nose is broken, he said it wasn't the first time, though. Amanda, sweetheart, has Josh done this to you before?"

Never had I wanted my parents to know how bad things had been in my life. I always wanted them to believe that I was happy and doing well. That fantasy had ended. It was time to tell the truth.

I nodded slowly, "This was not the first time."

"Oh, Amanda, why didn't you tell us? We would have helped you. Your dad and I would have done anything we could to have helped you. Don't you know that?" She squeezed my hand while tears ran down her cheeks.

"I was embarrassed to tell you. I thought he loved me, Mom. I really did. I thought it was just a phase and we would get past it." Hot tears ran down my swollen cheeks as I looked at her.

"Mandy, if he loved you, he would never have laid a hand on you. This is not something to be embarrassed about. It's not your fault." I watched as she closed her eyes attempting to hold back her own emotions. "We will talk more about this later, you rest now. The doctor said you can go home tomorrow." She squeezed my hand as she spoke.

I nodded. "Where is he?"

"He's in jail where he belongs. Now rest." She patted my hand and I closed my eyes.

Unlike before when I'd heard Josh had been arrested, this time, I did not feel guilt. He belonged behind bars, and I felt nothing but satisfaction at the news my mother had given me.

The next day, I went home to my parents' house. The doctor didn't want me being alone with the concussion, and I personally wasn't ready to be back in my apartment yet either.

On Monday morning, I lay in bed, wondering how I would deal with going back to work the next day. My face was a hot mess, bruised and swollen, showing the obvious signs of a battered woman. I hadn't been there long enough to have accrued any time off. Besides a day or two wasn't going to make much of a difference. I was already mortified at the thought of the looks that I would receive and the words that would be spoken behind my back.

I got out of bed and went to the mirror. Standing in front of it, I looked long and hard at the image reflected back. There stood a woman who had been torn down over and over again in her short adult life. I don't want to be that woman anymore, I thought to myself. I wanted to be someone strong, someone who could take care of herself, someone who would be worthy of love. I wanted a life of happiness; I didn't want to be afraid.

I made a decision as I stared at the image. I went looking for my mother once the decision was made. She was seated in the kitchen reading over the paper, drinking her coffee. She looked up as I entered. I saw the wince on her face even as she tried to force a smile.

"Hey, Mom, can you take me someplace? I need to go see someone." The look she gave me was concerned, but it softened as she took in my face. I knew my eyes were brighter now than they had been. While I had stood in front of the mirror, I had seen a change come over them myself.

"Sure, honey, whatever you need to do." I gave her a lopsided grin and turned to go back upstairs.

Three hours later, we pulled into a parking lot. I stared at the door. My mom had not questioned me on our destination. We sat there side by side, not speaking. My heart beat a wild cadence as I reached for the door handle. People walking in and out of the building didn't notice me, but I knew they would. I needed to do this, which meant having to face the stares and jaw drops.

As I pulled on the door handle, my mother put her hand on my arm. "Do you want me to go with you?"

"No, Mom, I need to do this by myself, but thanks." I squeezed her hand. Pushing open the door, I stepped out into the parking lot and inhaled deeply. I closed my eyes briefly, rolled my shoulders back, and stood up straight. The first step was the hardest, but I took it.

I walked to the door, keeping my head high when two people walked out. Both of their faces displayed horror as they looked at me, but I smiled the best I could, stepped around them, and entered. Whispers met my ears as the door closed, but it didn't matter anymore.

I searched the area for who I wanted, knowing people gawked at me. I saw him across the room. A child standing beside him reached over for his mother's hand. The woman gasped slightly as I walked up. The man beside her turned to look at me.

"Amanda! What happened to you?" He stepped towards me, but I stepped out of his reach. I wasn't ready for anyone to touch me.

I swallowed the bile in my throat and met his eyes. "My soon-to-be-ex-husband tried to kill me on Saturday. I'd like to sign up for classes, Zach."

CHAPTER THIRTY-ONE

AMANDA

*N*ine months ago I had walked in that front door. The same door I walked into now with my bag slung over my shoulder and a huge heartfelt smile on my face. Greeting people as I entered, I made my way to the locker rooms to change into my uniform.

Zach had been floored to learn that Josh had seen us together; he had tried to accept the fault as his. I explained to him several times that the blame lay with no one. I knew now that it would have eventually happened anyway. Josh had a problem, and it wasn't my fault.

I had been a victim, but I wasn't anymore.

I walked out to the floor, bowing to the flags as I stepped on to the mat to stretch. Zach was correct that I would love karate. I excelled at it in a way I could never have imagined, picking up the punches, kicks, and blocks like I was born to do them. My ability to do everything and focus on my formations so intently made belt testing easy, my goal to obtain my black belt.

Putting my feet at shoulder width, I leaned over and stretched to the floor; loosening my back and legs from sitting at a desk all day. I was always the first to arrive at class and well into stretching when more people made their way to the mat.

I had formed some great relationships with my classmates, friendships that I treasured. I turned my head when I heard a voice behind me. Zach walked onto the floor, smiling in my direction. Things hadn't worked out for us in a romantic sense, but we remained very close friends, still hiking and taking pictures at least twice a month.

In a way, he had saved my life, not physically, but mentally. He had introduced me to karate, a way to deal with my anger and a way to help me feel stronger not only outside, but inside. A confidence I had never known before blossomed in me.

I smiled as he walked by, and I tried to grab his foot to trip him up, but he was too good and jumped out of my reach, laughing.

Class was called; we all found our places on the line. I squared my shoulders, pulled in my focus, and looked at the mirror in front of me. No longer was I afraid to look into the reflective glass. I knew now that I was in charge of my life and I could do anything with it that I wanted to do.

My eyes held an energy they'd never had before, a rich deep confidence in myself and my abilities. I knew that I would never again be a victim like I had been. I would control what happened to me the best that I could. No man would raise his hand to me in anger, not ever again.

As our class began, I focused on my form in the mirror, realizing just how far I had come. I knew I still had a lot to overcome, but I would get there one day at a time, one step at a time.

Several of us went out to dinner after our class; I found myself laughing like I had never laughed before. A glance around the table made me realize how much I had missed in my young adult life, and I had a lot to make up for.

Parking my car at home, I pulled out my gym bag and glanced around the parking lot. I never allowed my eyes to drift to the ground as I walked to the mailbox. I kept my shoulders back, my head up, and my eyes constantly scanned around me. After getting my mail, I carried it to my apartment door and went inside. No longer did I try to read while I walked, I remained always aware. Dropping my bag in the corner away from the door, I flopped on the couch and flipped through the mail.

Electric bill, oh yeah, I thought. My fingers stopped, immediately trembling when I looked at the next envelope. The return address read from my attorney. I sat up to the edge of the couch, setting the other pieces of mail on the cushion beside me. With shaky hands, I tore open the flap. I slowly pulled out the three sheets of paper.

I unfolded the trifold, reading the top page. A letter explaining what was enclosed stared back at me, I didn't know if I should laugh or cry. A tragic chapter of my life was now closed. I flipped the page and saw the divorce decree on the second page.

A bubble of laughter escaped my mouth as I stared down at it. I was a single woman again; a single woman with her whole life ahead of her. No tears marred my vision; no longer did I feel those kinds of emotions about Josh.

The last time I had seen him had been in court. He had pled guilty to lesser charges and the state made arrangements for his probation to be moved so he could leave. He did thirty days in jail and then went back to Michigan. Our divorce agreement said he was to sell the house, and I was to get seventy-five percent of anything received over what was owed on the mortgage. I ended up with just over ten thousand. With the money banked, I was already looking at townhouses so I could have my own home.

Josh was under strict rules not to contact me at all, and the last time I saw him, I walked up to him and told him to stay out of my life for good. I filed for divorce the next day; his papers were served to him in jail.

The post office would deliver his letter soon; I wondered what would go through his mind. Had he gone back to that other woman or was he with someone else now? I didn't really care, but I wondered from time to time whose life he was making a living hell now.

I flipped over the paper to the third page and read the words. This time, my eyes did water up when I saw the words. My name had officially been changed back to my maiden name. I read the words over again.

Slowly leaning back into the couch, I saw another envelope sitting beside me. The return address caught my attention; I set the attorney's pages down on my lap to pick up the other letter. I stared at the cream envelope with the dark black print for a long time before I got the courage to pull it open.

The words jumped off the page in front of me. I stood up quickly, dropping the legal pages to the floor. Tears ran down my face as I read the words again.

"I got in," I said quietly. "I got in!"

Excitedly, I looked around the small living room, wanting to share my news. I swiped away the happy tears and yelled to myself, "I got in!" I jumped up and down, danced around the living room, and then I grabbed the phone.

Dialing as quickly as my excited fingers could, I called my mom. "Guess what!" I yelled as soon as she picked up the phone.

"Oh my gosh, Amanda, why are you screaming?"

I laughed because I couldn't contain it anymore. "I got into the police academy, Mom! I got in! Oh, and by the way, I'm not using my first name anymore. You can start calling me Nicole Nolan! Mom! I got in!"

CHAPTER THIRTY-TWO

FIVE AND A HALF POUNDS

*T*he snow had fallen slowly overnight and into the next day. Several inches had piled up along the ground, covering the world in pristine white. I walked out to my patrol car, looking around me. I had to admit that when the snow fell and covered up all the dead grass and trees, it did look rather pretty. I just wished it could do it without being so cold.

Inside my car, I checked my computer for any messages; none appeared, so I put the car in drive to pull out onto the road. Todd had called me a few minutes before, telling me he was heading down to the local convenience store to get us coffee. We were going to meet at the garage where we could stand inside and be warm while we drank.

I drove off in the opposite direction to make sure we didn't have any stranded motorists off in a ditch before I went to wait for him.

A slick spot on the asphalt made the back side of my car shift sideways. I eased off the gas, correcting the steering to keep the car on the road. As I headed west, the tones came over the radio, a shiver coursed through me that had nothing to do with the cold. The tones always announced something serious was happening and, while many times it was precautionary, there were times when those tones did actually mean life or death.

I put my hand to the knob to turn the radio up slightly just as my computer started beeping. Oh, crap! This call was ours, "Thirty-Seven units, you have a possible shooting."

There was nothing more adrenaline-pumping than knowing that someone might have a gun and that they might be using it on someone else. I flipped my computer screen up and looked at the address, 104 Whitehall Way.

"Oh shit, Rebecca." I pulled into a driveway to turn around as Todd answered the radio with his call number.

"Thirty-Seven units, a 911 call was received with an open line. Call takers could hear yelling in the background and then what sounded like shots being fired. The phone was disconnected; we got an answering machine on callback."

Todd responded that he was en route. I jumped on the radio right after him, and then heard two other officers from other jurisdictions say they would be responding also.

I drove as quickly as I could on the unsafe streets, praying I wouldn't lose control of my vehicle. I wondered where Todd was since he had been heading that direction for coffee. The roads were too hazardous for me to pull out my Nextel, so I flipped the radio to our side channel and called him there.

"Thirty-Seven Paul Three to Paul One on channel two." My hands were shaking as I held the radio waiting for his reply.

"Paul One, go ahead," his voice was anxious; he knew what the deal was.

"What's your location, Todd?" I asked, dropping the professional call signs automatically.

"About two minutes out with these roads. What's yours?" I could hear the tension in his voice even over the airwaves. I pushed the button on the side as soon as he clicked off.

"I'm about five out, stage and wait for me."

"Don't worry, I will." I clipped the mic back down and drove faster, feeling my tires give and take as the road dipped and curved.

Okay, God, get me there safely, I thought to myself, and please let her be alright.

Todd got on the radio about two minutes later, saying he was staged nearby. I told him I was still a few minutes out.

I was less than half a mile from the house when Todd yelled over the radio, "I got shots fired!"

If my heart hadn't been beating at hyper speed before, it was now. I pressed down on the accelerator as much as I dared and slid onto the road leading to the house.

Five and a half pounds of pressure is all it takes to pull the trigger on my Glock. That random thought raced through my mind as I grew closer to the scene. My partner's patrol car was parked back from the house as we normally did, his overhead lights off, the reflective striping on the side of his car caught my headlights and bounced back at me. It was nowhere as bright as the blasts of red-orange that were coming from either side of the vehicle: gunfire.

Approaching the scene, I pressed hard on the brake pedal; my left hand tight on the steering wheel trying to keep my car moving straight. My right hand reached down, and, for the first time in my twelve-year career, I pushed the tiny red button on my radio, next to the channel dial. This button was only the width of the tip of my finger and had the letters EMER written on top of it. We only pushed this button when we came to this point: When we were at the emergency of all emergencies, and we needed any and all help to respond.

Immediately, my dispatcher came over the radio, "Thirty-Seven Paul Three, we have your emergency identifier." I knew now that any and all radios on our system were listening to what was being said. This cut out anyone else and took priority over everything.

My eyes were trained on the flashes of red and orange in front of me, reflecting off the windows of the houses and the white snow that continued to fall softly around us.

My tires started to slide, but I braced myself and they finally grabbed the road again. My thumb connected with the button on my mic. I didn't even try to pick it up to my mouth as I depressed the button and yelled, "Paul One is under fire!" I released the mic from my hand. I heard it smack down on top of the radio as my car came to a stop thirty yards from the firefight in front of me.

Todd dropped to the ground beside his car firing over the hood as he moved, obviously trying to keep the engine block between him and the assailant. The subject was approaching him when my car finally came to a standstill. The nose of my car dipped low as the rear end rose up. I threw the column shifter into park as I reach my left hand over and unhooked my seatbelt. The belt started to slide up over my chest while my left hand reached for the door handle. I did not notice the sounds of the radio. I did not hear the words being spoken or the number of times my computer beeped as more units started our way. My focus was on exiting the vehicle and stopping the threat in front of me.

The door started to open, and I lifted my left leg to follow it. As my foot made contact with the ground, I felt it slip slightly in the newly-fallen snow. I planted it as solidly as I could and shifted my body weight onto that leg as the rest of my body exited the car, my right hand reaching down for my holster. My head cleared the door. My eyes watered from the cold wind smacking me in the face. My hand moved to my holster, my thumb found its mark.

I moved to stand upright beside my car, never taking my eyes off the threat in front of me. From the corner of my eye, I saw my partner fall backwards. He'd been the target before I arrived, and now he was down. My right hand gripped my pistol tightly while my thumb pushed down, releasing the safety lever. My thumb pushed forward and my firearm came up. It moved up and forward as I stepped back from my door. My right foot found purchase on the ground and I planted it there to steady myself for the shoot.

Todd lay on the ground; the threat turned to me. My handgun continued to move up, but it felt so slow, like I was moving through mud.

The subject turned toward me first with his head, and I saw the maniacal face of Jason Swift looking back at me. His body followed his line of vision, a long rifle held in his hands. I vaguely wondered where he'd gotten a firearm of that caliber as my gun leveled. I leaned my head to the right ever so slightly to look down my sights, my finger found the trigger and contact was made.

It sounded so simple in theory: Ready...aim...fire...but what actually transpired was so much more.

Yes, ready, well, whether I thought I was ready or not, this was not the time to contemplate that. Now was the time to act. This was the time I had trained for, the time we all prayed would never come; the time when protecting a life or taking a life was what we must decide to do or not— without much time for self-questioning.

I stared down my sights, perfectly lined up, the center one smack in between the rear ones, in a perfect row together. They glowed an eerie green in the darkness before me, reflecting the red and blue lights flashing at my side. How I noticed all of this, I will never know, but I did.

I started to pull that trigger, started to pull back with that simple five and a half pounds of pressure. I felt my finger against the ribbed piece of hard plastic pulling. As the trigger came back, the mechanism connected and the gun fired. There was no turning back now, I could not stop what I had begun, nor would I have.

The firing pin went into action; it slammed against the primer of my .40-caliber ammunition. The primer ignited and the blast propelled the bullet out of the casing and through the barrel of the gun. The fire of the blast expelled out the muzzle with the bullet causing a burst of orange and red to appear, but I didn't see the flash of flame. I saw through it. The bullet left the barrel traveling at around a thousand feet per second and found its target standing thirty yards away.

The firearm in my hand remained steady, despite the heavy adrenaline coursing through my veins. It helped to keep me in place when the gun wanted to jump up from the recoil of the blast. The slide moved back to expel the used casing and a new piece of ammunition took its place just as my finger pressed the trigger again. I saw the target start to lose his balance as the first bullet struck him, his eyes widened, his beard full of snow. The second bullet left my gun as he started to drop, hitting the target directly between the eyes.

I saw his head snap back just as I felt his bullet strike me in the chest, right above the edge of my vest. Surprise, pain, and the force of the bullet hitting me threw me off balance and I started falling. My right arm went up in the air as my left arm reached for something to stop my descent. I missed the door and my body continued to be pulled by gravity, stopping only when it made contact with the snow-covered ground. My head bounced off the cold asphalt, my gun tumbled from my hand.

Searing hot pain spread through my chest while the now-absent sounds of gunfire still echoed in my ears, filling my head with vibration. My eyes closed. I tried to breathe, but the air was so cold that it hurt to inhale. Never in my life had I felt this kind of pain. I opened my eyes slowly, turning my neck slightly to see my partner moving. He's alive, I thought to myself, and I changed the direction of my vision. I noticed the threat was now down and not moving. My job was done.

I turned my face to the sky and lay there, the black above me softened by the floating flakes. They fell on my cheeks and onto my lashes. Once cold to me, they felt refreshing against the searing pain in my chest. They took on the colors of my strobing lights and I watched them change between white, red, and blue as they fell quietly towards me.

I could just feel the cold wet snow soaking into my clothes as my body began to numb from head to toe. A shuddering breath escaped me, and my mind started to fade slowly as a stream of thoughts tried to hold me to the surface.

I didn't know whether I would live or die, but I did know that no matter what happened, I fought and I won. I became the person that I had always wanted to be. I was the type of person that people could look up to. I had made a life for myself and fought the evils of my past, not allowing myself to remain a victim, but becoming a survivor. I had stood strong and worked hard to protect those who could not defend themselves.

A small smile reached my face as the snowflakes gathered on my lashes. In the distance, I heard sirens coming my way. My chest ached with each breath I tried to take, but the rest of my body had gone numb.

The darkness began to take over, and my eyes closed of their own accord. I lay there remembering a time when I'd wanted to die, a time when a small voice in my mind had told me, No, you are worth it. I knew now that I was. I was someone I could be proud of. I was the woman I had always wanted to become.

THE END

A NOTE TO READERS:

Since *Whether I'll Live or Die* was released in 2012, I have read many reviews, and heard from many readers about their opinions on this book. Some people think Amanda was a weak person, or they couldn't relate to her. For that I am glad, for if you had been able to relate to her, then you yourself could have been a victim.

Amanda was not weak, she was brainwashed. She wanted to be loved, she believed in commitment, she believed that people could change. She was trained to believe that she was not worth anything, that she could do nothing right. Once she finally looked at herself in the mirror—long and hard—she realized how much of a lie it all was and she knew what she had to do. It was not an easy choice, I know. I was Amanda. I am Nicole.

Whether I'll Live or Die is a fictional account of my life when I was a young adult. While not everything that occurred in this book is true, the emotions, the fear, the anger, the will to live are *one hundred percent real*. I took what I knew, what I experienced and created a fictional story to show that no matter who you are, you can survive.

Writing this book was my attempt to purge my soul of the fear, anger, and self-hatred that I had within myself. There were times when I would write a sentence and then get up and walk away because the images of the incident would hit me so hard. Or I would finish a scene and find myself shaking, with tears running down my cheeks as I lived through the details all over again.

I hope that you never know such a world. That you are never touched by the hand of fear or anger the way I was. I hope that your life is filled with love, and that you feel safe in your relationships. You deserve that.

I deserved that. I know that now.

Stacy Eaton

P.S. as for the ending… what happens to her is up to you.

SNEAK PEEK - DISTORTED LOYALTY

Distorted Loyalty is a Romantic Suspense Novel
Chapter 1 - Rachel

*J*osh sucked on his straw so hard, he emptied his cup. His cheeks puckered while he drew in the last few drops. The loud slurp reminded me of the operating room. "Josh, I think you got it all." I eyed him over our almost-empty lunch tray as I spoke.

He grinned his boyish smile, and my heart tugged a bit in my chest—not that I would tell him his smile was boyish. At the age of sixteen, he was of the distinct impression that he was a man. My heart strings pulled a little tighter as I watched him eat the last of his fries. In a few years, he would be off to college, either near or far. At least I thought he was going to college, he hadn't mentioned doing anything else.

"Don't scrunch your face like that, Mom, it makes your wrinkles stand out." The surprised expression on my face must have entertained him because he belted out a laugh, "Just kidding."

I shook my head at him, "So why did you want me to come out shopping with you?" His laughter died quickly, and he glanced around the small café. I watched his nervous demeanor for a moment. "I'm not buying you anything expensive, Josh, Christmas is only a few weeks away."

He shook his head. "It's not for me."

I rested my elbows on the table and took a sip from my soda cup. I waited patiently for him to continue, and he searched every part of the room, except for where I was sitting. Well, someone is very nervous, I thought to myself.

"If it's not for you, who is it for?" I asked. I tried to ease his unease by busying myself as I set my cup down and wiped grains of salt off the edge of the table into my hand and dropped them onto my empty plate.

Josh studied me for a long moment, and I saw the boy behind the young man hiding in his blue eyes. He leaned across the table so he could speak softly. "You have to promise not to give me a hard time."

Oh boy, this should be good. "Alright," I said and waited for him.

"Um, see, there is this girl," he glanced around the room, and I followed his gaze.

When he hesitated, I chimed in, "Wait, what girl?"

He brought his attention back to me, "Her name is Jazlyn." I nodded for him to continue. I had heard the name before. "I, um, I," he stuttered for a moment.

"Josh, spit it out, what about the girl?" I watched him sitting in the hot seat, a little pink tint to his cheeks. It was obvious that he liked this Jazlyn, whoever she was.

He blew out a quick breath and rushed to speak before he lost his nerve, "I want to buy her a gift, but I don't know what to buy her, so I was thinking that you might be able to help me pick something out." His cheeks brightened.

"I didn't know you had a girlfriend," I stated, trying to keep the surprise out of my voice that he was seeing someone.

"I don't, but I have wanted to ask her out for a while. I thought maybe I could get her something small and ask her out, or ask her out and then give her a small gift over holiday break."

This was the first time that I could remember that Josh had wanted to buy a female, other than me, a gift, and it reminded me again that he was growing up—too fast.

"What does she like?"

He shrugged, "I don't know. I don't know her that well. That's why I needed your help."

Okay, what do you buy for a girl that you don't really know at the age of sixteen that doesn't cost an arm and a leg? "Is she a girly girl or is she athletic?"

His shoulder rose again. "She plays sports, but she wears nice clothes, so she is kinda both, I guess."

I looked out the window and scanned the shops that surrounded us in the Main Street Shopping Plaza. My eyes landed on a shop just down the way. Bingo! "Come on, I have the perfect idea."

To Read More Download a Copy from Amazon

ABOUT THE AUTHOR

Stacy Eaton is a USA Today Best Selling author and began her writing career in October of 2010. Stacy took an early retirement from law enforcement after over fifteen years of service in 2016, with her last three years in investigations and crime scene investigation to write full time.

Stacy resides in southeastern Pennsylvania with her husband, who works in law enforcement, and her teen daughter who is a second-degree black belt in Tae Kwon Do. She also has a son who is currently serving in the United States Navy.

Stacy is very involved in Domestic Violence Awareness and served on the Board of Directors for her local Domestic Violence Center for three years.

www.stacyeaton.com

ALSO BY STACY EATON

Paranormal Romance:

My Blood Runs Blue

Blue Blood for Life

Garda ~ Welcome to the Realm

Domestic Violence – Crime - Suspense:

Whether I'll Live or Die

Barbara's Plea

You're Not Alone

Romantic Suspense:

Liveon ~ No Evil

Second Shield

Second Shield II: The Return

Distorted Loyalty

Six Days of Memories

Contemporary Romance:

Tempt Me Too

Finding the Strength

Finding Love on Christmas Vacation

The Celebration Series:

Tangled in Tinsel, Book 1

Tears to Cheers, Book 2

Heathens & Hearts, Book 3

Rainbows bring Riches, Book 4

Sweet as Sugar, Book 5

Making Mom Mad, Book 6

Sparklers or Spankings, Book 7

Raffles to Rattles, Book 8

Flirting with Fireworks, Book 9

Working Under Wheels, Book 10

Masquerading at Midnight, Book 11

Blessings and Beans, Book 12

Velvet and Vows, Book 13

Heal Me Series:

Cured, Book 1

Revived, Book 2

Mended, Book 3

Heart of the Family Series:

(Celebration Spin-Off)

Mistletoe & Cocoa Kisses, Book 1

Roses & Champagne Kisses, Book 2

Orchids & Hurricane Kisses, Book 3

Pleasure Your Fantasies Series

(Celebration Spin-Off)

Mistletoe Fantasies, Book 1

The Twisted Love Series

Co-written with Amy Manemann

Love Lorn, Book 1 (Manemann)

Love Torn, Book 2 (Eaton

Love Inked, Book 3 (Manemann & Eaton - 2019)